Birthright

(1922)

By T. S. Stribling

**A FACSIMILE REPRODUCTION
WITH AN INTRODUCTION BY
EDWARD J. PIACENTINO**

**SCHOLARS' FACSIMILES & REPRINTS
DELMAR, NEW YORK, 1987**

SCHOLARS' FACSIMILES & REPRINTS
ISSN 0161-7729
SERIES ESTABLISHED 1936
VOLUME 424

Published by
Scholars' Facsimiles & Reprints, Inc.
Delmar, New York 12054-0344, U.S.A.

Library of Congress Cataloging-in-Publication Data

Stribling, T. S. (Thomas Sigismund), 1881-1965.

Birthright : 1922.

(Scholars' Facsimiles & Reprints, ISSN 0161-7729 ; v. 424)
Originally published: New York : Century, 1922.
Bibliography: p.
I. Title.
II. Series: Scholars' Facsimiles & Reprints (Series) ; v. 424.
PS3537.T836B5   1987   813'.52   87-23235
ISBN 0-8201-1424-3

Introduction

I

In the annals of literary history 1922 stands out as an *annus mirabilis*; it witnessed the publication of T. S. Eliot's *The Waste Land*, James Joyce's *Ulysses*, and Eugene O'Neill's *The Hairy Ape*. In this same year, a previously unknown and unheralded forty-one-year-old writer from Tennessee, T. S. Stribling, published his first serious social novel with a southern setting, *Birthright*, a book which represented a new departure in the treatment of race relations by a white southerner. Lauded by black critic William Stanley Braithwaite as "the most significant novel on the Negro written by a white American,"[1] *Birthright* launched Stribling's career as a daring new voice in southern letters, a pioneer in the southern literary renascence.[2]

Born in the Tennessee River village of Clifton in Wayne County, Tennessee, on 4 March 1881, Stribling spent his formative years in a provincial environment which would subsequently provide him with the subject matter for *Birthright* as well as for several social satires he would also write in the 1920s.[3] After finishing his primary and secondary education in Clifton and at Southern Normal College in Huntingdon, Tennessee, Stribling began his literary apprenticeship as a journalist, serving a brief stint as editor and chief writer for the *Clifton News*, a small weekly newspaper in his hometown. Yet Stribling's parents did not support his aspirations to be a writer and insisted that he continue his formal education to prepare himself for some more practical and lucrative endeavor.

Obedient to his parents' wishes, he entered the normal college in nearby Florence, Alabama, in 1902, and a year later completed the course of study requisite for entering the teaching profession. After graduating, Stribling taught for a year at a high school in Tuscaloosa, Alabama, hoping to earn enough money to enroll in the law school at the University of Alabama. He completed his legal studies in 1905, but he practiced law for only a short time. Still, it was long enough to acquire a keen understanding of the quirks and deficiencies of the

3

southern legal system, a subject which became a primary focus of satire in Stribling's seven southern novels.

The next stage of Stribling's literary apprenticeship was spent at the *Taylor-Trotwood Magazine*, a popular monthly published in Nashville, Tennessee. While on the staff of this magazine in 1907 and 1908, Stribling cultivated an interest in the fashionable, readily marketable Sunday school story, a formulaic, pedestrian mode that combined sentimentality, adventure, and didacticism. After mastering the formula, it did not take him long to discover that he could make easy money by writing such stories. At about this time he also wrote his first realistic stories, "The Imitator" and "The Thrall of the Green," both of which were published in the *Taylor-Trotwood Magazine*. And both exhibited the keen social consciousness he would later exploit in *Birthright* and his other serious novels in the 1920s and 1930s.

After moving to New Orleans in 1908, Stribling continued to pen Sunday school stories, veritably mass-producing them at the rate of seven per day. Most were eventually published in denominational magazines. For the next eight or nine years--a rather prolonged apprenticeship--Stribling continued to write Sunday school and adventure stories, many of the latter published in such popular periodicals as *American Boy*, *Holland's Magazine*, *Youth's Companion*, and *Everybody's Magazine*. Characterized by contrived and extremely sentimental plots, exotic and melodramatic descriptions, and obtrusive moralizing, these adventure stories let Stribling experiment with suspense and intrigue, which he subsequently used in his novels with foreign settings. The first of these, *The Cruise of the Dry Dock* (1917), was a melodramatic sea adventure. Others included *Fombombo* (1923), *Red Sand* (1924), and *Strange Moon* (1929)--each set in Venezuela and based on events Stribling had observed on visits to that country both before and after the First World War. *East Is East* (1928) was set in Algiers and treated the conflict of American and Algerian cultures. *Clues of the Caribbees* (1929), a collection of five mystery stories previously published in *Adventure Magazine* and featuring an amateur detective named Henry Poggioli, who investigates a series of bizarre crimes committed in the Caribbean islands, also falls into this light, sensational category. Stribling continued to write detective stories for the remainder of his literary career.

These novels and stories were composed hurriedly, and they were intended primarily to entertain. But Stribling's reputation as a pioneer of modern southern literature does not depend on these works. Rather, it is by his serious novels, such as *Birthright*, which focus on the problems of the Piedmont South, that we must measure his primary contributions as a writer.

Besides *Birthright* (1922), Stribling wrote six other southern novels. *Teeftallow* (1926) and a sequel, *Bright Metal* (1928), are satires that assaulted small-town society of middle Tennessee after the manner of Sinclair Lewis's *Main Street*. Also, in 1928 Stribling collaborated with David Wallace on a play entitled *Rope*, a dramatization of *Teeftallow*. The play, which opened at New York's Biltmore Theatre in February of 1928, closed less than a month later, after a run of only thirty-two performances. The novel *Backwater*, which combines melodrama and satire to expose the hypocrisies and lawlessness of rural Arkansas, was published in 1930, the same year that Stribling married Lou Ella Kloss, a talented violinist and fellow resident of Clifton. His next three novels--*The Forge* (1931), *The Store* (1932), and *Unfinished Cathedral* (1934)--comprised his iconoclastic trilogy of the South, a work which collectively has been regarded as his premier literary production, his most ambitious and significant contribution to modern southern literature. Using a large gallery of characters drawn from all segments of society and tracing the changes affecting the lives of three generations of a southern family which resides in northern Alabama, these novels cover a period in southern social history from the beginning of the Civil War through the boom years of the twenties. *The Store*, the second part of the trilogy, was awarded a Pulitzer Prize in 1933.

Stribling's final two novels--*The Sound Wagon* (1935) and *These Bars of Flesh* (1938)--are both set in the North. Whereas *The Sound Wagon* indicts the shortcomings of political life in Washington, D.C. and New York City, *These Bars of Flesh*, set in New York City, exposes the foibles and hypocrisies of life in a metropolitan university.

Although Stribling continued to write after 1938, he had passed his prime. His most frequent literary efforts were detective stories, published in magazines such as *Ellery Queen*, *Smashing Detective Stories*, *Saint Detective*, and *Famous Detective*. Some were subsequently collected and posthumously published in *Best Dr. Poggioli Detective Stories* in 1975. In addition, in 1940, at the age of fifty-nine, Stribling began his memoirs, a project he worked on periodically for the remainder of his life. Posthumously published in 1982 and titled *Laughing Stock*, this autobiography provides an engaging and zestful account of Stribling's life up to 1938.

A trailblazer in the southern literary renascence of the 1920s and early 1930s, Stribling contributed to the development of the serious social novel in the South. Yet by the early 1960s, the last years of his life, he had been largely forgotten and his pioneering efforts, which had been harshly criticized by the South's Agrarian New Critics in the 1930s, were unappreciated. After a brief illness Stribling died in Florence, Alabama, on 8 July 1965, at the age of eighty-four.

II

Birthright, Stribling's first serious southern social novel, was something of a literary landmark in the realistic delineation of an educated southern black man. According to Stribling, the novel grew out of a series of short stories he had begun writing in 1920. "After I had finished three stories," he disclosed in an interview in 1938, "I saw that they made three chapters for a novel. The stories sort of welded themselves together and became a novel with very little effort on my part."[4] He acknowledged that *Birthright* was based on actual experience, the way of life and the people he had known in Clifton in the early 1900s.[5] His educated black protagonist, Peter Siner, was modeled on a young Negro victimized by racial prejudice.[6]

Stribling completed *Birthright* in the spring of 1921 before departing for an extended tour of South America. Feeling *Birthright*'s controversial subject matter and stark realism would make it difficult to find a publisher, Stribling decided to leave his manuscript with Joe Cox, a New York friend, hoping that Cox would find a publisher willing to consider it. While in the West Indies Stribling received a cable from the Century Company in New York, expressing the desire not only to publish *Birthright* in book form but to serialize it first in *Century Magazine*, beginning in the fall of 1921.[7] Impressed by Century's generous offer of $7,000, Stribling accepted, and *Birthright* was serialized in seven installments from October 1921 through April 1922.[8] In the spring of 1922, Century published the book form in a modest edition of 5,000 copies. Realizing that the book's publication initiated a new direction in his career, Stribling later remarked that "*Birthright* made it fairly easy for me to get an editorial hearing in any American magazine or book publishing house."[9] Much later Stribling disclosed that *Birthright* was intended to be the first part of a Negro trilogy he hoped to write, but this ambitious project never materialized.[10]

Birthright represented a forthright repudiation of the "treacly sentimentalities" that the editors of the New Orleans *Double-Dealer* complained had predominated in southern depictions of race relations.[11] Stribling dared to portray the black man and his plight sympathetically, emphatically showing him to be a helpless object of hatred and oppression, an individual denied political and social equality. Commenting on the portrayal of blacks in southern fiction by some of Stribling's nineteenth-century predecessors, many of whom wrote in the local-color mode, Louis D. Rubin has perceptively observed that "however vivid the human characterization they created, however free they may have been from the limitations of their time and place, none of [these] . . . Southern novelists could consistently view the situation of the Negro from the standpoint of the Negro; they could not recognize in his circumstance a full and sustaining metaphor for their own."[12] Even several of Stribling's southern contemporaries, Dubose Heyward and Julia Peterkin, never portrayed their black characters as human beings in their own right. Typically their novels delineated blacks as "exotic primitives" who lived happily and innocently in their picturesque surroundings. In *Porgy* (1925), for example, Heyward consciously refrains from blaming Charleston aristocrats (of whom he was one) for the injustices inflicted on the Negro.

In contrast, Stribling in *Birthright* sharply disparages all his white characters, making it emphatically clear that they are responsible for the black man's dehumanized existence. Unlike Heyward, Stribling seems not to have cared that his iconoclastic depiction of the abuses in a small southern town, abuses stemming from the perpetuation of a racist caste system, would probably offend the pride and arouse the ire of many white southerners. "Until the time I wrote it," Stribling asserted in explaining the effect that writing *Birthright* had on him, "I had looked upon the Negroes in the South precisely as the great majority of Southerners looked upon them, as a slightly subhuman folk. . . . But by the time I had written the life and adventures of my brown hero, it dawned on me that the Negroes were people just like everybody else."[13]

III

Some contemporary southern readers of *Birthright* were quite disturbed and harshly condemned Stribling for his depiction of black experience. Some even conjectured that Stribling might be a Negro himself. Mrs. Mary Anne Bleecher of Camp Benning, Georgia, wrote the editor of *Century Magazine* a typical white southern reaction:

> At best I a very poorly educated and my vocabulary is small. However, if it were a hundred times larger than it really is, I could never, never, express the horrible thoughts I have about Mr. Stribling's story, *Birthright*.
> Personally, I think that the author might be an octoroon himself.[14]

Contemporary reviewers treated *Birthright* much more judiciously and objectively. Desda Garner has counted at least 187 reviews of *Birthright*,[15] and while all did not praise it, some recognized that Stribling's novel presented a fresh examination of bigotry and narrow-mindedness in a small southern town. H. W. Boynton, who criticized Stribling for not providing a well-rounded picture of southern life in *Birthright*, pronounced the novel "a frank and unsentimentalized study of the modern Negro in the South, though the plight of his white neighbors does not come into it."[16] In commenting on the starkly realistic delineation of black life in H. A. Shands's *White and Black* and in *Birthright*, Sarah N. Cleghorn remarked that in neither novel "do we receive a hint of racial *noblesse oblige*. The garment of our race relations has been pulled off us wrong side out, and here are the seams showing."[17] Although she disapproved of Stribling's generalizations about race relations, Martha Gruening, an English critic, still praised *Birthright* as "a first novel of unusual distinction, power and sincerity, in a field in which these qualities have heretofore been conspicuously lacking."[18] And Herschel Brickell, who berated Stribling for his heavy-handed propagandizing, saw merit in his treatment of Peter Siner, the novel's black protagonist. "It is when Mr. Stribling is writing about the plight of Peter as a refined, educated man in a seemingly hopeless environment," Brickell affirmed, "that the book is at its best."[19]

IV

Stribling quite possibly might not have written the kind of novel that he did in 1921 had Sinclair Lewis not published *Main Street* in

1920. Indeed, Carl Van Doren in 1921 aptly designated the stories *Main Street* spawned "the revolt from the village."[20] Several reviewers noted *Birthright*'s similarities to Lewis's best seller. Heywood Broun asserted that *Birthright* was "profoundly moving and interesting. Even Sinclair Lewis has no greater facility for bringing to the reader the physical aspect of a place. Indeed the book concerns another Main Street, but this time it is the thoroughfare of the Negro quarter in a small town in Tennessee."[21] Another reviewer noted that "Mr. Stribling, who, as a Southerner, knows his Hooker's Bend [the novel's principal setting] as Mr. Lewis knows his Gopher Prairie, has been as ruthless, and almost as patient, as the recorder of the life of Main Street. If his novel is not as completely done, the lack is due, it would seem, to a more pressing interest in analysis than possessed Lewis in his bestseller."[22]

"A Negro *Main Street*," as the Nashville Agrarian Donald Davidson called it, *Birthright* may be regarded as a southern rendition of Lewis's novel,[23] for *Birthright* exposes to acerbic satiric scrutiny some of the same shortcomings associated with provincial village life. In an effort to show the blighting and dehumanizing effects of life in a small Tennessee town, Stribling satirizes bigotry, materialism, complacency, conventional thinking, smugness, narrow-mindedness, and hypocrisy. Moreover, Stribling's protagonist, Peter Siner, shares affinities with Lewis's Carol Kennicott, the central character in *Main Street*, and functions in the narrative in much the same way. Like Carol, Peter is young, idealistic, and college-educated. Sharing Carol's messianic impulse, he attempts to engender social understanding and good will between blacks and whites in Hooker's Bend, his hometown, as well as to initiate economic reforms, in an effort to eliminate the long-standing wretched conditions under which the village's blacks have been forced to live. Yet Peter's well-intentioned plans fare no better than Carol's in Gopher Prairie because the townspeople, black as well as white, accept the racial status quo. Like Carol Kennicott, Peter becomes disillusioned and frustrated, unable to break down the solid barriers of prejudice, conformity, materialism, hatred, and mistrust that dominate the community. At the end of *Birthright*, as in the conclusion of *Main Street*, practicality triumphs over idealism and altruism. Just as Carol's worldly wise husband forces her to recognize that her schemes to make Gopher Prairie a haven of beauty and culture will not work, so Peter Siner's girlfriend, Cissie Dildine, manages to persuade him that his aspirations to sway the complacent whites and blacks of Hooker's Bend are futile. Stribling offers no workable solution for terminating the problems of racial prejudice. Peter and Cissie withdraw to the North, hoping to find there the equality and opportunity that have eluded them in Hooker's Bend. Yet even their migration offers no definite guarantees for a better, more fulfilling life.

Stribling retreats to a safe, noncontroversial position, advocating the "autonomous development" of both races, a reasserting of the southern white conservative stance on race relations, what Frank Durham has aptly described as "separate and unequal:"[24]

> And yet there is no such thing as absolute morals. Morals are as transitory as the sheen on a blackbird's wing; they change perpetually with the necessities of the race. Any people with an abounding vitality will naturally practise customs which a less vital people must shun.
>
> Morals are nothing more than the engines controlling the stream of energy that propel a race on its course. All engines are not alike, nor are all races bound for the same port.
>
> Here Peter Siner made the amazing discovery that although he had spent four years in Harvard, he had come out, just as he went in, a negro (308-9).

Stribling shows in painstaking detail that narrow-mindedness, seen chiefly as the white man's bigotry toward the Negro, and the pursuance of economic self-interest, prompted by greed and a desire to dominate village society, are formidable and apparently ineradicable forces. In developing this theme Stribling employs various village character types who reflect attitudes and who behave despicably, not unlike their counterparts in *Main Street*. To describe Henry Hooker, the cashier of the Planter's Bank, Stribling uses overtly pejorative terms: this "shabby little banker," with a "hatchet face, close-set eyes, harsh, straight hair and squeaky voice [which] made him seem like some prickly, dried up gnome a man sees in a fever" (63), resembles Ezra Stowbody, the avaricious, unscrupulous Gopher Prairie banker in *Main Street* who discriminates against and exploits Scandinavian farmers. Priding himself on his ability to fool blacks, Hooker is a scoundrel and a hypocrite, who while altruistically supporting missionary efforts to assist African blacks, at the same time swindles the docile and naive blacks of Hooker's Bend:

Peter knew that the banker subscribed liberally to foreign missions; indeed, at the cashier's behest, the white church of Hooker's Bend kept a paid missionary on the upper Congo. But the banker had sold some village lots to the negroes, and in two instances, where a streak of commercial phosphate had been discovered on the properties, the lots had reverted to the Hooker estate. There had been in the deed something concerning a mineral reservation that the negro purchasers knew nothing about until the phosphate was discovered. The whole matter had been perfectly legal (9).

Dawson Bobbs, the town peace officer, is "a big, fleshy, red-faced man, with chilly blue eyes and a little straight slit of a mouth in his wide face" (24). Bobbs shares the uncompromising prejudice of Hooker and most of the townspeople against blacks and delights in sadistically exploiting and defrauding them in order to serve his own advantage and to preserve the racial status quo.

In Captain Milt Renfrew, who appears to be Peter Siner's unacknowledged white father, Stribling presents the class and caste system of the antebellum South. In fact, Renfrew's personal library may be regarded as a veritable repository of racist propaganda--"an attorney's special pleading against the equality of man" (219). In addition, Renfrew is writing a literary memoir eulogizing "the picturesqueness and stateliness of the old slave regime" (211). Renfrew's obsessive defense of the "peculiar institution," a reiteration of standard Old South arguments supporting slavery under the plantation system, seems absurdly anachronistic and hence an easy target of Stribling's satire. In debunking such traditionalism, another force contributing to Hooker's Bend's moral degeneration, Stribling again echoes a concern that Lewis attacked in *Main Street*.

V

Like other American writers of the twenties Stribling also employs several stylistic strategies which resemble some that Lewis used in *Main Street*.[25] He consciously accentuates the ugly, disagreeable, and unpleasant aspects of small-town life. By concentrating on the nether side of southern village experience, Stribling probably hoped to shock the reader from fear and complacency, to awaken revulsion and disgust. To accomplish this task, Stribling appealed directly to the reader's emotions. In a national radio broadcast in 1935, Stribling attempted to explain the rationale behind his composition:

> Propaganda, the spreading of ideas by emotion mixed or unmixed with reason, is the only instrument that will move a democracy. And the more completely democratic any country becomes the more completely will it depend on propaganda. I am speaking now not as an idealist looking forward to a millennium of an educated citizenry, but as a realist to the here and now.[26]

That Stribling's purpose in *Birthright* is propagandistic becomes immediately apparent. He consciously paints an unrelievedly dismal picture of village life, emphasizing its ugly, repugnant, and oppressive aspects. When Peter Siner returns to the town after graduating from Harvard, the reader sees what Peter himself observes:

> It was stony in places, muddy in places, strewn with goods-boxes, broken planking, excelsior, and straw that had been used for packing. Charred rubbish-piles lay in front of every store, which the clerks had swept out and attempted to burn. Hogs roamed the thoroughfare, picking up decaying fruit and parings, and nosing tin cans that had been thrown out by the merchants. The stores that Peter had once looked upon as showplaces were poor two-story brick or frame buildings, defiled by time and wear and weather. The white merchants were coatless, listless men who sat in chairs on the brick pavements before their stores and who moved slowly when a customer entered their doors (22).

Here in the hub of the town's business establishment and in the neighboring residential areas, racial prejudice has been nurtured, has thrived, and has become the accepted way of life. This squalid physical and social environment is the product of a society where complacency, negligence, and meanness prevail.

Stribling treats equally harshly the sordid, repugnant features of Hooker's Bend's black community, a place known to whites and blacks alike as Niggertown. In Niggertown, Stribling writes, "there are perhaps not two upright buildings" and "the grimy cabins lean at crazy angles, some propped with poles, while others hold out against gravitation at a hazard" (26). The most conspicuous image of Hooker's Bend's overall moral and physical degradation is the public well, where rainfall flowing under Niggertown's pig sties, stables, and outhouses collects and from which the the town's three or four hundred black residents regularly draw their water. More a cesspool than anything else, this well causes many of the diseases that devastate Niggertown residents:

> The inhabitants of Niggertown suffer from divers diseases; they develop strange ailments that no amount of physicking will overcome; young wives grow sickly for no apparent cause. Although only three or four hundred persons live in Niggertown, two or three negroes are always slowly dying of tuberculosis; winter brings pneumonia; summer, malaria. About once a year the state health officer visits Hooker's Bend and forces the white soda-water dispensers on the other side of the hill to sterilize their glasses in the name of the sovereign State of Tennessee (27).

Stribling also employs a selective omniscient point of view, with Peter Siner observing or reflecting on the key scenes and events. To have the principal character function as a surrogate author permitted Stribling to communicate his message naturally and unobtrusively. While this technique may be condemned as indirect editorializing, Peter's astute perceptions are credibly motivated and expressed in language consonant with his background. All the same, Peter's perceptions reflect some of Stribling's as well. Here Peter considers the system under which black domestics in Hooker's Bend work:

> The wage of cooks in small Southern villages is a pittance--and what they can steal. The tragedy of the mothers of a whole race working for their board and thievings came over Peter with a rising grimness. And there was no public sentiment against such practice. It was accepted everywhere as natural and inevitable. The negresses were never prosecuted; no effort was made to regain the stolen goods. The employers realized that what they paid would not keep body and soul together; that it was steal or perish. . . . The whole system was the lees of slavery, and was surely the most demoralizing, the most grotesque method of hiring service in the whole civilized world. It was so absurd that its mere relation lapses into humor, that bane of black folk (247-48).

VI

It has been justly claimed that T. S. Stribling was in the forefront

INTRODUCTION

"in turning to the starker actualities of Negro [life]" in *Birthright*,[27] that he broke new ground in depicting "an unsentimentalized, objective view of the problem of being a Negro in the South."[28] But given the more subtle, complex treatment of race relations by other modern southern writers such as Richard Wright, Ralph Ellison, William Styron, Ernest J. Gaines, Alice Walker, and especially of the major artificer of twentieth-century southern letters, William Faulkner--all of whose major works treating this subject appeared after *Birthright*--it is easy in retrospect to berate Stribling for not going far enough. While *Birthright* was actually in the vanguard in its realistic and sympathetic portrayal of a sensitive, educated black man, some still misconstrue Stribling's effort. Frank Durham has noted, "*Birthright* is a racist novel, accepting the inferiority of the Negro, perpetuating the comic and bestial stereotypes, repeating the ancient truisms about the Negro -- indolence, dishonesty, odor, barbaric love of color, emotionalism, sexual promiscuity . . . as inherent in race. . . ."[29] Although he was a white southerner living in a region where conservative attitudes toward race prevailed, Stribling unequivocally shows, except in a few isolated situations, that in a racist society blacks who choose to or have to remain there must necessarily dissemble, thus compromising their humanity by playing humiliating, stereotypical roles in order to survive.

Even with this rationale *Birthright* may never completely escape being perceived as a novel whose racial views reflect a conservative white southern bias. And while not a novel of major magnitude, *Birthright* may still be viewed as a work of some historical and cultural significance in the development of the serious social novel in the South. Coming as it did in serial form just one year after Sinclair Lewis's *Main Street*, *Birthright* was one of the first southern novels to use iconoclastic social realism to reveal the more despicable aspects of a provincial southern village. As a social satirist, Stribling employed the strategies that *Main Street* made popular, thereby emerging as a transitional figure, who opened the way for further critical scrutiny of the southern Piedmont by more talented writers of the region who would soon follow the path that he explored first.

EDWARD J. PIACENTINO

High Point College

14

NOTES

1. William Stanley Braithwaite, "The Negro in Literature," *Crisis*, 28 (Sept. 1924), 206.

2. Hershel Brickell, "The Literary Awakening in the South," *The Bookman*, 66 (Oct. 1927), 141.

3. All biographical information on Stribling, unless otherwise noted, comes from my essay in the *Dictionary of Literary Biography* series, "T. S. Stribling," in *American Novelists 1900-1945*, ed. James J. Martine (Detroit: Gale Research Co., 1981), pp. 72-78.

4. Roberta G. Moore, "A Study of the Background and of the Mechanics of the Stribling Novels," (M.A. thesis, Ohio University, 1938), p. 4.

5. T. S. Stribling, *Laughing Stock*, eds. R. K. Cross and J. T. McMillan (Memphis: St. Luke's Press, 1982), p. 176.

6. Moore, "A Study of the Background," p. 6.

7. "Stribling Sees Himself as Others Don't," *Knoxville News-Sentinel*, 1 June 1930, p. 1c.

8. Wilton Eckley, "The Novels of T. S. Stribling: A Socio-Literary Study," (Ph.D diss., Western Reserve University, 1965), p. 44.

9. Charles C. Baldwin, *The Men Who Make Our Novels* (New York: Dodd, Mead and Co., 1924), p. 472.

10. Stribling, *Laughing Stock*, p. 177.

11. "Southern Letters," *The Double-Dealer*, 1 (June 1921), 214.

12. Louis D. Rubin, Jr., "Southern Local Color and the Black Man," *The Southern Review*, NS 6 (Oct. 1970), 1030.

13. Stribling, *Laughing Stock*, p. 177.

14. Quoted in Thomas D. Jarrett, "Stribling's Novels," *Phylon*, 4 (1943), p. 345.

15. Desda Garner, "Intimate Study of the Life and Writings of Thomas Sigismund Stribling,"(M.A. thesis, George Peabody College for Teachers, 1934), p. 17.

16. H. W. Boynton, "Yellow Is Black," *The Independent*, 13 May 1922, p. 459.

17. Sarah N. Cleghorn, Review of *Birthright*, by T. S. Stribling, and *White and Black*, by H. A. Shands, *The Nation*, 26 Apr. 1922, p. 498.

18. Martha Gruening, "Aspects of the Race Question," *The Freeman*, 26 July 1922, p. 476.

19. Hershel Brickell, "The New Negro in Fiction," *Literary Review of the New York Evening Post*, 22 Apr. 1922, p. 596.

20. Carl Van Doren, "The Revolt from the Village: 1920," *The*

NOTES

Nation, 12 Oct. 1921, pp. 407-12.

21. Heywood Broun, Review of *Birthright*, by T. S. Stribling, *New York World*, 29 Mar. 1922, p. 22.

22. Review of *Birthright*, by T. S. Stribling, *Dial*, 72 (June 1922), 648.

23. Donald Davidson, "The Trend in Literature: A Partisan View," in *Culture in the South*, ed. W. T. Couch (Chapel Hill: University of North Carolina Press, 1934), p. 190.

24. Frank Durham, "The Reputed Demises of Uncle Tom; or, the Treatment of the Negro in Fiction by White Southern Authors in the 1920's," *Southern Literary Journal*, 2 (Spring 1970), 36.

25. The standard study on the principal phase of the literary assault on the American small town is Anthony Channel Hilfer's *The Revolt from the Village, 1915-1930* (Chapel Hill: University of North Carolina Press, 1969).

26. "Literature and Life," *America's Town Meeting of the Air*, No. 9, ed. Lyman Bryson (New York: The American Book Co., 1935), p. 24.

27. James S. Wilson, "Poor-White and Negro," *Virginia Quarterly Review*, 8 (Oct. 1932), 621.

28. Wilton Eckley, *T. S. Stribling* (Boston: Twayne Publishers, 1975), p. 31.

29. Durham, "The Reputed Demises of Uncle Tom," pp. 36-37.

SELECTED BIBLIOGRAPHY

Becker, George J. "T. S. Stribling: Pattern in Black and White." *American Quarterly*, 4 (Fall 1952), 203-13.

Bryson, Lyman, ed. *America's Town Meeting of the Air*, No. 9. New York: American Book Co., 1935.

Durham, Frank. "The Reputed Demises of Uncle Tom; or, the Treatment of the Negro in Fiction by White Southern Authors in the 1920's." *Southern Literary Journal*, 2 (Spring 1970), 26-50.

Eckley, Wilton. *T. S. Stribling*. Boston: Twayne Publishers, 1975.

Hilfer, Anthony Channell. *The Revolt from the Village, 1915-1930*. Chapel Hill: University of North Carolina Press, 1969.

Piacentino, Edward J. "The *Main Street* Mode in Selected Minor Southern Novels of the 1920's." *Sinclair Lewis Newsletter*, 7 & 8 (1975-1976), 18-22.

——. "No More 'Treachy Sentimentalities': The Legacy of T. S. Stribling to the Southern Literary Renascence." *Southern Studies: An Interdisciplinary Journal of the South*, 20 (Spring 1981): 67-83.

——, ed. "Selected Letters of T. S. Stribling, 1910-1934." *Mississippi Quarterly*, 38 (Fall 1985), 447-70.

Salpeter, Harry. "Stribling the Novelist of the South." *Boston Evening Transcript*, 3 Dec. 1932, pp. 1, 3.

Stribling, T. S. *Laughing Stock*. Ed. Randy K. Cross and John T. McMillan. Memphis: St. Luke's Press, 1982.

Walsh, Ulysses. "Read and Write and Burn." *The Writer*, 45 (May 1932), 127-29.

Warren, Robert Penn. "T. S. Stribling: A Paragraph in the History of Critical Realism." *American Review*, 2 (Feb. 1934), 463-86.

BIRTHRIGHT

"Yes, Cissie, I understand now"

BIRTHRIGHT

A NOVEL

BY
T. S. STRIBLING

Illustrated by
F. Luis Mora

NEW YORK
THE CENTURY CO.
1922

PRINTED IN U. S. A.

TO MY MOTHER
AMELIA WAITS STRIBLING

LIST OF ILLUSTRATIONS

BIRTHRIGHT

BIRTHRIGHT

CHAPTER I

A T Cairo, Illinois, the Pullman-car conductor asked
Peter Siner to take his suitcase and traveling-bag
and pass forward into the Jim Crow car. The request
came as a sort of surprise to the negro. During Peter
Siner's four years in Harvard the segregation of black
folk on Southern railroads had become blurred and
reminiscent in his mind; now it was fetched back into
the sharp distinction of the present instant. With a
certain sense of strangeness, Siner picked up his bags,
and saw his own form, in the car mirrors, walking
down the length of the sleeper. He moved on through
the dining-car, where a few hours before he had had
dinner and talked with two white men, one an Oregon
apple-grower, the other a Wisconsin paper-manufac-
turer. The Wisconsin man had furnished cigars, and
the three had sat and smoked in the drawing-room,
indeed, had discussed this very point; and now it was
upon him.

At the door of the dining-car stood the porter of his
Pullman, a negro like himself, and Peter mechanically
gave him fifty cents. The porter accepted it silently,

without offering the amenities of his whisk-broom and shoe-brush, and Peter passed on forward.

Beyond the dining-car and Pullmans stretched twelve day-coaches filled with less-opulent white travelers in all degrees of sleepiness and dishabille from having sat up all night. The thirteenth coach was the Jim Crow car. Framed in a conspicuous place beside the entrance of the car was a copy of the Kentucky state ordinance setting this coach apart from the remainder of the train for the purposes therein provided.

The Jim Crow car was not exactly shabby, but it was unkept. It was half filled with travelers of Peter's own color, and these passengers were rather more noisy than those in the white coaches. Conversation was not restrained to the undertones one heard in the other day-coaches or the Pullmans. Near the entrance of the car two negroes in soldiers' uniforms had turned a seat over to face the door, and now they sat talking loudly and laughing the loose laugh of the half intoxicated as they watched the inflow of negro passengers coming out of the white cars.

The windows of the Jim Crow car were shut, and already it had become noisome. The close air was faintly barbed with the peculiar, penetrating odor of dark, sweating skins. For four years Peter Siner had not known that odor. Now it came to him not so much offensively as with a queer quality of intimacy and reminiscence. The tall, carefully tailored negro spread his wide nostrils, vacillating whether to sniff it out with disfavor or to admit it for the sudden mental associations it evoked.

It was a faint, pungent smell that played in the back of his nose and somehow reminded him of his mother, Caroline Siner, a thick-bodied black woman whom he remembered as always bending over a wash-tub. This was only one unit of a complex. The odor was also connected with negro protracted meetings in Hooker's Bend, and the Harvard man remembered a lanky black preacher waving long arms and wailing of hell-fire, to the chanted groans of his dark congregation; and he, Peter Siner, had groaned with the others. Peter had known this odor in the press-room of Tennessee cotton-gins, over a river packet's boilers, where he and other roustabouts were bedded, in bunk-houses in the woods. It also recalled a certain octoroon girl named Ida May, and an intimacy with her which it still moved and saddened Peter to think of. Indeed, it resurrected innumerable vignettes of his life in the negro village in Hooker's Bend; it was linked with innumerable emotions, this pungent, unforgetable odor that filled the Jim Crow car.

Somehow the odor had a queer effect of appearing to push his conversation with the two white Northern men in the drawing-room back to a distance, an indefinable distance of both space and time.

The negro put his suitcase under the seat, hung his

overcoat on the hook, and placed his hand-bag in the rack overhead; then with some difficulty he opened a window and sat down by it.

A stir of travelers in the Cairo station drifted into the car. Against a broad murmur of hurrying feet, moving trucks, and talking there stood out the thin, flat voice of a Southern white girl calling good-by to some one on the train. Peter could see her waving a bright parasol and tiptoeing. A sandwich boy hurried past, shrilling his wares. Siner leaned out, with fifteen cents, and signaled to him. The urchin hesitated, and was about to reach up one of his wrapped parcels, when a peremptory voice shouted at him from a lower car. With a sort of start the lad deserted Siner and went trotting down to his white customer. A moment later the train bell began ringing, and the Dixie Flier puffed deliberately out of the Cairo station and moved across the Ohio bridge into the South.

Half an hour later the blue-grass fields of Kentucky were spinning outside of the window in a vast green whirlpool. The distant trees and houses moved forward with the train, while the foreground, with its telegraph poles, its culverts, section-houses, and shrubbery, rushed backward in a blur. Now and then into the Jim Crow window whipped a blast of coal smoke and hot cinders, for the engine was only two cars ahead.

Peter Siner looked out at the interminable spin of the landscape with a certain wistfulness. He was coming back into the South, into his own country.

Here for generations his forebears had toiled endlessly and fruitlessly, yet the fat green fields hurtling past him told with what skill and patience their black hands had labored.

The negro shrugged away such thoughts, and with a certain effort replaced them with the constructive idea that was bringing him South once more. It was a very simple idea. Siner was returning to his native village in Tennessee to teach school. He planned to begin his work with the ordinary public school at Hooker's Bend, but, in the back of his head, he hoped eventually to develop an institution after the plan of Tuskeegee or the Hampton Institute in Virginia.

To do what he had in mind, he must obtain aid from white sources, and now, as he traveled southward, he began conning in his mind the white men and white women he knew in Hooker's Bend. He wanted first of all to secure possession of a small tract of land which he knew adjoined the negro school-house over on the east side of the village.

Before the negro's mind the different villagers passed in review with that peculiar intimacy of vision that servants always have of their masters. Indeed, no white Southerner knows his own village so minutely as does any member of its colored population. The colored villagers see the whites off their guard and just as they are, and that is an attitude in which no one looks his best. The negroes might be called the black recording angels of the South. If what they

know should be shouted aloud in any Southern town,
its social life would disintegrate. Yet it is a strange
fact that gossip seldom penetrates from the one race
to the other.

So Peter Siner sat in the Jim Crow car musing over
half a dozen villagers in Hooker's Bend. He thought
of them in a curious way. Although he was now a
B. A. of Harvard University, and although he knew
that not a soul in the little river village, unless it was
old Captain Renfrew, could construe a line of Greek
and that scarcely two had ever traveled farther north
than Cincinnati, still, as Peter recalled their names and
foibles, he involuntarily felt that he was telling over a
roll of the mighty. The white villagers came marching
through his mind as beings austere, and the very cranks
and quirks of their characters somehow held that austerity. There were the Brownell sisters, two old
maids, Molly and Patti, who lived in a big brick house
on the hill. Peter remembered that Miss Molly Brownell always doled out to his mother, at Monday's wash-
day dinner, exactly one biscuit less than the old negress
wanted to eat, and she always paid her in old clothes.
Peter remembered, a dozen times in his life, his mother
coming home and wondering in an impersonal way how
it was that Miss Molly Brownell could skimp every
meal she ate at the big house by exactly one biscuit.
It was Miss Brownell's thin-lipped boast that she
understood negroes. She had told Peter so several
times when, as a lad, he went up to the big house on

errands. Peter Siner considered this remembrance
without the faintest feeling of humor, and mentally removed Miss Molly Brownell from his list of possible
subscribers. Yet, he recalled, the whole Brownell
estate had been reared on negro labor.

Then there was Henry Hooker, cashier of the
village bank. Peter knew that the banker subscribed
liberally to foreign missions; indeed, at the cashier's
behest, the white church of Hooker's Bend kept a paid
missionary on the upper Congo. But the banker had
sold some village lots to the negroes, and in two instances, where a streak of commercial phosphate had
been discovered on the properties, the lots had reverted
to the Hooker estate. There had been in the deed
something concerning a mineral reservation that the
negro purchasers knew nothing about until the phosphate was discovered. The whole matter had been
perfectly legal.

A hand shook Siner's shoulder and interrupted his
review. Peter turned, and caught an alcoholic breath
over his shoulder, and the blurred voice of a Southern
negro called out above the rumble of the car and the
roar of the engine:

" 'Fo' Gawd, ef dis ain't Peter Siner I 's been lookin'
at de las' twenty miles, an' not knowin' him wid sich
skeniptious clo'es on! Wha you fum, nigger?"

Siner took the enthusiastic hand offered him and
studied the heavily set, powerful man bending over
the seat. He was in a soldier's uniform, and his broad

nutmeg-colored face and hot black eyes brought Peter
a vague sense of familiarity; but he never would have
identified his impression had he not observed on the
breast of the soldier's uniform the Congressional military medal for bravery on the field of battle. Its glint
furnished Peter the necessary clew. He remembered
his mother's writing him something about Tump Pack
going to France and getting "crowned" before the
army. He had puzzled a long time over what she
meant by "crowned" before he guessed her meaning.
Now the medal aided Peter in reconstructing out of
this big umber-colored giant the rather spindling Tump
Pack he had known in Hooker's Bend.

Siner was greatly surprised, and his heart warmed
at the sight of his old playmate.

"What have you been doing to yourself, Tump?"
he cried, laughing, and shaking the big hand in sudden
warmth. "You used to be the size of a dime in a
jewelry store."

"Been in 'e army, nigger, wha I 's been fed," said
the grinning brown man, delightedly. "I sho is picked
up, ain't I?"

"And what are you doing here in Cairo?"

"Tryin' to bridle a lil white mule." Mr. Pack
winked a whisky-brightened eye jovially and touched
his coat to indicate that some of the "white mule" was
in his pocket and had not been drunk.

"How 'd you get here?"

"Wucked my way down on de St. Louis packet an'

got paid off at Padjo [Paducah, Kentucky]; 'n 'en I
thought I 'd come on down heah an' roll some bones.
Been hittin' 'em two days now, an' I sho come putty
nigh bein' cleaned; but I put up lil Joe heah, an' won
'em all back, 'n 'en some." He touched the medal
on his coat, winked again, slapped Siner on the leg,
and burst into loud laughter.

Peter was momentarily shocked. He made a place
on the seat for his friend to sit. "You don't mean you
put up your medal on a crap game, Tump?"

"Sho do, black man." Pack became soberer.
"Dat 's one o' de great benefits o' bein' dec'rated. Dey
ain't a son uv a gun on de river whut kin win lil Joe;
dey all tried it."

A moment's reflection told Peter how simple and
natural it was for Pack to prize his military medal as
a good-luck piece to be used as a last resort in crap
games. He watched Tump stroke the face of his
medal with his fingers.

"My mother wrote me about your getting it, Tump.
I was glad to hear it."

The brown man nodded, and stared down at the
bit of gold on his barrel-like chest.

"Yas-suh, dat 'uz guv to me fuh bravery. You
know whut a skeery lil nigger I wuz roun' Hooker's
Ben'; well, de sahgeant tuk me an' he drill ever' bit o'
dat right out 'n me. He gimme a baynit an' learned
me to stob dummies wid it over at Camp Oglethorpe,
ontil he felt lak I had de heart to stob anything; 'n' 'en

he sont me acrost. I had to git a new pair breeches ever' three weeks, I growed so fas'." Here he broke out into his big loose laugh again, and renewed the alcoholic scent around Peter.

"And you made good?"

"Sho did, black man, an', 'fo' Gawd, I 'serve a medal ef any man ever did. Dey gimme dish-heah fuh stobbin fo' white men wid a baynit. 'Fo' Gawd, nig-ger, I never felt so quare in all my born days as when I wuz a-jobbin' de livers o' dem white men lak de sahgeant tol' me to." Tump shook his head, be-wildered, and after a moment added, "Yas-suh, I never wuz mo' surprised in all my life dan when I got dis medal fuh stobbin' fo' white men."

Peter Siner looked through the Jim Crow window at the vast rotation of the Kentucky landscape on which his forebears had toiled; presently he added soberly:

"You were fighting for your country, Tump. It was war then; you were fighting for your country."

At Jackson, Tennessee, the two negroes were forced to spend the night between trains. Tump Pack piloted Peter Siner to a negro café where they could eat, and later they searched out a negro lodging-house on Gate Street where they could sleep. It was a grimy, smelly place, with its own odor spiked by a phosphate-reduc-ing plant two blocks distant. The paper on the wall of the room Peter slept in looked scrofulous. There was no window, and Peter's four-years régime of open windows and fresh-air sleep was broken. He arranged his clothing for the night so it would come in contact with nothing in the room but a chair back. He felt dull next morning, and could not bring himself either to shave or bathe in the place, but got out and hunted up a negro barber-shop furnished with one greasy red-plush barber-chair.

A few hours later the two negroes journeyed on down to Perryville, Tennessee, a village on the Tennessee River where they took a gasolene launch up to Hooker's Bend. The launch was about fifty feet long and had two cabins, a colored cabin in front of, and a white cabin behind, the engine-room.

This unremitting insistence on his color, this continual shunting him into obscure and filthy ways, gradually gave Peter a loathly sensation. It increased the unwashed feeling that followed his lack of a morning bath. The impression grew upon him that he was being handled with tongs, along back-alley routes; that he and his race were something to be kept out of sight as much as possible, as careful housekeepers manœuver their slops.

At Perryville a number of passengers boarded the up-river boat; two or three drummers; a yellowed old hill woman returning to her Wayne County home; a red-headed peanut-buyer; a well-groomed white girl in a tailor suit; a youngish man barely on the right side of middle age who seemed to be attending her; and some negro girls with lunches. The passengers trailed from the railroad station down the river bank through a slush of mud, for the river had just fallen and had left a layer of liquid mud to a height of about twenty feet all along the littoral. The passengers picked their way down carefully, stepping into one another's tracks in the effort not to ruin their shoes. The drummers grumbled. The youngish man piloted the girl down, holding her hand, although both could have managed better by themselves.

Following the passengers came the trunks and grips on a truck. A negro deck-hand, the truck-driver, and the white master of the launch shoved aboard the big sample trunks of the drummers with grunts, profanity, and much stamping of mud. Presently, without the formality of bell or whistle, the launch clacked away from the landing and stood up the wide, muddy river.

The river itself was monotonous and depressing. It was perhaps half a mile wide, with flat, willowed mud banks on one side and low shelves of stratified limestone on the other.

Trading-points lay at ten- or fifteen-mile intervals along the great waterway. The typical landing was a dilapidated shed of a store half covered with tin tobacco signs and ancient circus posters. Usually, only one man met the launch at each landing, the merchant, a democrat in his shirt-sleeves and without a tie. His voice was always a flat, weary drawl, but his eyes, wrinkled against the sun, usually held the shrewdness of those who make their living out of two-penny trades.

At each place the red-headed peanut-buyer slogged up the muddy bank and bargained for the merchant's peanuts, to be shipped on the down-river trip of the first St. Louis packet. The loneliness of the scene embraced the trading-points, the river, and the little gasolene launch struggling against the muddy current. It permeated the passengers, and was a finishing touch to Peter Siner's melancholy.

The launch clacked on and on interminably. Sometimes it seemed to make no headway at all against the heavy, silty current. Tump Pack, the white captain, and the negro engineer began a game of craps in the negro cabin. Presently, two of the white drummers came in from the white cabin and began betting on the throws. The game was listless. The master of the launch pointed out places along the shores where wildcat stills were located. The crap-shooters, negro and white, squatted in a circle on the cabin floor, snapping their fingers and calling their points monotonously. One of the negro girls in the negro cabin took an apple out of her lunch sack and began eating it, holding it in her palm after the fashion of negroes rather than in her fingers, as is the custom of white women.

Both doors of the engine-room were open, and Peter Siner could see through into the white cabin. The old hill woman was dozing in her chair, her bonnet bobbing to each stroke of the engines. The youngish man and the girl were engaged in some sort of intimate lovers' dispute. When the engines stopped at one of the landings, Peter discovered she was trying to pay him what he had spent on getting her baggage trucked down at Perryville. The girl kept pressing a bill into the man's hand, and he avoided receiving the money. They kept up the play for sake of occasional contacts.

When the launch came in sight of Hooker's Bend toward the middle of the afternoon, Peter Siner experienced one of the profoundest surprises of his life. Somehow, all through his college days he had remembered Hooker's Bend as a proud town with important stores and unapproachable white residences. Now he saw a skum of negro cabins, high piles of lumber, a sawmill, and an ice-factory. Behind that, on a little rise, stood the old Brownell manor, maintaining a certain shabby dignity in a grove of oaks. Behind and westward from the negro shacks and lumber-piles ranged the village stores, their roofs just visible over the top of the bank. Moored to the shore, lay the wharf-boat in weathered greens and yellows. As a background for the whole scene rose the dark-green height of what was called the "Big Hill," an eminence that separated the negro village on the east from the white village on the west. The hill itself held no houses, but appeared a solid green-black with cedars.

The ensemble was merely another lonely spot on the south bank of the great somnolent river. It looked dead, deserted, a typical river town, unprodded even by the hoot of a jerk-water railroad.

As the launch chortled toward the wharf, Peter Siner

stood trying to orient himself to this unexpected and amazing minifying of Hooker's Bend. He had left a metropolis; he was coming back to a tumble-down village. Yet nothing was changed. Even the two scraggly locust-trees that clung perilously to the brink of the river bank still held their toe-hold among the strata of limestone.

The negro deck-hand came out and pumped the hand-power whistle in three long discordant blasts. Then a queer thing happened. The whistle was answered by a faint strain of music. A little later the passengers saw a line of negroes come marching down the river bank to the wharf-boat. They marched in military order, and from afar Peter recognized the white aprons and the swords and spears of the Knights and Ladies of Tabor, a colored burial association.

Siner wondered what had brought out the Knights and Ladies of Tabor. The singing and the drumming gradually grew upon the air. The passengers in the white cabin came out on the guards at this unexpected fanfare. As soon as the white travelers saw the marching negroes, they began joking about what caused the demonstration. The captain of the launch thought he knew, and began an oath, but stopped it out of deference to the girl in the tailor suit. He said it was a dead nigger the society was going to ship up to Savannah.

The girl in the tailor suit was much amused. She said the darkies looked like a string of caricatures marching down the river bank. Peter noticed her

Northern accent, and fancied she was coming to Hooker's Bend to teach school.

One of the drummers turned to another.

"Did you ever hear Bob Taylor's yarn about Uncle 'Rastus's funeral? Funniest thing Bob ever got off." He proceeded to tell it.

Every one on the launch was laughing except the captain, who was swearing quietly; but the line of negroes marched on down to the wharf-boat with the unshakable dignity of black folk in an important position. They came singing an old negro spiritual. The women's sopranos thrilled up in high, weird phrasing against an organ-like background of male voices.

But the black men carried no coffin, and suddenly it occurred to Peter Siner that perhaps this celebration was given in honor of his own home-coming. The mulatto's heart beat a trifle faster as he began planning a suitable response to this ovation.

Sure enough, the singing ranks disappeared behind the wharf-boat, and a minute later came marching around the stern and lined up on the outer guard of the vessel. The skinny, grizzly-headed negro commander held up his sword, and the Knights and Ladies of Tabor fell silent.

The master of the launch tossed his head-line to the wharf-boat, and yelled for one of the negroes to make it fast. One did. Then the commandant with the sword began his address, but it was not directed to Peter. He said:

Peter recognized the white aprons and the swords and spears
of the Knights and Ladies of Tabor

"Brudder Tump Pack, we, de Hooker's Ben' lodge uv de Knights an' Ladies uv Tabor, welcome you back to yo' native town. We is proud uv you, a colored man, who brings back de highes' crown uv bravery dis Newnighted States has in its power to bestow.

"Two yeahs ago, Brudder Tump, we seen you marchin' away fum Hooker's Ben' wid thirteen udder boys, white an' colored, all marchin' away togedder. Fo' uv them boys is already back home; three, we heah, is on de way back, but six uv yo' brave comrades, Brudder Pack, is sleepin' now in France, an' ain't never goin' to come home no mo'. When we honors you, we honors them all, de libin' an' de daid, de white an' de black, who fought togedder fuh one country, fuh one flag."

Gasps, sobs from the line of black folk, interrupted the speaker. Just then a shriveled old negress gave a scream, and came running and half stumbling out of the line, holding out her arms to the barrel-chested soldier on the gang-plank. She seized him and began shrieking:

"Bless Gawd! my son 's done come home! Praise de Lawd! Bless His holy name!" Here her laudation broke into sobbing and choking and laughing, and she squeezed herself to her son.

Tump patted her bony black form.

"I 's heah, Mammy," he stammered uncertainly. "I 's come back, Mammy."

Half a dozen other negroes caught the joyful

hysteria. They began a religious shouting, clapping
their hands, flinging up their arms, shrieking.

One of the drummers grunted:

"Good God! all this over a nigger getting back!"

At the extreme end of the dark line a tall cream-
colored girl wept silently. As Peter Siner stood
blinking his eyes, he saw the octoroon's shoulders
and breasts shake from the sobs, which her white
blood repressed to silence.

A certain sympathy for her grief and its suppression
kept Peter's eyes on the young woman, and then, with
the queer effect of one picture melting into another,
the strange girl's face assumed familiar curves and
softnesses, and he was looking at Ida May.

A quiver traveled deliberately over Peter from his
crisp black hair to the soles of his feet. He started
toward her impulsively.

At that moment one of the drummers picked up his
grip, and started down the gang-plank, and with its
leathern bulk pressed Tump Pack and his mother out
of his path. He moved on to the shore through the
negroes, who divided at his approach. The captain
of the launch saw that other of his white passengers
were becoming impatient, and he shouted for the
darkies to move aside and not to block the gangway.
The youngish man drew the girl in the tailor suit close
to him and started through with her. Peter heard him
say, "They won't hurt you, Miss Negley." And Miss
Negley, in the brisk nasal intonation of a Northern

woman, replied: "Oh, I'm not afraid. We waste a lot of sympathy on them back home, but when you see them—"

At that moment Peter heard a cry in his ears and felt arms thrown about his neck. He looked down and saw his mother, Caroline Siner, looking up into his face and weeping with the general emotion of the negroes and this joy of her own. Caroline had changed since Peter last saw her. Her eyes were a little more wrinkled, her kinky hair was thinner and very gray.

Something warm and melting moved in Peter Siner's breast. He caressed his mother and murmured incoherently, as had Tump Pack. Presently the master of the launch came by, and touched the old negress, not ungently, with the end of a spike-pole.

"You 'll have to move, Aunt Ca'line," he said. "We 're goin' to get the freight off now."

The black woman paused in her weeping. "Yes, Mass' Bob," she said, and she and Peter moved off of the launch onto the wharf-boat.

The Knights and Ladies of Tabor were already up the river bank with their hero. Peter and his mother were left alone. Now they walked around the guards of the wharf-boat to the bank, holding each other's arms closely. As they went, Peter kept looking down at his old black mother, with a growing tenderness. She was so worn and heavy! He recognized the very dress she wore, an old black silk which she had "washed out" for Miss Patti Brownell when he was a boy. It had been then, it was now, her best dress. During the years the old negress had registered her increasing bulk by letting out seams and putting in panels. Some of the panels did not agree with the original fabric either in color or in texture, and now the seams were stretching again and threatening a rip. Peter's own immaculate clothes reproached him, and he wondered for the hundredth, or for the thousandth time how his mother had obtained certain remittances which she had forwarded him during his college years.

As Peter and his mother crept up the bank of the river, stopping occasionally to let the old negress rest, his impression of the meanness and shabbiness of the whole village grew. From the top of the bank the single business street ran straight back from the river. It was stony in places, muddy in places, strewn with goods-boxes, broken planking, excelsior, and straw that had been used for packing. Charred rubbish-piles lay in front of every store, which the clerks had swept out and attempted to burn. Hogs roamed the thoroughfare, picking up decaying fruit and parings, and nosing tin cans that had been thrown out by the merchants. The stores that Peter had once looked upon as show-places were poor two-story brick or frame buildings, defiled by time and wear and weather. The white merchants were coatless, listless men who sat in chairs on the brick pavements before their stores and who moved slowly when a customer entered their doors.

And, strange to say, it was this fall of his white townsmen that moved Peter Siner with a sense of the greatest loss. It seemed fantastic to him, this sudden land-slide of the mighty.

As Peter and his mother came over the brow of the river bank, they saw a crowd collecting at the other end of the street. The main street of Hooker's Bend is only a block long, and the two negroes could easily hear the loud laughter of men hurrying to the focus of interest and the blurry expostulations of negro voices. The laughter spread like a contagion. Merchants as far up as the river corner became infected, and moved toward the crowd, looking back over their shoulders at every tenth or twelfth step to see that no one entered their doors.

Presently, a little short man, fairly yipping with laughter, stumbled back up the street to his store with tears of mirth in his eyes. A belated merchant stopped him by clapping both hands on his shoulders and shaking some composure into him.

"What is it? What's so funny? Damn it! I miss ever'thing!"

"I-i-it's that f-fool Tum-Tump Pack. Bobbs's arrested him!"

The inquirer was astounded.

"How the hell can he arrest him when he hit town this minute?"

"Wh-why, Bobbs had an old warrant for crap-shooting—three years old—before the war. Just as Tump was a-coming down the street at the head of the coons, out steps Bobbs—" Here the little man was overcome.

The merchant from the corner opened his eyes.

"Arrested him on an old crap charge?"

The little man nodded. They gazed at each other. Then they exploded simultaneously.

Peter left his obese mother and hurried to the corner. Dawson Bobbs, the constable, had handcuffs on Tump's wrists, and stood with his prisoner amid a crowd of arguing negroes.

Bobbs was a big, fleshy, red-faced man, with chilly blue eyes and a little straight slit of a mouth in his wide face. He was laughing and chewing a sliver of toothpick.

"O Tump Pack," he called loudly, "you kain't git away from me! If you roll bones in Hooker's Bend, you'll have to divide your winnings with the county." Dawson winked a chill eye at the crowd in general.

"But hit's out o' date, Mr. Bobbs," the old gray-headed minister, Parson Ranson, was pleading.

"May be that, Parson, but hit's easier to come up before the J. P. and pay off than to fight it through the circuit court."

Siner pushed his way through the crowd. "How much do you want, Mr. Bobbs?" he asked briefly.

The constable looked with reminiscent eyes at the tall, well-tailored negro. He was plainly going through some mental card-index, hunting for the name of Peter Siner on some long-forgotten warrant. Apparently, he discovered nothing, for he said shortly:

"How do I know before he's tried? Come on, Tump!"

The procession moved in a long noisy line up Pillow Street, the white residential street lying to the west. It stopped before a large shaded lawn, where a number of white men and women were playing a game with cards. The cards used by the lawn party were not ordinary playing-cards, but had figures on them instead of spots, and were called "rook" cards. The party of white ladies and gentlemen were playing "rook." On a table in the middle of the lawn glittered some pieces of silver plate which formed the first, second, and third prizes for the three leading scores.

The constable halted his black company before the lawn, where they stood in the sunshine patiently waiting for the justice of the peace to finish his game and hear the case of the State of Tennessee, plaintiff, versus Tump Pack, defendant.

CHAPTER II

O N the eastern edge of Hooker's Bend, drawn in a rough semicircle around the Big Hill, lies Niggertown. In all the half-moon there are perhaps not two upright buildings. The grimy cabins lean at crazy angles, some propped with poles, while others hold out against gravitation at a hazard.

Up and down its street flows the slow negro life of the village. Here children of all colors from black to cream fight and play; deep-chested negresses loiter to and fro, some on errands to the white section of the village on the other side of the hill, where they go to scrub or cook or wash or iron. Others go down to the public well with a bucket in each hand and one balanced on the head.

The public well itself lies at the southern end of this miserable street, just at a point where the drainage of the Big Hill collects. The rainfall runs down through Niggertown, under its sties, stables, and outdoor toilets, and the well supplies the negroes with water for cooking, washing, and drinking. Or, rather, what was once a well supplies this water, for it is a well no longer. Its top and curbing caved in long ago, and now there is simply a big hole in the soft, water-soaked clay, about fifteen feet wide, with water standing at the bottom.

Here come the unhurried colored women, who throw in their buckets, and with a dexterity that comes of long practice draw them out full of water. Black mothers shout at their children not to fall into this pit, and now and then, when a pig fails to come up for its evening slops, a black boy will go to the public well to see if perchance his porker has met misfortune there.

The inhabitants of Niggertown suffer from divers diseases; they develop strange ailments that no amount of physicking will overcome; young wives grow sickly from no apparent cause. Although only three or four hundred persons live in Niggertown, two or three negroes are always slowly dying of tuberculosis; winter brings pneumonia; summer, malaria. About once a year the state health officer visits Hooker's Bend and forces the white soda-water dispensers on the other side of the hill to sterilize their glasses in the name of the sovereign State of Tennessee.

The Siner home was a three-room shanty about midway in the semicircle. Peter Siner stood in the sunlight just outside the entrance, watching his old mother clean the bugs out of a tainted ham that she had bought for a pittance from some white housekeeper in the village. It had been too high for white people to eat. Old Caroline patiently tapped the honeycombed meat to scare out the last of the little green householders, and then she washed it in a solution of soda to freshen it up.

The sight of his bulky old mother working at the spoiled ham and of the negro women in the street moving to and from the infected well filled Peter Siner with its terrible pathos. Although he had seen these surroundings all of his life, he had a queer impression that he was looking upon them for the first time. During his boyhood he had accepted all this without question as the way the world was made. During his college days a criticism had arisen in his mind, but it came slowly, and was tempered by that tenderness every one feels for the spot called home. Now, as he stood looking at it, he wondered how human beings lived there at all. He wondered if Ida May used water from the Niggertown well.

He turned to ask old Caroline, but checked himself with a man's instinctive avoidance of mentioning his intimacies to his mother. At that moment, oddly enough, the old negress brought up the topic herself.

"Ida May wuz 'quirin' 'bout you las' night, Peter."

A faint tingle filtered through Peter's throat and chest, but he asked casually enough what she had said.

"Did n' say; she wrote."

Peter looked around, frankly astonished.

"Wrote?"

"Yeah; co'se she wrote."

"What made her write?" a fantasy of Ida May dumb flickered before the mulatto.

Up and down its street flows the slow negro life of the village

"Why, Ida May's in Nashville." Caroline looked at Peter. "She wrote to Cissie, astin' 'bout you. She ast is you as bright in yo' books as you is in yo' color." The old negress gave a pleased abdominal chuckle as she admired her broad-shouldered brown son.

"But I saw Ida May standing on the wharf-boat the day I came home," protested Peter, still bewildered.

"No you ain't. I reckon you seen Cissie. Dey looks kind o' like when you is fur off."

"Cissie?" repeated Peter. Then he remembered a smaller sister of Ida May's, a little, squalling, yellow, wet-nosed nuisance that had annoyed his adolescence. So that little spoil-sport had grown up into the girl he had mistaken for Ida May. This fact increased his sense of strangeness—that sense of great change that had fallen on the village in his absence which formed the groundwork of all his renewed associations.

Peter's prolonged silence aroused certain suspicions in the old negress. She glanced at her son out of the tail of her eyes.

"Cissie Dildine is Tump Pack's gal," she stated defensively, with the jealousy all mothers feel toward all sons.

A diversion in the shouts of the children up the mean street and a sudden furious barking of dogs drew Peter from the discussion. He looked up, and saw a negro girl of about fourteen coming down the curved street, with long, quick steps and an occasional glance over her shoulder.

From across the thoroughfare a small chocolate-colored woman, with her wool done in outstanding spikes, thrust her head out at the door and called:

"Whut's de matter, Ofeely?"

The girl lifted a high voice:

"Oh, Miss Nan, it's that constable goin' th'ugh the houses!" The girl veered across the street to the safety of the open door and one of her own sex.

"Good Lawd!" cried the spiked one in disgust, "ever' time a white pusson gits somp'n misplaced—" She moved to one side to allow the girl to enter, and continued staring up the street, with the whites of her eyes accented against her dark face, after the way of angry negroes.

Around the crescent the dogs were furious. They were Niggertown dogs, and the sight of a white man always drove them to a frenzy. Presently in the hullabaloo, Peter heard Dawson Bobbs's voice shouting:

"Aunt Mahaly, if you kain't call off this dawg, I'm shore goin' to kill him."

Then an old woman's scolding broke in and complicated the mêlée. Presently Peter saw the bulky form of Dawson Bobbs come around the curve, moving methodically from cabin to cabin. He held some legal-looking papers in his hands, and Peter knew what the constable was doing. He was serving a blanket search-warrant on the whole black population of Hooker's Bend. At almost every cabin a dog ran out to blaspheme at the intruder, but a wave of the man's pistol sent them yelping under the floors again.

When the constable entered a house, Peter could hear him bumping and rattling among the furnishings, while the black householders stood outside the door and watched him disturb their housekeeping arrangements.

Presently Bobbs came angling across the street toward the Siner cabin. As he entered the rickety gate, old Caroline called out:

"Whut is you after, anyway, white man?"

Bobbs turned cold, truculent eyes on the old negress. "A turkey roaster," he snapped. "Some o' you niggers stole Miss Lou Arkwright's turkey roaster."

"Tukky roaster!" cried the old black woman, in great disgust. "Whut you s'pose us niggers is got to roast in a tukky roaster?"

The constable answered shortly that his business was to find the roaster, not what the negroes meant to put in it.

"I decla'," satirized old Caroline, savagely, "dish-heah Niggertown is a white man's pocket. Ever' time he misplace somp'n, he feel in his pocket to see ef it ain't thaiuh. Don'-chu turn over dat sody-water, white man! You know dey ain't no tukky roaster under dat sody-water. I 'cla' 'fo' Gawd, ef a white man wuz to eat a flapjack, an' it did n' give him de belly-ache, I 'cla' 'fo' Gawd he 'd git out a search-wa'nt to see ef some nigger had n' stole dat flapjack goin' down his th'oat."

"Mr. Bobbs has to do his work, Mother," put in Peter. "I don't suppose he enjoys it any more than we do."

"Den let 'im git out'n dis business an' git in anudder," scolded the old woman. "Dis sho is a mighty po' business."

The ponderous Mr. Bobbs finished with a practised thoroughness his inspection of the cabin, and then the inquisition proceeded down the street, around the crescent, and so out of sight and eventually out of hearing.

Old Caroline snapped her chair back beside her greasy table and sat down abruptly to her spoiled ham again.

"Dat make me mad," she grumbled. "Ever' time a white pusson fail to lay dey han' on somp'n, dey comes an' turns over ever'thing in my house." She paused a moment, closed her eyes in thought, and then mused aloud: "I wonder who is got Miss Arkwright's roaster."

The commotion of the constable's passing died in his wake, and Niggertown resumed its careless existence. Dogs reappeared from under the cabins and stretched in the sunshine; black children came out of hiding and picked up their play; the frightened Ophelia came out of Nan's cabin across the street and went her way; a lanky negro youth in blue coat and pin-striped trousers appeared, coming down the squalid thoroughfare whistling the "Memphis Blues" with bird-like virtuosity. The lightness with which Niggertown accepted the moral side glance of a blanket search-warrant depressed Siner.

Caroline called her son to dinner, as the twelve-o'clock meal is called in Hooker's Bend, and so ended his meditation. The Harvard man went back into the kitchen and sat down at a rickety table covered with a red-checked oil-cloth. On it were spread the spoiled ham, a dish of poke salad, a corn pone, and a pot of weak coffee. A quaint old bowl held some brown sugar. The fat old negress made a slight, habitual settling movement in her chair that marked the end of her cooking and the beginning of her meal. Then she bent her grizzled, woolly head and mumbled off one of those queer old-fashioned graces which consist of a swift string of syllables without pauses between either words or sentences.

Peter sat watching his mother with a musing gaze. The kitchen was illuminated by a single small square window set high up from the floor. Now the disposition of its single ray of light over the dishes and the bowed head of the massive negress gave Peter one of those sharp, tender apprehensions of formal harmony that lie back of the genre in art. It stirred his emotion in an odd fashion. When old Caroline raised her head, she found her son staring with impersonal eyes not at herself, but at the whole room, including her. The old woman was perplexed and a little apprehensive.

"Why, son!" she ejaculated, "did n' you bow yo' haid while yo' mammy ast de grace?"

Peter was a little confused at his remissness. Then he leaned a little forward to explain the sudden glamour which for a moment had transfigured the interior of their kitchen. But even as he started to speak, he realized that what he meant to say would only confuse his mother; therefore he cast about mentally for some other explanation of his behavior, but found nothing at hand.

"I hope you ain't forgot yo' 'ligion up at de 'versity, son."

"Oh, no, no, indeed, Mother, but just at that moment, just as you bowed your head, you know, it struck me that—that there is something noble in our race." That was the best he could put it to her.

"Noble—"

"Yes. You know," he went on a little quickly, "sometimes I—I 've thought my father must have been a noble man."

The old negress became very still. She was not looking quite at her son, or yet precisely away from him.

"Uh—uh noble nigger,"—she gave her abdominal chuckle. "Why—yeah, I reckon yo' father wuz putty noble as—as niggers go." She sat looking at her son, oddly, with a faint amusement in her gross black face, when a careful voice, a very careful voice, sounded in the outer room, gliding up politely on the syllables:

"Ahnt Carolin'! oh, Ahnt Carolin', may I enter?"

The old woman stirred.

"Da' 's Cissie, Peter. Go ast her in to de fambly-room."

When Siner opened the door, the vague resemblance of the slender, creamy girl on the threshold to Ida May again struck him; but Cissie Dildine was younger, and her polished black hair lay straight on her pretty head, and was done in big, shining puffs over her ears in a way that Ida May's unruly curls would never have permitted. Her eyes were the most limpid brown Peter had ever seen, but her oval face was faintly unnatural from the use of negro face powder, which colored women insist on, and which gives their yellows and browns a barely perceptible greenish hue. Cissie wore a fluffy yellow dress some three shades deeper than the throat and the glimpse of bosom revealed at the neck.

The girl carried a big package in her arms, and now she manipulated this to put out a slender hand to Peter.

"This is Cissie Dildine, Mister Siner." She smiled up at him. "I just came over to put my name down on your list. There was such a mob at the Benevolence Hall last night I could n't get to you."

The girl had a certain finical precision to her English that told Peter she had been away to some school, and had been taught to guard her grammar very carefully as she talked.

Peter helped her inside amid the handshake and said he would go fetch the list. As he turned, Cissie offered her bundle. "Here is something I thought might be a little treat for you and Ahnt Carolin'." She paused, and then explained remotely, "Sometimes it is hard to get good things at the village market."

Peter took the package, vaguely amused at Cissie's patronage of the Hooker's Bend market. It was an attitude instinctively assumed by every girl, white or black, who leaves the village and returns. The bundle was rather large and wrapped in newspapers. He carried it into the kitchen to his mother, and then returned with the list.

The sheet was greasy from the handling of black fingers. The girl spread it on the little center-table with a certain daintiness, seated herself, and held out her hand for Peter's pencil. She made rather a graceful study in cream and yellow as she leaned over the table and signed her name in a handwriting as perfect and as devoid of character as a copy-book. She began discussing the speech Peter had made at the Benevolence Hall.

"I don't know whether I am in favor of your project or not, Mr. Siner," she said as she rose from the table.

"No?" Peter was surprised and amused at her attitude and at her precise voice.

"No, I'm rather inclined toward Mr. DuBois's

theory of a literary culture than toward Mr. Washington's plan for a purely industrial training."

Peter broke out laughing.

"For the love of Mike, Cissie, you talk like the instructor in Sociology B! And have n't we met before somewhere? This 'Mister Siner' stuff—"

The girl's face warmed under its faint, greenish powder.

"If I are n't careful with my language, Peter," she said simply, "I 'll be talking just as badly as I did before I went to the seminary. You know I never hear a proper sentence in Hooker's Bend except my own."

A certain resignation in the girl's soft voice brought Peter a qualm for laughing at her. He laid an impulsive hand on her young shoulder.

"Well, that 's true, certainly, but it won't always be like that, Cissie. More of us go off to school every year. I do hope my school here in Hooker's Bend will be of some real value. If I could just show our people how badly we fare here, how ill fed, ill housed, and unsanitary—"

The girl pressed Peter's fingers with a woman's optimism for a man.

"You 'll succeed, Peter, I know you will. Some day the name Siner will mean the same thing to colored people as Tanner and Dunbar and Braithwaite do. Anyway, I 've put my name down for ten dollars to help out." She returned the pencil. "I 'll have

Tump Pack come around and pay you my subscription, Peter."

"I 'll watch out for Tump," promised Peter in a lightening mood, "—and make him pay."

"He 'll do it."

"I don't doubt it. You ought to have him under perfect control. I meant to tell you what a pretty frock you have on."

The girl dimpled, and dropped him a little curtsy, half ironical and wholly graceful.

Peter was charmed.

"Now keep that way, Cissie, smiling and human, not so grammatical. I wish I had a brooch."

"A brooch?"

"I 'd give it to you. Your dress needs a brooch, an old gold brooch at the bosom, just a glint there to balance your eyes."

Cissie flushed happily, and made the feminine movement of concealing the V-shaped opening at her throat.

"It 's a pleasure to doll up for a man like you, Peter. You see a girl's good points—if she has any," she tacked on demurely.

"Oh, just any man—"

"Don't think it! Don't think it!" waved down Cissie, humorously.

"But, Cissie, how is it possible—"

"Just blind." Cissie rippled into a boarding-school laugh. "I could wear the whole rue del Opera here in Niggertown, and nobody would ever see it but you."

Cissie was moving toward the door. Peter tried to detain her. He enjoyed the implication of Tump Pack's stupidity, in their badinage, but she would not stay. He was finally reduced to thanking her for her present, then stood guard as she tripped out into the grimy street. In the sunshine her glossy black hair and canary dress looked as trim and brilliant as the plumage of a chaffinch.

Peter Siner walked back into the kitchen with the fixed smile of a man who is thinking of a pretty girl. The black dowager in the kitchen received him in silence, with her thick lips pouted. When Peter observed it, he felt slightly amused at his mother's resentment.

"Well, you sho had a lot o' chatter over signin' a lil ole paper."

"She signed for ten dollars," said Peter, smiling.

"Huh! she 'll never pay it."

"Said Tump Pack would pay it."

"Huh!" The old negress dropped the subject, and nodded at a huge double pan on the table. "Dat's whut she brung you." She grunted disapprovingly.

"And it 's for you, too, Mother."

"Ya-as, I 'magine she brung somp'n fuh me."

Peter walked across to the double pans, and saw they held a complete dinner—chicken, hot biscuits, cake, pickle, even ice-cream.

The sight of the food brought Peter a realization that he was keenly hungry. As a matter of fact, he had not eaten a palatable meal since he had been evicted from the white dining-car at Cairo, Illinois. Siner served his own and his mother's plate.

The old woman sniffed again.

"Seems to me lak you is mighty onobsarvin' fuh a nigger whut 's been off to college."

"Anything else?" Peter looked into the pans again.

"Ain't you see whut it 's all in?"

"What it 's in?"

"Yeah; whut it 's in. You heared whut I said."

"What is it in?"

"Why, it 's in Miss Arkwright's tukky roaster, dat 's whut it 's in." The old negress drove her point home with an acid accent.

Peter Siner was too loyal to his new friendship with Cissie Dildine to allow his mother's jealous suspicions to affect him; nevertheless the old woman's observations about the turkey roaster did prevent a complete and care-free enjoyment of the meal. Certainly, there were other turkey roasters in Hooker's Bend than Mrs. Arkwright's. Cissie might very well own a roaster. It was absurd to think that Cissie, in the midst of her almost pathetic struggle to break away from the uncouthness of Niggertown, would stoop to— Even in his thoughts Peter avoided nominating the charge.

And then, somehow, his memory fished up the fact that years ago Ida May, according to village rumor, was "light-fingered." At that time in Peter's life

"light-fingeredness" carried with it no opprobrium
whatever. It was simply a fact about Ida May, as
were her sloe eyes and curling black hair. His
reflections renewed his perpetual sense of queerness
and strangeness that hall-marked every phase of
Niggertown life since his return from the North.

Cissie Dildine's contribution tailed out the one
hundred dollars that Peter needed, and after he had
finished his meal, the mulatto set out across the Big
Hill for the white section of the village, to complete
his trade.

It was Peter's program to go to the Planter's Bank,
pay down his hundred, and receive a deed from one
Elias Tomwit, which the bank held in escrow. Two
or three days before Peter had tried to borrow the
initial hundred from the bank, but the cashier, Henry
Hooker, after going into the transaction, had declined
the loan, and therefore Siner had been forced to await
a meeting of the Sons and Daughters of Benevolence.
At this meeting the subscription had gone through
promptly. The land the negroes purposed to purchase for an industrial school was a timbered tract
lying southeast of Hooker's Bend on the head-waters
of Ross Creek. A purchase price of eight hundred dollars had been agreed upon. The timber on the tract,
sold on the stump, would bring almost that amount.
It was Siner's plan to commandeer free labor in
Niggertown, work off the timber, and have enough

money to build the first unit of his school. A number of negro men already had subscribed a certain number of days' work in the timber. It was a modest and entirely practical program, and Peter felt set up over it.

The brown man turned briskly out into the hot afternoon sunshine, down the mean semicircular street, where piccaninnies were kicking up clouds of dust. He hurried through the dusty area, and presently turned off a by-path that led over the hill, through a glade of cedars, to the white village.

The glade was gloomy, but warm, for the shade of cedars somehow seems to hold heat. A carpet of needles hushed Siner's footfalls and spread a Sabbatical silence through the grove. The upward path was not smooth, but was broken with outcrops of the same reddish limestone that marks the whole stretch of the Tennessee River. Here and there in the grove were circles eight or ten feet in diameter, brushed perfectly clean of all needles and pebbles and twigs. These places were crap-shooters' circles, where black and white men squatted to shoot dice.

Under the big stones on the hillside, Peter knew, was cached illicit whisky, and at night the boot-leggers carried on a brisk trade among the gamblers. More than that, the glade on the Big Hill was used for still more demoralizing ends. It became a squalid grove of Ashtoreth; but now, in the autumn evening, all the petty obscenities of white and black sloughed away amid the religious implications of the dark-green aisles.

The sight of a white boy sitting on an outcrop of limestone with a strap of school-books dropped at his feet rather surprised Peter. The negro looked at the hobbledehoy for several seconds before he recognized in the lanky youth a little Arkwright boy whom he had known and played with in his pre-college days. Now there was such an exaggerated wistfulness in young Arkwright's attitude that Peter was amused.

"Hello, Sam," he called. "What you doing out here?"

The Arkwright boy turned with a start.

"Aw, is that you, Siner?" Before the negro could reply, he added: "Was you on the Harvard football team, Siner? Guess the white fellers have a pretty gay time in Harvard, don't they, Siner? Geemenettie! but I git tired o' this dern town! D' reckon I could make the football team? Looks like I could if a nigger like you could, Siner."

None of this juvenile outbreak of questions required answers. Peter stood looking at the hobbledehoy without smiling.

"Aren't you going to school?" he asked.

Arkwright shrugged.

"Aw, hell!" he said self-consciously. "We got marched down to the protracted meetin' while ago—whole school did. My seat happened to be close to a window. When they all stood up to sing, I crawled out and skipped. Don't mention that, Siner."

"I won't."

"When a fellow goes to college he don't git marched to preachin', does he, Siner?"

"I never did."

"We-e-ll," mused young Sam, doubtfully, "you're a nigger."

"I never saw any white men marched in, either."

"Oh, hell! I wish I was in college."

"What are you sitting out here thinking about?" inquired Peter of the ingenuous youngster.

"Oh—football and—women and God and—how to stack cards. You think about ever'thing, in the woods. Damn it! I got to git out o' this little jay town. D' reckon I could git in the navy, Siner?"

"Don't see why you could n't, Sam. Have you seen Tump Pack anywhere?"

"Yeah; on Hobbett's corner. Say, is Cissie Dildine at home?"

"I believe she is."

"She cooks for us," explained young Arkwright, "and Mammy wants her to come and git supper, too."

The phrase "get supper, too," referred to the custom in the white homes of Hooker's Bend of having only two meals cooked a day, breakfast and the twelve-o'clock dinner, with a hot supper optional with the mistress.

Peter nodded, and passed on up the path, leaving young Arkwright seated on the ledge of rock, a prey to all the boiling, erratic impulses of adolescence. The negro sensed some of the innumerable difficulties of this white boy's life, and once, as he walked on over the silent needles, he felt an impulse to turn back and talk to young Sam Arkwright, to sit down and try to explain to the youth what he could of this hazardous adventure called Life. But then, he reflected, very likely the boy would be offended at a serious talk from a negro. Also, he thought that young Arkwright, being white, was really not within the sphere of his ministry. He, Peter Siner, was a worker in the black world of the South. He was part of the black world which the white South was so meticulous to hide away, to keep out of sight and out of thought.

A certain vague sense of triumph trickled through some obscure corner of Peter's mind. It was so subtle that Peter himself would have been the first, in all good faith, to deny it and to affirm that all his motives were altruistic. Once he looked back through the cedars. He could still see the boy hunched over, chin in fist, staring at the mat of needles.

As Peter turned the brow of the Big Hill, he saw at its eastern foot the village church, a plain brick building with a decaying spire. Its side was perforated by four tall arched windows. Each was a memorial window of stained glass, which gave the building a black look from the outside. As Peter walked down the hill toward the church he heard the confused and somewhat nasal singing of uncultivated white voices mingled with the snoring of a reed organ.

When he reached Main Street, Peter found the whole business portion virtually deserted. All the stores were closed, and in every show-window stood a printed notice that no business would be transacted between the hours of two and three o'clock in the afternoon during the two weeks of revival then in progress. Beside this notice stood another card, giving the minister's text for the current day. On this particular day it read:

GO YE INTO ALL THE WORLD
Come hear Rev. E. B. Blackwater's great
Missionary Address on
CHRISTIANIZING AFRICA
ELOQUENT, PROFOUND, HEART-SEARCHING.
ILLUSTRATED WITH SLIDES.

Half a dozen negroes lounged in the sunshine on Hobbett's corner as Peter came up. They were amusing themselves after the fashion of blacks, with mock fights, feints, sudden wrestlings. They would seize one another by the head and grind their knuckles into one another's wool. Occasionally, one would leap up and fall into one of those grotesque shuffles called "breakdowns." It all held a certain rawness, an irrepressible juvenility.

As Peter came up, Tump Pack detached himself from the group and gave a pantomime of thrusting.

He was clearly reproducing the action which had won for him his military medal. Then suddenly he fell down in the dust and writhed. He was mimicking with a ghastly realism the death-throes of his four victims. His audience howled with mirth at this dumb show of the bayonet-fight and of killing four men. Tump himself got up out of the dust with tears of laughter in his eyes. Peter caught the end of his sentence, "Sho put it to 'em, black boy. Fo' white men—"

His audience roared again, swayed around, and pounded one another in an excess of mirth.

Siner shouted from across the street two or three times before he caught Tump's attention. The ex-soldier looked around, sobered abruptly.

"Whut-chu want, nigger?" His inquiry was not over-cordial.

Peter nodded him across the street.

The heavily built black in khaki hesitated a moment, then started across the street with the dragging feet of a reluctant negro. Peter looked at him as he came up.

"What's the matter, Tump?" he asked playfully.

"Ain't nothin' matter wid me, nigger."

Peter made a guess at Tump's surliness.

"Look here, are you puffed up because Cissie Dildine struck you for a ten?"

Tump's expression changed.

"Is she struck me fuh a ten?"

"Yes; on that school subscription."

"Is dat whut you two niggers wuz a-talkin' 'bout over thaiuh in yo' house?"

"Exactly." Peter showed the list, with Cissie's name on it. "She told me to collect from you."

Tump brightened up.

"So dat wuz whut you two niggers wuz a-talkin' 'bout over at yo' house." He ran a fist down into his khaki, and drew out three or four one-dollar bills and about a pint of small change. It was the usual crap-shooter's offering. The two negroes sat down on the ramshackle porch of an old jeweler's shop, and Tump began a complicated tally of ten dollars.

By the time he had his dimes, quarters, and nickels in separate stacks, services in the village church were finished, and the congregation came filing up the street. First came the school-children, running and chattering and swinging their books by the straps; then the business men of the hamlet, rather uncomfortable in coats and collars, hurrying back to their stores; finally came the women, surrounding the preacher.

Tump and Peter walked on up to the entrance of the Planter's Bank and there awaited Mr. Henry Hooker, the cashier. Presently a skinny man detached himself from the church crowd and came angling across the dirty street toward the bank. Mr. Hooker wore somewhat shabby clothes for a banker; in fact, he never could recover from certain personal habits formed during a penurious boyhood. He had a thin hatchet face which just at this moment was shining as though from some inward glow. Although he was an unhandsome little man, his expression was that of one at peace with man and God and was pleasant to see. He had been so excited by the minister that he was constrained to say something even to two negroes. So as he unlocked the little one-story bank, he told Tump and Peter that he had been listening to a man who was truly a man of God. He said Blackwater could touch the hardest heart, and, sure enough, Mr. Hooker's rather popped and narrow-set eyes looked as though he had been crying.

All this encomium was given in a high, cracked voice as the cashier opened the door and turned the negroes into the bank. Tump, who stood with his hat off, listening to all the cashier had to say, said he thought so, too.

The shabby interior of the little bank, the shabby little banker, renewed that sense of disillusion that pervaded Peter's home-coming. In Boston the mulatto had done his slight banking business in a white marble structure with tellers of machine-like briskness and neatness.

Mr. Hooker strolled around into his grill-cage; when he was thoroughly ensconced he began business in his high voice:

"You came to see me about that land, Peter?"

"Yes, sir."

"Sorry to tell you, Peter, you are not back in time to get the Tomwit place."

Peter came out of his musing over the Boston banks with a sense of bewilderment.

"How's that? why, I bought that land—"

"But you paid nothing for your option, Siner."

"I had a clear-cut understanding with Mr. Tomwit—"

Mr. Hooker smiled a smile that brought out sharp wrinkles around the thin nose on his thin face.

"You should have paid him an earnest, Siner, if you wanted to bind your trade. You colored folks are always stumbling over the law."

Peter stared through the grating, not knowing what to do.

"I'll go see Mr. Tomwit," he said, and started uncertainly for the door.

The cashier's falsetto stopped him:

"No use, Peter. Mr. Tomwit surprised me, too, but no use talking about it. I didn't like to see such an important thing as the education of our colored people held up, myself. I've been thinking about it."

"Especially when I had made a fair square trade," put in Peter, warmly.

"Exactly," squeaked the cashier. "And rather than let your project be delayed, I'm going to offer you the old Dillihay place at exactly the same price, Peter —eight hundred."

"The Dillihay place?"

"Yes; that's west of town; it's bigger by twenty acres than old man Tomwit's place."

Peter considered the proposition.

"I'll have to carry this before the Sons and Daughters of Benevolence, Mr. Hooker."

The cashier repeated the smile that bracketed his thin nose in wrinkles.

"That's with you, but you know what you say goes with the niggers here in town, and, besides, I won't promise how long I'll hold the Dillihay place. Real estate is brisk around here now. I didn't want to delay a good work on account of not having a location." Mr. Hooker turned away to a big ledger on a breast-high desk, and apparently was about to settle himself to the endless routine of bank work.

Peter knew the Dillihay place well. It lacked the timber of the other tract; still, it was fairly desirable. He hesitated before the tarnished grill.

"What do you think about it, Tump?"

"You won't make a mistake in buying," answered the high voice of Mr. Hooker at his ledger.

"I don' think you'll make no mistake in buyin', Peter," repeated Tump's bass.

Peter turned back a little uncertainly, and asked how long it would take to fix the new deed. He had a notion of making a flying canvass of the officers of the Sons and Daughters in the interim. He was surprised to find that Mr. Hooker already had the deed and the notes ready to sign, in anticipation of

Peter's desires. Here the banker brought out the set of papers.

"I 'll take it," decided Peter; "and if the lodge does n't want it, I 'll keep the place myself."

"I like to deal with a man of decision," piped the cashier, a wrinkled smile on his sharp face.

Peter pushed in his bag of collections, then Mr. Hooker signed the deed, and Peter signed the land notes. They exchanged the instruments. Peter received the crisp deed, bound in blue manuscript cover. It rattled unctuously. To Peter it was his first step toward a second Tuskegee.

The two negroes walked out of the Planter's Bank filled with a sense of well-doing. Tump Pack was openly proud of having been connected, even in a casual way, with the purchase. As he walked down the steps, he turned to Peter.

"Don' reckon nobody could git a deed off on you wid stoppers in it, does you?"

"We don't know any such word as 'stop,' Tump," declared Peter, gaily.

For Peter was gay. The whole incident at the bank was beginning to please him. The meeting of a sudden difficulty, his quick decision—it held the quality of leadership. Napoleon had it.

The two colored men stepped briskly through the afternoon sunshine along the mean village street. Here and there in front of their doorways sat the merchants, yawning and talking, or watching pigs root in the piles of waste.

In Peter's heart came a wonderful thought. He would make his industrial institution such a model of neatness that the whole village of Hooker's Bend would catch the spirit. The white people should see that something clean and uplifting could come out of Niggertown. The two races ought to live for a mutual benefit. It was a fine, generous thought. For some reason, just then, there flickered through Peter's mind a picture of the Arkwright boy sitting hunched over in the cedar glade, staring at the needles.

All this musing was brushed away by the sight of old Mr. Tomwit crossing the street from the east side to the livery-stable on the west. That human desire of wanting the person who has wronged you to know that you know your injury moved Peter to hurry his steps and to speak to the old gentleman.

Mr. Tomwit had been a Confederate cavalryman in the Civil War, and there was still a faint breeze and horsiness about him. He was a hammered-down old gentleman, with hair thin but still jet-black, a seamed, sunburned face, and a flattened nose. His voice was always a friendly roar. Now, when he saw Peter turning across the street to meet him, he halted and called out at once:

"Now, Peter, I know what's the matter with you. I did n't do you right."

Peter went closer, not caring to take the whole village into his confidence.

"How came you to turn down my proposition, Mr. Tomwit," he asked, "after we had agreed and drawn up the papers?"

"We-e-ell, I had to do it, Peter," explained the old man, loudly.

"Why, Mr. Tomwit?"

"A white neighbor wanted me to, Peter," boomed the cavalryman.

"Who, Mr. Tomwit?"

"Henry Hooker talked me into it, Peter. It was a mean trick, Peter. I done you wrong." He stood nodding his head and rubbing his flattened nose in an impersonal manner. "Yes, I done you wrong, Peter," he acknowledged loudly, and looked frankly into Peter's eyes.

The negro was immensely surprised that Henry Hooker had done such a thing. A thought came that perhaps some other Henry Hooker had moved into town in his absence.

"You don't mean the cashier of the bank?"

Old Mr. Tomwit drew out a plug of Black Mule tobacco, set some gapped, discolored teeth into a corner, nodded at Peter silently, at the same time utilizing the nod to tear off a large quid. He rolled this about with his tongue and after a few moments adjusted it so that he could speak.

"Yeah," he proceeded in a muffled tone, "they ain't

but one Henry Hooker; he is the one and only Henry.
He said if I sold you my land, you'd put up a nigger
school and bring in so many blackbirds you'd run me
clean off my farm. He said it'd ruin the whole town,
a nigger school would."

Peter was astonished.

"Why, he didn't talk that way to me!"

"Natchelly, natchelly," agreed the old cavalryman,
dryly. "Henry has a different way to talk to ever'
man, Peter."

"In fact," proceeded Peter, "Mr. Hooker sold me
the old Dillihay place in lieu of the deal I missed with
you."

Old Mr. Tomwit moved his quid in surprise.

"The hell he did!"

"That at least shows he doesn't think a negro
school would ruin the value of his land. He owns
farms all around the Dillihay place."

Old Mr. Tomwit turned his quid over twice and
spat thoughtfully.

"That your deed in your pocket?" With the air of
a man certain of being obeyed he held out his hand for
the blue manuscript cover protruding from the mulatto's pocket. Peter handed it over. The old gentleman unfolded the deed, then moved it carefully to and
from his eyes until the typewriting was adjusted to
his focus. He read it slowly, with a movement of
his lips and a drooling of tobacco-juice. Finally he
finished, remarked, "I be damned!" in a deliberate

voice, returned the deed, and proceeded across the street to the livery-stable, which was fronted by an old mulberry-tree, with several chairs under it. In one of these chairs he would sit for the remainder of the day, making an occasional loud remark about the weather or the crops, and watching the horses pass in and out of the stable.

Siner had vaguely enjoyed old Mr. Tomwit's discomfiture over the deed, if it was discomfiture that had moved the old gentleman to his sententious profanity. But the negro did not understand Henry Hooker's action at all. The banker had abused his position of trust as holder of a deed in escrow by snapping up the sale himself; then he had sold Peter the Dillihay place. It was a queer shift.

Tump Pack caught his principal's mood with that chameleon-like mental quality all negroes possess.

"Dat Henry Hooker," criticized Tump, "allus wuz a lil ole dried-up snake in de grass."

"He abused his position of trust," said Peter, gloomily; "I must say, his motives seem very obscure to me."

"Dat sho am a fine way to put hit," said Tump, admiringly.

"Why do you suppose he bought in the Tomwit tract and sold me the Dillihay place?"

Asked for an opinion, Tump began twiddling his military medal and corrugated the skin on his inch-high brow.

"Now you puts it to me lak dat, Peter," he answered with importance, "I wonders ef dat gimlet-haided white man ain't put some stoppers in dat deed he guv you. He mout of."

Such remarks as that from Tump always annoyed Peter. Tump's intellectual method was to talk sense just long enough to gain his companion's ear, and then produce something absurd and quash the tentative interest.

Siner turned away from him and said, "Piffle."

Tump was defensive at once.

"'T ain't piffle, either! I's talkin' sense, nigger."

Peter shrugged, and walked a little way in silence, but the soldier's nonsense stuck in his brain and worried him. Finally he turned, rather irritably.

"Stoppers—what do you mean by stoppers?"

Tump opened his jet eyes and their yellowish whites. "I means nigger-stoppers," he reiterated, amazed in his turn.

"Negro-stoppers—" Peter began to laugh sardonically, and abruptly quit the conversation.

Such rank superiority irritated the soldier to the nth power.

"Look heah, black man, I knows I *is* right. Heah, lemme look at dat-aiuh deed. Maybe I can find 'em. I knows I suttinly is right."

Peter walked on, paying no attention to the request until Tump caught his arm and drew him up short.

"Look heah, nigger," said Tump, in a different

tone, "I faded dad deed fuh ten iron men, an' I reckon I got a once-over comin' fuh my money."

The soldier was plainly mobilized and ready to attack. To fight Tump, to fight any negro at all, would be Peter's undoing; it would forfeit the moral leadership he hoped to gain. Moreover, he had no valid grounds for a disagreement with Tump. He passed over the deed, and the two negroes moved on their way to Niggertown.

Tump trudged forward with eyes glued to paper, his face puckered in the unaccustomed labor of reading. His thick lips moved at the individual letters, and constructed them bunglingly into syllables and words. He was trying to uncover the verbal camouflage by which the astute white brushed away all rights of all black men whatsoever.

To Peter there grew up something sadly comical in Tump's efforts. The big negro might well typify all the colored folk of the South, struggling in a web of law and custom they did not understand, misplacing their suspicions, befogged and fearful. A certain penitence for having been irritated at Tump softened Peter.

"That's all right, Tump; there 's nothing to find."

At that moment the soldier began to bob his head.

"Eh! eh! eh! W-wait a minute!" he stammered. "Whut dis? B'lieve I done foun' it! I sho is! Heah she am! Heah 's dis nigger-stopper, jes lak I tol' you!" Tump marked a sentence in the guaranty of the deed with a rusty forefinger and looked up at Peter in mixed triumph and accusation.

Peter leaned over the deed, amused.

"Let 's see your mare's nest."

"Well, she 'fo' God is thaiuh, an' you sho let loose a hundud dollars uv our 'ciety's money, an' got nothin' fuh hit but a piece o' paper wid a nigger-stopper on hit!"

Tump's voice was so charged with contempt that Peter looked with a certain uneasiness at his find. He read this sentence switched into the guaranty of the indenture:

Be it further understood and agreed that no negro, black man, Afro-American, mulatto, quadroon, octoroon, or any person whatsoever of colored blood or lineage, shall enter upon, seize, hold, occupy, reside upon, till, cultivate, own or possess any part or parcel of said property, or garner, cut, or harvest therefrom, any of the usufruct, timber, or emblements thereof, but shall by these presents be estopped from so doing forever."

Tump Pack drew a shaken, unhappy breath.

"Now, I reckon you see whut a nigger-stopper is."

Peter stood in the sunshine, looking at the estoppel clause, his lips agape. Twice he read it over. It held something of the quality of those comprehensive curses that occur in the Old Testament. He moistened his lips and looked at Tump.

"Why, that can't be legal." His voice sounded empty and shallow.

"Legal! 'Fo' Gawd, nigger, whauh you been to school all dese yeahs, never to heah uv a nigger-stopper befo'!"

"But—but how can a stroke of the pen, a mere gesture, estop a whole class of American citizens forever?" cried Peter, with a rising voice. "Turn it around. Suppose they had put in a line that no white man should own that land. It—it's empty! I tell you, it's mere words!"

Tump cut into his diatribe: "No use talkin' lak dat. Our 'ciety thought you wuz a aidjucated nigger. We did n't think no white man could put nothin' over on you."

"Education!" snapped Siner. "Education is n't supposed to keep you away from shysters!"

"Keep you away fum 'em!" cried Tump, in a scandalized voice. "'Fo' Gawd, nigger, you don' know nothin'! O' co'se a aidjucation ain't to keep you away fum shysters; hit's to mek you one 'uv 'em!"

Peter stood breathing irregularly, looking at his deed. A determination not to be cheated grew up and hardened in his nerves. With unsteady hands he refolded his deed and put it into his pocket, then he turned about and started back up the village street toward the bank.

Tump stared after him a moment and presently called out:

"Heah, nigger, whut you gwine do?" A moment

later he repeated to his friend's back: "Look heah, nigger, I 'vise you ag'inst anything you's gwine do, less 'n you's ready to pass in yo' checks!" As Peter strode on he lifted his voice still higher: "Peter! Hey, Peter, I sho' 'vise you 'g'inst anything you's 'gwine do!"

A pulse throbbed in Siner's temples. The wrath of the cozened heated his body. His clothes felt hot. As he strode up the trash-piled street, the white merchants lolling in their doors began smiling. Presently a laugh broke out at one end of the street and was caught up here and there. It was the undying minstrel jest, the comedy of a black face. Dawson Bobbs leaned against the wide brick entrance of the livery-stable, his red face balled into shining convexities by a quizzical smile.

"Hey, Peter," he drawled, winking at old Mr. Tomwit, "been investin' in real estate?" and broke into Homeric laughter.

As Peter passed on, the constable dropped casually in behind the brown man and followed him up to the bank.

To Peter Siner the walk up to the bank was an emotional confusion. He had a dim consciousness that voices said things to him along the way and that there was laughter. All this was drowned by desperate thoughts and futile plans to regain his lost money, flashing through his head. The cashier would exchange the money for the deed; he would enter suit and carry it to the Supreme Court; he would show the money had not been his, he had had no right to buy; he would beg the cashier. His head seemed to spin around and around.

He climbed the steps into the Planter's Bank and opened the screen-door. The cashier glanced up briefly, but continued busily at his ledger.

Peter walked shakenly to the barred window in the grill.

"Mr. Hooker."

"Very busy now, Peter," came the high voice.

"I want to know about this deed."

The banker was nimbly setting down long rows of figures. "No time to explain deeds, Peter."

"But—but there is a clause in this deed, Mr. Hooker, estopping colored persons from occupying the Dillihay place."

"Precisely. What about it?" Mr. Hooker snapped out his inquiry and looked up suddenly, catching Peter full in the face with his narrow-set eyes. It was the equivalent of a blow.

"According to this, I—I can't establish a school on it."

"You cannot."

"Then what can I do with it?" cried Peter.

"Sell it. You have what lawyers call a cloud on the title. Sell it. I'll give you ten dollars for your right in it, just to clear up my title."

A queer trembling seized Peter. The little banker turned into a fantastic caricature of a man. His hatchet face, close-set eyes, harsh, straight hair, and squeaky voice made him seem like some prickly, dried-up gnome a man sees in a fever.

At that moment the little wicket-door of the window opened under the pressure of Peter's shoulder. Inside, on the desk, lay neat piles of bills of all denominations, ready to be placed in the vault. In a nervous tremor Peter dropped in his blue-covered deed and picked up a hundred-dollar bill.

"I—I won't trade," he jibbered. "It—it was n't my money. Here's your deed!" Peter was moving away. He felt a terrific impulse to run, but he walked.

The banker straightened abruptly. "Stop there, Peter!" he screeched.

At that moment Dawson Bobbs lounged in at the door, with his perpetual grin balling up his broad red face. He had a toothpick in his mouth.

"'S matter?" he asked casually.

"Peter there," said the banker, with a pale, sharp face, "does n't want to stick to his trade. He is just walking off with one of my hundred-dollar bills."

"Sick o' yo' deal, Peter?" inquired Bobbs, smiling and shifting the toothpick. He bit down on it. "Well, whut-chu want done, Henry?"

"Oh," hesitated the cashier in a quandary, "nothing, I suppose. Siner was excited; you know how niggers are. We can't afford to send every nigger to the pen that breaks the law." He stood studying Peter out of his close-set eyes. "Here's your deed, Peter." He shoved it back under the grill. "And lemme give you a little friendly advice. I'd just run an ordinary nigger school if I was you. This higher education don't seem to make a nigger much smarter when he comes back than when he starts out." A faint smile bracketed the thin nose.

Dawson Bobbs roared with sudden appreciation, took the bill from Peter's fingers, and pushed it back under the grill.

The cashier picked up the money, casually. He considered a moment, then reached for a long envelop. As he did so, the incident with Peter evidently passed from his mind, for his hatchet face lighted up as with some inward illumination.

"Bobbs," he said warmly, "that was a great sermon Brother Blackwater preached. It made me want to help according as the Lord has blessed me. Couldn't you spare five dollars, Bobbs, to go along with this?"

The constable tried to laugh and wriggle away, but the cashier's gimlet eyes kept boring him, and eventually he fished out a five-dollar bill and handed it in. Mr. Hooker placed the two bills in the envelop, sealed it, and handed it to the constable.

"Jest drop that in the post-office as you go down the street, Bobbs," he directed in his high voice.

Peter caught a glimpse of the type-written address.
It was

Rev. Lemuel Hardiman,
c/o United Missions,
Katuako Post,
Bahr el Ghazal,
Sudan,
East Africa.

CHAPTER III

THE white population of Hooker's Bend was much amused and gratified at the outcome of the Hooker-Siner land deal. Every one agreed that the cashier's chicanery was a droll and highly original turn to give to a negro exclusion clause drawn into a deed. Then, too, it involved several legal points highly congenial to the Hooker's Bend intellect. Could the Sons and Daughters of Benevolence recover their hundred dollars? Could Henry Hooker force them to pay the remaining seven hundred? Could not Siner establish his school on the Dillihay place regardless of the clause, since the cashier would be estopped from obtaining an injunction by his own instrument?

As a matter of fact, the Sons and Daughters of Benevolence sent a committee to wait on Mr. Hooker to see what action he meant to take on the notes that paid for his spurious deed. This brought another harvest of rumors. Street gossip reported that Henry had compromised for this, that, and the other amount, that he would not compromise, that he had persuaded the fool niggers into signing still other instruments. Peter never knew the truth. He was not on the committee.

But high above the legal phase of interest lay the warming fact that Peter Siner, a negro graduate of

Harvard, on his first tilt in Hooker's Bend affairs had ridden to a fall. This pleased even the village women, whose minds could not follow the subtle trickeries of legal disputation. The whole affair simply proved what the white village had known all along: you can't educate a nigger. Hooker's Bend warmed with pleasure that half of its population was ineducable.

White sentiment in Hooker's Bend reacted strongly on Niggertown. Peter Siner's prestige was no more. The cause of higher education for negroes took a mighty slump. Junius Gholston, a negro boy who had intended to go to Nashville to attend Fisk University, reconsidered the matter, packed away his good clothes, put on overalls, and shipped down the river as a roustabout instead.

In the Siner cabin old Caroline Siner berated her boy for his stupidity in ever trading with that low-down, twisting snake in the grass, Henry Hooker. She alternated this with floods of tears. Caroline had no sympathy for her offspring. She said she had thrown away years of self-sacrifice, years of washing, a thousand little comforts her money would have bought, all for nothing, for less than nothing, to ship a fool nigger up North and to ship him back.

Of all Niggertown, Caroline was the most unforgiving because Peter had wounded her in her pride. Every other negro in the village felt that genial satisfaction in a great man's downfall that is balm to small souls. But the old mother knew not this consolation.

Peter was her proxy. It was she who had fallen.

The only person in Niggertown who continued amiable to Peter Siner was Cissie Dildine. The octoroon, perhaps, had other criteria by which to judge a man than his success or mishap in dealing with a pettifogger.

Two or three days after the catastrophe, Cissie made an excursion to the Siner cabin with a plate of cookies. Cissie was careful to place her visit on exactly a normal footing. She brought her little cakes in the rôle of one who saw no evil, spoke no evil, and heard no evil. But somehow Cissie's visit increased the old woman's wrath. She remained obstinately in the kitchen, and made remarks not only audible, but arresting, through the thin partition that separated it from the poor living-room.

Cissie was hardly inside when a voice stated that it hated to see a gal running after a man, trying to bait him with a lot of fum-diddles.

Cissie gave Peter a single wide-eyed glance, and then attempted to ignore the bodiless comment.

"Here are some cookies, Mr. Siner," began the girl, rather nervously. "I thought you and Ahnt Carolin'—"

"Yeah, I 'magine dey's fuh me!" jeered the spectral voice.

"Might like them," concluded the girl, with a little gasp.

"I suttinly don' want no light-fingered hussy ma'yin'

In the Siner cabin old Caroline Siner berated her boy

my son," proceeded the voice, "an' de whole Dildine fambly 'll bear watchin'."

"Won't you have a seat?" asked Peter, exquisitely uncomfortable.

Cissie handed him her plate in confusion.

"Why, no, Mr. Siner," she hastened on, in her careful grammar, "I just—ran over to—"

"To fling herse'f in a nigger's face 'cause he 's been North and got made a fool uv," boomed the hidden censor.

"I must go now," gasped Cissie.

Peter made a harried gesture.

"Wait—wait till I get my hat."

He put the plate down with a swift glance around for his hat. He found it, and strode to the door, following the girl. The two hurried out into the street, followed by indistinct strictures from the kitchen. Cissie breathed fast, with open lips. They moved rapidly along the semicircular street almost with a sense of flight. The heat of the early autumn sun stung them through their clothes. For some distance they walked in a nervous silence, then Cissie said:

"Your mother certainly hates me, Peter."

"No," said Peter, trying to soften the situation; "it 's me; she 's terribly hurt about—" he nodded toward the white section—"that business."

Cissie opened her clear brown eyes.

"Your own mother turned against you!"

"Oh, she has a right to be," began Peter, defensively. "I ought to have read that deed. It's amazing I did n't, but I—I really was n't expecting a trick. Mr. Hooker seemed so—so sympathetic—" He came to a lame halt, staring at the dust through which they picked their way.

"Of course you were n't expecting tricks!" cried Cissie, warmly. "The whole thing shows you 're a gentleman used to dealing with gentlemen. But of course these Hooker's Bend negroes will never see that!"

Peter, surprised and grateful, looked at Cissie. Her construction of the swindle was more flattering than any apology he had been able to frame for himself.

"Still, Cissie, I ought to have used the greatest care—"

"I 'm not talking about what you 'ought,'" stated the octoroon, crisply; "I 'm talking about what you are. When it comes to 'ought,' we colored people must get what we can, any way we can. We fight from the bottom." The speech held a viperish quality which for a moment caught the brown man's attention; then he said:

"One thing is sure, I 've lost my prestige, whatever it was worth."

The girl nodded slowly.

"With the others you have, I suppose."

Peter glanced at Cissie. The temptation was strong

to give the conversation a personal turn, but he continued on the general topic:

"Well, perhaps it's just as well. My prestige was a bit too flamboyant, Cissie. All I had to do was to mention a plan. The Sons and Daughters did n't even discuss it. They put it right through. That was n't healthy. Our whole system of society, all democracies are based on discussion. Our old Witenagemot—"

"But it was n't *our* old Witenagemot," said the girl.

"Well—no," admitted the mulatto, "that's true."

They moved along for some distance in silence, when the girl asked:

"What are you going to do now, Peter?"

"Teach, and keep working for that training-school," stated Peter, almost belligerently. "You did n't expect a little thing like a hundred dollars to stop me, did you?"

"No-o-o," conceded Cissie, with some reserve of judgment in her tone. Presently she added, "You could do a lot better up North, Peter."

"For whom?"

"Why, yourself," said the girl, a little surprised.

Siner nodded.

"I thought all that out before I came back here, Cissie. A friend of mine named Farquhar offered me a place with him up in Chicago,—a string of garages. You'd like Farquhar, Cissie. He's a materialist with an absolutely inexorable brain. He mechanizes the universe. I told him I could n't take his offer. 'It's like this,' I argued: 'if every negro with a little ability leaves the South, our people down there will never progress.' It's really that way, Cissie, it takes a certain mental atmosphere to develop a people as a whole. A few individuals here and there may have the strength to spring up by themselves, but the run of the people —no. I believe one of the greatest curses of the colored race in the South is the continual draining of its best individuals North. Farquhar argued—" Just then Peter saw that Cissie was not attending his discourse. She was walking at his side in a respectful silence. He stopped talking, and presently she smiled and said:

"You have n't noticed my new brooch, Peter." She lifted her hand to her bosom, and twisted the face of the trinket toward him. "You ought n't to have made me show it to you after you recommended it yourself." She made a little *moue* of disappointment.

It was a pretty bit of old gold that complimented the creamy skin. Peter began admiring it at once, and, negro fashion, rather overstepped the limits white beaux set to their praise, as he leaned close to her.

At the moment the two were passing one of the oddest houses in Niggertown. It was a two-story cabin built in the shape of a steamboat. A little cupola represented a pilot-house, and two iron chimneys served for smoke-stacks.

This queer building had been built by a negro stevedore because of a deep admiration for the steamboats on which he had made his living. Instead of steps at the front door, this boat-like house had a stage-plank. As Peter strolled down the street with Cissie, admiring her brooch, and suffused with a sense of her nearness, he happened to glance up, and saw Tump Pack walk down the stage-plank, come out, and wait for them at the gate.

There was something grim in the ex-soldier's face and in the set of his gross lips as the two came up, but the aura of the girl prevented Peter from paying much attention to it. As the two reached Tump, Peter had just lifted his hand to his hat when Tump made a quick step out at the gate, in front of them, and swung a furious blow at Peter's head.

Cissie screamed. Siner staggered back with flames dancing before his eyes. The soldier lunged after his toppling man with gorilla-like blows. Hot pains shot through Peter's body. His head roared like a gong. The sunlight danced about him in flashes. The air was full of black fists smashing him, and not five feet away, the bullet head of Tump Pack bobbed this way and that in the rapid shifts of his attack. A stab of pain cut off Peter's breath. He stood with his diaphragm muscles tense and paralyzed, making convulsive efforts to breathe. At that moment he glimpsed the convexity of Tump's stomach. He drop-kicked at it with foot-ball desperation. Came a loud explosive groan. Tump seemed to rise a foot or two in air, turned over, and thudded down on his shoulders in the dust. The soldier made no attempt to rise, but curled up, twisting in agony.

Peter stood in the dust-cloud, wabbly, with roaring head. His open mouth was full of dust. Then he became aware that negroes were running in from every direction, shouting. Their voices whooped out what had happened, who it was, who had licked. Tump Pack's agonized spasms brought howls of mirth from the black fellows. Negro women were in the crowd, grinning, a little frightened, but curious. Some were in Mother-Hubbards; one had her hair half combed, one side in a kinky mattress, the other lying flat and greased down to her scalp.

When Peter gradually became able to breathe and could think at all, there was something terrible to him in Tump's silent attack and in this extravagant black mirth over mere suffering. Cissie was gone,—had fled, no doubt, at the beginning of the fight.

The prostrate man's tortured abdomen finally allowed him to twist around toward Peter. His eyes were popped, and seemed all yellows and streaked with swollen veins.

"I 'll git you fuh dis," he wheezed, spitting dust. "You did n' fight fair, you—"

The black chorus rolled their heads and pounded one another in a gale of merriment.

Peter Siner turned away toward his home filled with sick thought. He had never realized so clearly the open sore of Niggertown life and its great need of healing, yet this very episode would further bar him, Peter, from any constructive work. He foresaw, too plainly, how the white town and Niggertown would react to this fight. There would be no discrimination in the scandal. He, Peter Siner, would be grouped with the boot-leggers and crap-shooters and women-chasers who filled Niggertown with their brawls. As a matter of simple fact, he had been fighting with another negro over a woman. That he was subjected to an attack without warning or cause would never become a factor in the analysis. He knew that very well.

Two of Peter's teeth were loose; his left jaw was swelling; his head throbbed. With that queer perversity of human nerves, he kept biting his sore teeth together as he walked along.

When he reached home, his mother met him at the door. Thanks to the swiftness with which gossip spreads among black folk, she had already heard of the fight, and incidentally had formed her judgment of the matter. Now she looked in exasperation at her son's swelling face.

"I 'cla' 'fo' Gawd!—ain't been home a week befo' he 's fightin' over a nigger wench lak a roustabout!"

Peter's head throbbed so he could hardly make out the details of Caroline's face.

"But, Mother—" he began defensively, "I—"

"Me sweatin' over de wash-pot," the negress went on, "so 's you could go up North an' learn a lil sense; heah you comes back chasin' a dutty slut!"

"But, Mother," he begged thickly, "I was simply walking home with Miss Dildine."

"Miss Dildine! Miss Dildine!" exploded the ponderous woman, with an erasing gesture. "Ef you means dat stuck-up fly-by-night Cissie Dildine, say so, and don' stan' thaiuh mouthin', 'Miss Dildine, Miss Dildine'!"

"Mother," asked Peter, thickly, through his swelling mouth, "do you want to know what did happen?"

"I knows. I tol' you to keep away fum dat hussy. She's a fool 'bout her bright color an' straight hair. Need n't be givin' herse'f no airs!"

Peter stood in the doorway, steadying himself by the jamb. The world still swayed from the blows he had received on the head.

"What girl would you be willing for me to go with?" he asked in faint satire.

"Heah in Niggertown?"

Peter nodded. The movement increased his headache.

"None a-tall. No Niggertown wench a-tall. When you mus' ma'y, I's 'speckin' you to go off summuhs an' pick yo' gal, lak you went off to pick yo' aidjucation." She swung out a thick arm, and looked at Peter out of the corner of her eyes, her head tilted to one side, as negresses do when they become dramatically serious:

Peter left his mother to her stare and went to his own room. This constant implication among Niggertown inhabitants that Niggertown and all it held was worthless, mean, and unhuman depressed Peter. The mulatto knew the real trouble with Niggertown was it had adopted the white village's estimate of it. The sentiment of the white village was overpowering among the imitative negroes. The black folk looked into the eyes of the whites and saw themselves reflected as chaff and skum and slime, and no human being ever suggested that they were aught else.

Peter's room was a rough shed papered with old newspapers. All sorts of yellow scare-heads streaked his walls. Hanging up was a crayon enlargement of his mother, her broad face as unwrinkled as an egg and drawn almost white, for the picture agents have discovered the only way to please their black patrons is to make their enlargements as nearly white as possible.

In one corner, on a home-made book-rack, stood Peter's library,—a Greek book or two, an old calculus, a sociology, a psychology, a philosophy, and a score of other volumes he had accumulated in his four college years. As Peter, his head aching, looked at these, he realized how immeasurably removed he was from the cool abstraction of the study.

The brown man sat down in an ancient rocking-chair by the window, leaned back, and closed his eyes. His blood still whispered in his ears from his fight. Notwithstanding his justification, he gradually became filled with self-loathing. To fight—to hammer and kick in Niggertown's dust—over a girl! It was an indignity.

Peter shifted his position in his chair, and his thoughts took another trail. Tump's attack had been sudden and silent, much like a bulldog's. The possibility of a simple friendship between a woman and a man never entered Tump's head; it never entered any Niggertown head. Here all attraction was reduced to the simplest terms of sex. Niggertown held no delicate intimacies or reserves. Two youths could not go with the same girl. Black women had no very great powers of choice over their suitors. The strength of a man's arm isolated his sweetheart. That did not seem right, resting the power of successful mating entirely upon brawn.

As Peter sat thinking it over, it came to him that the progress of any race depended, finally, upon the woman having complete power of choosing her mate. It is woman alone who consistently places the love accent upon other matters than mere flesh and muscle. Only woman has much sex selectiveness, or is inclined to select individuals with qualities of mind and spirit.

For millions of years these instinctive spiritualizers of human breeding stock have been hampered in their choice of mates by the unrestrained right of the fighting male. Indeed, the great constructive work of chivalry in the middle ages was to lay, unconsciously, the corner-stone of modern civilization by resigning to the woman the power of choosing from a group of males.

Siner stirred in his chair, surprised at whither his reverie had lead him. He wondered how he had stumbled upon these thoughts. Had he read them in a book? In point of fact, a beating administered by Tump Pack had brought the brown man the first original idea he had entertained in his life.

By this time, Peter's jaw had reached its maximum swelling and was eased somewhat. He looked out of his little window, wondering whether Cissie Dildine would choose him—or Tump Pack.

Peter was surprised to find blue dusk peering through his panes. All the scare-heads on his walls had lapsed into a common obscurity. As he rose slowly, so as not to start his head hurting again, he heard three rapid pistol shots in the cedar glade between Niggertown and the white village. He knew this to be the time-honored signal of boot-leggers announcing that illicit whisky was for sale in the blackness of the glade.

CHAPTER IV

NEXT day the Siner-Pack fight was the focus of
news interest in Hooker's Bend. White mistresses extracted the story from their black maids, and
were amused by it or deprecated Cissie Dildine's
morals as the mood moved them.

Along Main Street in front of the village stores, the
merchants and hangers-on discussed the affair. It
was diverting that a graduate of Harvard should come
back to Hooker's Bend and immediately drop into such
a fracas. Old Captain Renfrew, one-time attorney at
law and representative of his county in the state legislature, sat under the mulberry in front of the livery-
stable and plunged into a long monologue, with old Mr.
Tomwit as listener, on the uneducability of the black
race.

"Take a horse, sir," expounded the captain; "a horse
can be trained to add and put its name together out of
an alphabet, but no horse could ever write a promissory
note and figure the interest on it, sir. Take a dog.
I 've known dogs, sir, that could bring your mail from
the post-office, but I never saw a dog stop on the way
home, sir, to read a post-card."

Here the old ex-attorney spat and renewed the tobacco in a black brier, then proceeded to draw the

parallel between dogs and horses and Peter Siner newly returned from Harvard.

"God'lmighty has set his limit on dogs, horses, and niggers, Mr. Tomwit. Thus far and no farther. Take a nigger baby at birth; a nigger baby has no fontanelles. It has no window toward heaven. Its skull is sealed up in darkness. The nigger brain can never expand and absorb the universe, sir. It can never rise on the wings of genius and weigh the stars, nor compute the swing of the Pleiades. Thus far and no farther! It's congenital.

"Now, take this Peter Siner and his disgraceful fight over a nigger wench. Would you expect an educated stud horse to pay no attention to a mare, sir? You can educate a stud till—"

"But hold on!" interrupted the old cavalryman. "I've known as gentlemanly stallions as—as anybody!"

The old attorney cleared his throat, momentarily taken aback at this failure of his metaphor. However he rallied with legal suppleness:

"You are talking about thoroughbreds, sir."

"I am, sir."

"Good God, Tomwit! you don't imagine I'm comparing a nigger to a thoroughbred, sir!"

On the street corners, or piled around on cotton-bales down on the wharf, the negro men of the village discussed the fight. It was for the most part a purely technical discussion of blows and counters and kicks, and of the strange fact that a college education failed to enable Siner utterly to annihilate his adversary. Jim Pink Staggs, a dapper gentleman of ebony blackness, of pin-stripe flannels and blue serge coat— altogether a gentleman of many parts—sat on one of the bales and indolently watched an old black crone fishing from a ledge of rocks just a little way below the wharf-boat. Around Jim Pink lounged and sprawled black men and youths, stretching on the cotton-bales like cats in the sunshine.

Jim Pink was discussing Peter's education.

"I 'fo' Gawd kain't see no use goin' off lak dat an' den comin' back an' lettin' a white man cheat you out'n yo' hide an' taller, an' lettin' a black man beat you up tull you has to kick him in the spivit. Ef a aidjucation does you any good a-tall, you 'd be boun' to beat de white man at one en' uv de line, or de black man at de udder. Ef Peter ain't to be foun' at eider en', wha is he?"

"Um-m-m!" "Eh-h-h!" "You sho spoke a moufful, Jim Pink!" came an assenting chorus from the bales.

Eventually such gossip died away and took another flurry when a report went abroad that Tump Pack was carrying a pistol and meant to shoot Peter on sight. Then this in turn ceased to be news and of human interest. It clung to Peter's mind longer than to any other person's in Hooker's Bend, and it presented to the brown man a certain problem in casuistry.

Should he accede to Tump Pack's possession of Cissie Dildine and give up seeing the girl? Such a course cut across all his fine-spun theory about women having free choice of their mates. However, the Harvard man could not advocate a socialization of courtship when he himself would be the first beneficiary. The prophet whose finger points selfward is damned. Furthermore, all Niggertown would side with Tump Pack in such a controversy. It was no uncommon thing for the very negro women to fight over their beaux and husbands. As for any social theory changing this régime, in the first place the negroes could n't understand the theory; in the second, it would have no effect if they could. Actions never grow out of theories; theories grow out of actions. A theory is a looking-glass that reflects the past and makes it look like the future, but the glass really hides the future, and when humanity comes to a turn in its course, there is always a smash-up, and a blind groping for the lost path.

Now, in regard to Cissie Dildine, Peter was not precisely afraid of Tump Pack, but he could not clear his mind of the fact that Tump had been presented with a medal by the Congress of the United States for killing four men. Good sense and a care for his reputation and his skin told Peter to abandon his theory of free courtship for the time being. This meant a renunciation of Cissie Dildine; but he told himself he renounced very little. He had no reason to think that Cissie cared a picayune about him.

Peter's work kept him indoors for a number of days

following the encounter. He was reviewing some primary school work in order to pass a teacher's examination that would be held in Jonesboro, the county seat, in about three weeks.

To the uninitiated it may seem strange to behold a Harvard graduate stuck down day after day poring over a pile of dog-eared school-books—third arithmetics, primary grammars, beginners' histories of Tennessee, of the United States, of England; physiology, hygiene. It may seem queer. But when it comes to standing a Wayne County teacher's examination, the specific answers to the specific questions on a dozen old examination slips are worth all the degrees Harvard ever did confer.

So, in his newspapered study, Peter Siner looked up long lists of questions, and attempted to memorize the answers. But the series of missteps he had made since returning to Hooker's Bend besieged his brain and drew his thoughts from his catechism. It seemed strange that in so short a time he should have wandered so far from the course he had set for himself. His career in Niggertown formed a record of slight mistakes, but they were not to be undone, and their combined force had swung him a long way from the course he had plotted for himself. There was no way to explain. Hooker's Bend would judge him by the sheer surface of his works. What he had meant to do, his dreams and altruisms, they would never surmise. That was the irony of the thing.

Then he thought of Cissie Dildine who did understand him. This thought might have been Cissie's cue
to enter the stage of Peter's mind. Her oval, creamy
face floated between Peter's eyes and the dog-eared
primer. He thought of Cissie wistfully, and of her
lonely fight for good English, good manners, and good
taste. There was a pathos about Cissie.

Peter got up from his chair and looked out at his
high window into the early afternoon. He had been
poring over primers for three days, stuffing the most
heterogeneous facts. His head felt thick and slightly
feverish. Through his window he saw the side of
another negro cabin, but by looking at an angle east-
ward he could see a field yellow with corn, a valley, and,
beyond, a hill wooded and glowing with the pageantry
of autumn. He thought of Cissie Dildine again, of
walking with her among the burning maples and the
golden elms. He thought of the restfulness such a
walk with Cissie would bring.

As he mused, Peter's soul made one of those sharp
liberating movements that occasionally visit a human
being. The danger of Tump Pack's jealousy, the loss
of his prestige, the necessity of learning the specific
answers to the examination questions, all dropped away
from him as trivial and inconsequent. He turned from
the window, put away his books and question-slips,
picked up his hat, and moved out briskly through his
mother's room toward the door.

The old woman in the kitchen must have heard him,

for she called to him through the partition, and a moment later her bulky form filled the kitchen entrance. She wiped her hands on her apron and looked at him accusingly.

"Wha you gwine, son?"

"For a walk."

The old negress tilted her head aslant and looked fixedly at him.

"You 's gwine to dat Cissie Dildine's, Peter."

Peter looked at his mother, surprised and rather disconcerted that she had guessed his intentions from his mere footsteps. The young man changed his plans for his walk, and began a diplomatic denial:

"No, I 'm going to walk by myself. I 'm tired; I 'm played out."

"Tired?" repeated his mother, doubtfully. "You ain't done nothin' but set an' turn th'ugh books an' write on a lil piece o' paper."

Peter was vaguely amused in his weariness, but thought that he concealed his mirth from his mother.

"That gets tiresome after a while."

She grunted her skepticism. As Peter moved for the door she warned him:

"Peter, you knows ef Tump Pack sees you, he 's gwine to shoot you sho!"

"Oh, no he won't; that 's Tump's talk."

"Talk! talk! Whut 's matter wid you, Peter? Dat nigger done git crowned fuh killin' fo' men!" She stood staring at him with white eyes. Then she urged, "Now, look heah, Peter, come along an' eat yo' supper."

"No, I really need a walk. I won't walk through Niggertown. I 'll walk out in the woods."

"I jes made some salmon coquettes fuh you whut 'll spile ef you don' eat 'em now."

"I did n't know you were making croquettes," said Peter, with polite interest.

"Well, I is. I gotta can o' salmon fum Miss Mollie Brownell she 'd opened an' could n't quite use. I doctered 'em up wid a lil vinegar an' sody, an' dey is 'bout as pink as dey ever wuz."

A certain uneasiness and annoyance came over Peter at this persistent use of unwholesome foods.

"Look here, Mother, you 're not using old canned goods that have been left over?"

The old negress stood looking at him in silence, but lost her coaxing expression.

"I 've told and told you about using any tainted or impure foods that the white people can't eat."

"Well, whut ef you is?"

"If it 's too bad for them, it 's too bad for you!"

Caroline made a careless gesture.

"Good Lawd, boy! I don' 'speck to eat whut 's good fuh me! All I says is, 'Grub, keep me alive. Ef you do dat, you done a good day's wuck.' "

Peter was disgusted and shocked at his mother's flippancy. Modern colleges are atheistic, but they do exalt three gods,—food, cleanliness, and exercise.

Now here was Peter's mother blaspheming one of his trinity.

"I wish you'd let me know when you want anything, Mother. I'll get it fresh for you." His words were filial enough, but his tone carried his irritation.

The old negress turned back to the kitchen.

"Huh, boy! you been fotch up on lef'-overs," she said, and disappeared through the door.

Peter walked to the gate, let himself out, and started off on his constitutional. His tiff with his mother renewed all his nervousness and sense of failure. His litany of mistakes renewed their dolor in his mind.

An autumn wind was blowing, and long plumes of dust whisked up out of the curving street and swept over the ill-kept yards, past the cabins, and toward the sere fields and chromatic woods. The wind beat at the brown man; the dust whispered against his clothes, made him squint his eyes to a crack and tickled his nostrils at each breath.

When Peter had gone two or three hundred yards, he became aware that somebody was walking immediately behind him. Tump Pack popped into his mind. He looked over his shoulder and then turned. Through the veils of flying dust he made out some one, and a moment later identified not Tump Pack, but the gangling form of Jim Pink Staggs, clad in a dark-blue sack-coat and white flannel trousers with pin stripes. It was the sort of costume affected by interlocutors of minstrel shows; it had a minstrel trigness about it.

As a matter of fact, Jim Pink was a sort of semi-professional minstrel. Ordinarily, he ran a pressing-shop in the Niggertown crescent, but occasionally he impressed all the dramatic talent of Niggertown and really did take the road with a minstrel company. These barn-storming expeditions reached down into Alabama, Mississippi, and Arkansas. Sometimes they proved a great success, and the darkies rode back several hundred dollars ahead. Sometimes they tramped back.

Jim Pink hailed Peter with a wave of his hand and a grotesque displacement of his mouth to one side of his face, which he had found effective in his minstrel buffoonery.

"Whut you raisin' so much dus' about?" he called out of the corner of his mouth, while looking at Peter out of one half-closed eye.

Peter shook his head and smiled.

"Thought it mout be Mister Hooker deliverin' dat lan' you bought." Jim Pink flung his long, flexible face into an imitation of convulsed laughter, then next moment dropped it into an intense gravity and declared, " 'Dus' thou art, to dus' returnest.' " The quotation seemed fruitless and silly enough, but Jim Pink tucked his head to one side as if listening intently to himself, then repeated sepulchrally, " 'Dus' thou art, to dus' returnest.' By the way, Peter," he broke off cheerily, "you ain't happen to see Tump Pack, is you?"

"No," said Peter, unamused.

"Is he borrowed a gun fum you?" inquired the minstrel, solemnly.

"No-o." Peter looked questioningly at the clown through half-closed eyes.

"Huh, now dat's funny." Jim Pink frowned, and pulled down his loose mouth and seemed to study. He drew out a pearl-handled knife, closed his hand over it, blew on his fist, then opened the other hand, and exhibited the knife lying in its palm, with the blade open. He seemed surprised at the change and began cleaning his finger-nails. Jim Pink was the magician at his shows.

Peter waited patiently for Jim Pink to impart his information, "Well, what's the idea?" he asked at last.

"Don' know. 'Pears lak dat knife won't stay in any one han'." He looked at it, curiously.

"I mean about Tump," said Peter, impatiently.

"O-o-oh, yeah; you mean 'bout Tump. Well, I thought Tump mus' uv borrowed a gun fum you. He lef' Hobbett's corner wid a great big forty-fo', inquirin' wha you is." Just then he glanced up, looked penetratingly through the dust-cloud, and added, "Why, I b'lieve da' 's Tump now."

With a certain tightening of the nerves, Peter followed his glance, but made out nothing through the fogging dust. When he looked around at Jim Pink again, the buffoon's face was a caricature of immense mirth. He shook it sober, abruptly, minstrel fashion.

"Maybe I's mistooken," he said solemnly. "Tump

did start over heah wid a gun, but Mister Dawson
Bobbs done tuk him up fuh ca'yin' concealed squid-
julums; so Tump's done los' dat freedom uv motion
in de pu'suit uv happiness gua'anteed us niggers an'
white folks by the Constitution uv de Newnighted
States uv America." Here Jim Pink broke into genuine laughter, which was quite a different thing from his
stage grimaces. Peter stared at the fool astonished.

"Has he gone to jail?"

"Not prezactly."

"Well—confound it!—exactly what did happen, Jim
Pink?"

"He gone to Mr. Cicero Throgmartins'."

"What did he go there for?"

"Could n't he'p hisse'f."

"Look here, you tell me what's happened."

"Mr. Bobbs ca'ied Tump thaiuh. Y' see, Mr.
Throgmartin tried to hire Tump to pick cotton. Tump
did n't haf to, because he'd jes shot fo' natchels in a
crap game. So to-day, when Tump starts over heah
wid his gun, Mr. Bobbs 'resses Tump. Mr. Throgmartin bails him out, so now Tump's gone to pick
cotton fuh Mr. Throgmartin to pay off'n his fine."
Here Jim Pink yelped into honest laughter at Tump's
undoing, so that dust got into his nose and mouth and
set him sneezing and coughing.

"How long's he up for?" asked Peter, astonished
and immensely relieved at this outcome of Tump's
expedition against himself.

Jim Pink controlled his coughing long enough to gasp:

"Th-thutty days, ef he don' run off," and fell to laughing again.

Peter Siner, long before, had adopted the literate man's notion of what is humorous, and Tump's mishap was slap-stick to him. Nevertheless, he did smile. The incident filled him with extraordinary relief and buoyancy. At the next corner he made some excuse to Jim Pink, and turned off up an alley.

Peter walked along with his shoulders squared and the dust peppering his back. Not till Tump was lifted from his mind did he realize what an incubus the soldier had been. Peter had been forced into a position where, if he had killed Tump, he would have been ruined; if he had not, he would probably have been murdered. Now he was free—for thirty days.

He swung along briskly in the warm sunshine toward the multicolored forest. The day had suddenly become glorious. Presently he found himself in the back alleys near Cissie's house. He was passing chicken-houses and stables. Hogs in open pens grunted expectantly at his footsteps.

Peter had not meant to go to Cissie's at all, but now, when he saw he was right behind her dwelling, she seemed radiantly accessible to him. Still, it struck him that it would not be precisely the thing to call on Cissie immediately after Tump's arrest. It might look as if— Then the thought came that, as a neighbor, he should stop and tell Cissie of Tump's misfortune. He really ought to offer his services to Cissie, if he could do anything. At Cissie's request he might even aid Tump Pack himself. Peter got himself into a generous glow as he charged up a side alley, around to a rickety front gate. Let Niggertown criticize as it would, he was braced by a high altruism.

Peter did not shout from the gate, as is the fashion of the crescent, but walked up a little graveled path lined with dusty box-shrubs and tapped at the unpainted door.

Doors in Niggertown never open straight away to visitors. A covert inspection first takes place from the edges of the window-blinds.

Peter stood in the whipping dust, and the caution of the inmates spurred his impatience to see Cissie. At last the door opened, and Cissie herself was in the entrance. She stood quite still a moment, looking at Peter with eyes that appeared frightened.

"I—I was n't expecting to see you," she stammered.

"No? I came by with news, Cissie."

"News?" She seemed more frightened than ever. "Peter, you—you have n't—" She paused, regarding him with big eyes.

"Tump Pack's been arrested," explained Peter, quickly, sensing the tragedy in her thoughts. "I came by to tell you. If there's anything I can do for you —or him, I'll do it."

His altruistic offer sounded rather foolish in the actual saying.

He could not tell from her face whether she was glad or sorry.

"What did they arrest him for?"

"Carrying a pistol."

She paused a moment.

"Will he—get out soon?"

"He's sentenced for thirty days."

Cissie dropped her hands with a hopeless gesture.

"Oh, isn't this all sickening!—sickening!" she exclaimed. She looked tired. Ghosts of sleepless nights circled her eyes. Suddenly she said, "Come in. Oh, do come in, Peter." She reached out and almost pulled him in. She was so urgent that Peter might have fancied Tump Pack at the gate with his automatic. He did glance around, but saw nobody passing except the Arkwright boy. The hobbledehoy walked down the other side of the street, hands thrust in pockets, with the usual discontented expression on his face.

Cissie slammed the door shut, and the two stood rather at a loss in the sudden gloom of the hall. Cissie broke into a brief, mirthless laugh.

"Peter, it's hard to be nice in Niggertown. I—I just happened to think how folks would gossip—you coming here as soon as Tump was arrested."

"Perhaps I'd better go," suggested Peter, uncomfortably.

Cissie reached up and caught his lapel.

"Oh, no, don't feel that way! I'm glad you came, really. Here, let's go through this way to the arbor. It isn't a bad place to sit."

She led the way silently through two dark rooms. Before she opened the back door, Peter could hear Cissie's mother and a younger sister moving around the outside of the house to give up the arbor to Cissie and her company.

The arbor proved a trellis of honeysuckle over the back door, with a bench under it. A film of dust lay over the dense foliage, and a few withered blooms pricked its grayish green. The earthen floor of the arbor was beaten hard and bare by the naked feet of children.

Cissie sat down on the bench and indicated a place beside her.

"I've been so uneasy about you! I've been wondering what on earth you could do about it."

"It's a snarl, all right," he said, and almost immediately began discussing the peculiar *impasse* in which his difficulty with Tump had landed him. Cissie sat listening with a serious, almost tragic face, giving a little nod now and then. Once she remarked in her precise way:

"The trouble with a gentleman fighting a rowdy, the gentleman has all to lose and nothing to gain. If you don't live among your own class, Peter, your life will simmer down to an endless diplomacy."

"You mean deceit, I suppose."

"No, I mean diplomacy. But that is n't a very healthy frame of mind,—always to be suppressing and guarding yourself."

Peter did n't know about that. He was inclined to argue the matter, but Cissie would n't argue. She seemed to assume that all of her statements were axioms, truths reduced to the simplest possible mental terms, and that proof was unnecessary, if not impossible. So the topic went into the discard.

"Been baking my brains over a lot of silly little exam. questions," complained Peter. "Can you trace the circulation of the blood? I think it leaves the grand central station through the right aorta, and then, after a schedule run of nine minutes, you can hear it coming up the track through the left ventricle, with all the passengers eager to get off and take some refreshment at the lungs. I have the general idea, but the exact routing gets me.'"

Cissie laughed accommodatingly.

"I wonder why it 's necessary for everybody to know that once. I did. I could follow the circulation the right way or backward."

"Must have been harder backward, going against the current."

Cissie laughed again. A girl's part in a witty conversation might seem easy at first sight. She has only to laugh at the proper intervals. However, these intervals are not always distinctly marked. Some girls take no chances and laugh all the time,

Cissie's appreciation was the sedative Peter needed. The relief of her laughter and her presence ran along his nerves and unkinked them, like a draft of Kentucky Special after a debauch. The curves of her cheek, the tilt of her head, and the lift of her dull-blue blouse at the bosom wove a great restfulness about Peter. The brooch of old gold glinted at her throat. The heavy screen of the arbor gave them a sweet sense of privacy. The conversation meandered this way and that, and became quite secondary to the feeling of the girl's nearness and sympathy. Their talk drifted back to Peter's mission here in Hooker's Bend, and Cissie was saying:

"The trouble is, Peter, we are out of our *milieu.*" Some portion of Peter's brain that was not basking in the warmth and invitation of the girl answered quite logically:

"Yes, but if I could help these people, Cissie, reconstruct our life here culturally—"

Cissie shook her head. "Not culturally."

This opposition shunted more of Peter's thought to the topic in hand. He paused interrogatively.

"Racially," said Cissie.

"Racially?" repeated the man, quite lost.

Cissie nodded, looking straight into his eyes. "You know very well, Peter, that you and I are not—are not anything near full bloods. You know that racially we don't belong in—Niggertown."

Peter never knew exactly how this extraordinary

sentence had come about, but in a kind of breath he realized that he and this almost white girl were not of Niggertown. No doubt she had been arguing that he, Peter, who was one sort of man, was trying to lead quite another sort of men moved by different racial impulses, and such leading could only come to confusion. He saw the implications at once.

It was an extraordinary idea, an explosive idea, such as Cissie seemed to have the faculty of touching off. He sat staring at her.

It was the white blood in his own veins that had sent him struggling up North, that had brought him back with this flame in his heart for his own people. It was the white blood in Cissie that kept her struggling to stand up, to speak an unbroken tongue, to gather around her the delicate atmosphere and charm of a gentlewoman. It was the Caucasian in them buried here in Niggertown. It was their part of the tragedy of millions of mixed blood in the South. Their common problem, a feeling of their joint isolation, brought Peter to a sense of keen and tingling nearness to the girl.

She was talking again, very earnestly, almost tremulously:

"Why don't you go North, Peter? I think and think about you staying here. You simply can't grow up and develop here. And now, especially, when everybody doubts you. If you 'd go North—"

"What about you, Cissie? You say we're together—"

"Oh, I'm a woman. We have n't the chance to do as we will."

A kind of titillation went over Peter's scalp and body.

"Then you are going to stay here and marry— Tump?" He uttered the name in a queer voice.

Tears started in Cissie's eyes; her bosom lifted to her quick breathing.

"I—I don't know what I'm going to do," she stammered miserably.

Peter leaned over her with a drumming heart; he heard her catch her breath.

"You don't care for Tump?" he asked with a dry mouth.

She gasped out something, and the next moment Peter felt her body sink limply in his groping arms. They clung together closely, quiveringly. Three nights of vigil, each thinking miserably and wistfully of the other, had worn the nerves of both man and girl until they were ready to melt together at a touch. Her soft body clinging to his own, the little nervous pressures of her arms, her eased breathing at his neck, wiped away Siner's long sense of strain. Strength and peace seemed to pour from her being into his by a sort of spiritual osmosis. She resigned her head to his palm in order that he might lift her lips to his when he pleased. After all, there is no way for a man to rest without a woman. All he can do is to stop work.

For a long time they sat transported amid the dusty honeysuckles and withered blooms, but after a while they began talking a little at a time of the future, their future. They felt so indissolubly joined that they could not imagine the future finding them apart. There was no need for any more trouble with Tump Pack. They would marry quietly, and go away North to live. Peter thought of his friend Farquhar. He wondered if Farquhar's attitude would be just the same toward Cissie as it was toward him.

"North," was the burden of the octoroon's dreams. They would go North to Chicago. There were two hundred and fifty thousand negroes in Chicago, a city within itself three times the size of Nashville. Up North she and Peter could go to theaters, art galleries, could enter any church, could ride in street-cars, rail-road-trains, could sleep and eat at any hotel, live authentic lives.

It was Cissie planning her emancipation, planning to escape her lifelong disabilities.

"Oh, I'll be so glad! so glad! so glad!" she sobbed, and drew Peter's head passionately down to her deep bosom.

CHAPTER V

PETER SINER walked home from the Dildine cabin that night rather dreading to meet his mother, for it was late. Cissie had served sandwiches and coffee on a little table in the arbor, and then had kept Peter hours afterward. Around him still hung the glamour of Cissie's little supper. He could still see her rounded elbows that bent softly backward when she extended an arm, and the glimpses of her bosom when she leaned to hand him cream or sugar. She had accomplished the whole supper in the white manner, with all poise and daintiness. In fact, no one is more exquisitely polite than an octoroon woman when she desires to be polite, when she elevates the subserviency of her race into graciousness.

However, the pleasure and charm of Cissie were fading under the approaching abuse that Caroline was sure to pour upon the girl. Peter dreaded it. He walked slowly down the dark semicircle, planning how he could best break to his mother the news of his engagement. Peter knew she would begin a long bill of complaints,—how badly she was treated, how she had sacrificed herself, her comfort, how she had washed and scrubbed. She would surely charge Cissie with being a thief and a drab, and all the announcements of engagements that Peter could make would never induce the old woman to soften her abuse. Indeed, they would make her worse.

So Peter walked on slowly, smelling the haze of dust that hung in the blackness. Out on the Big Hill, in the glade, Peter caught an occasional glimmer of light where crap-shooters and boot-leggers were beginning their nightly carousal.

These evidences of illicit trades brought Peter a thrill of disgust. In a sort of clear moment he saw that he could not keep Cissie in such a sty as this. He could not rear in such a place as this any children that might come to him and Cissie. His thoughts drifted back to his mother, and his dread of her tongue.

The Siner cabin was dark and tightly shut when Peter let himself in at the gate and walked to the door. He stood a moment listening, and then gently pressed open the shutter. A faint light burned on the inside, a night-lamp with an old-fashioned brass bowl. It sat on the floor, turned low, at the foot of his mother's bed. The mean room was mainly in shadow. The old-style four-poster in which Caroline slept was an indistinct mound. The air was close and foul with the bad ventilation of all negro sleeping-rooms. The brass lamp, turned low, added smoke and gas to the tight quarters.

The odor caught Peter in the nose and throat, and once more stirred up his impatience with his mother's disregard of hygiene. He tiptoed into the room and decided to remove the lamp and open the high, small window to admit a little air. He moved noiselessly and had stooped for the lamp when there came a creaking and a heavy sigh from the bed, and the old negress asked:

"Is dat you, son?"

Peter was tempted to stand perfectly still and wait till his mother dozed again, thus putting off her inevitable tirade against Cissie; but he answered in a low tone that it was he.

"Whut you gwine do wid dat lamp, son?"

"Go to bed by it, Mother."

"Well, bring hit back." She breathed heavily, and moved restlessly in the old four-poster. As Peter stood up he saw that the patched quilts were all askew over her shapeless bulk. Evidently, she had not been resting well.

Peter's conscience smote him again for worrying his mother with his courtship of Cissie, yet what could he do? If he had wooed any other girl in the world, she would have been equally jealous and grieved. It was inevitable that she should be disappointed and bitter; it was bound up in the very part and parcel of her sacrifice. A great sadness came over Peter. He almost wished his mother would berate him, but she continued to lie there, breathing heavily under her disarranged covers. As Peter passed into his room, the old negress called after him to remind him to bring the light back when he was through with it.

This time something in her tone alarmed Peter. He paused in the doorway.

"Are you sick, Mother?" he asked.

The old woman gave a yawn that changed to a groan.

"I—I ain't feelin' so good."

"What 's the matter, Mother?"

"My stomach, my—" But at that moment her sentence changed to an inarticulate sound, and she doubled up in bed as if caught in a spasm of acute agony.

Peter hurried to her, thoroughly frightened, and saw sweat streaming down her face. He stared down at her.

"Mother, you are sick! What can I do?" he cried, with a man's helplessness.

She opened her eyes with an effort, panting now as the edge of the agony passed. There was a movement under the quilts, and she thrust out a rubber hot-water bottle.

"Fill it—fum de kittle," she wheezed out, then relaxed into groans, and wiped clumsily at the sweat on her shining black face.

Peter seized the bottle and ran into the kitchen. There he found a brisk fire popping in the stove and a kettle of water boiling. It showed him, to his further alarm, that his mother had been trying to minister to herself until forced to bed.

The man scalded a finger and thumb pouring water into the flared mouth, but after a moment twisted on the top and hurried into the sick-room.

He reached the old negress just as another knife of pain set her writhing and sweating. She seized the hot-water bottle, pushed it under the quilts, and pressed it to her stomach, then lay with eyes and teeth clenched tight, and her thick lips curled in a grin of agony.

Peter set the lamp on the table, said he was going for the doctor, and started.

The old woman hunched up in bed. With the penuriousness of her station and sacrifices, she begged Peter not to go; then groaned out, "Go tell Mars' Renfrew," but the next moment did not want Peter to leave her.

Peter said he would get Nan Berry to stay while he was gone. The Berry cabin lay diagonally across the street. Peter ran over, thumped on the door, and shouted his mother's needs. As soon as he received an answer, he started on over the Big Hill toward the white town.

Peter was seriously frightened. His run to Dr. Jallup's, across the Big Hill, was a series of renewed strivings for speed. Every segment of his journey seemed to seize him and pin him down in the midst of the night like a bug caught in a black jelly. He seemed to progress not at all.

Now he was in the cedar glade. His muffled flight

drove in the sentries of the crap-shooters, and the gamesters blinked out their lights and listened to his feet stumbling on through the darkness.

After an endless run in the glade, Peter found himself on top of the hill, amid boulders and outcrops of limestone and cedar-shrubs. His flash-light picked out these objects, limned them sharply against the blackness, then dropped them into obscurity again.

He tried to run faster. His impatience subdivided the distance into yards and feet. Now he was approaching that boulder, now he was passing it; now he was ten feet beyond, twenty, thirty. Perhaps his mother was dying, alone save for stupid Nan Berry.

Now he was going down the hill past the white church. All that was visible was its black spire set against a web of stars. He was making no speed at all. He panted on. His heart hammered. His legs drummed with Lilliputian paces. Now he was among the village stores, all utterly black. At one point the echo of his feet chattered back at him, as if some other futile runner strained amid vast spaces of blackness.

After a long time he found himself running up a residential street, and presently, far ahead, he saw the glow of Dr. Jallup's porch light. Its beam had the appearance of coming from a vast distance. When he reached the place, he flung his breast against the top panel of the doctor's fence and held on, exhausted. He drew in his breath, and began shouting, "Hello, Doctor!"

Peter called persistently, and as he commanded more breath, he called louder and louder, "Hello, Doctor! Hello, Doctor! Hello, Doctor!" in tones edging on panic.

The doctor's house might have been dead. Somewhere a dog began barking. High in the Southern sky a star looked down remotely on Peter's frantic haste. The black man stood in the black night with his cries: "Hello, Doctor! Hello, Doctor! Hello, Doctor!"

At last, in despair, he tried to think of other doctors. He thought of telephoning to Jonesboro. Just as he decided he must turn away there came a stirring in the dead house, a flicker of light appeared on the inside now here, now there; it steadied into a tiny beam and approached the door. The door opened, and Dr. Jallup's head and breast appeared, illuminated against the black interior.

"My mother's sick, Doctor," began Peter, in immense relief.

"Who is it?" inquired the half-clad man, impassively.

"Caroline Siner; she's been taken with a—"

The physician lifted his light a trifle in an effort to see Peter.

"Lemme see: she's that fat nigger woman that lives in a three-roomed house—"

"I'll show you the way," said Peter. "She's very ill."

The half-dressed man shook his head.

"No, Ca'line Siner owes me a five-dollar doctor's bill already. Our county medical association made a rule that no niggers should—"

With a drying mouth, Peter Siner stared at the man of medicine.

"But, my God, Doctor," gasped the son, "I 'll pay you—"

"Have you got the money there in your pocket?" asked Jallup, impassively.

A sort of chill traveled deliberately over Peter's body and shook his voice.

"N-no, but I can get it—"

"Yes, you can all get it," stated the physician in dull irritation. "I 'm tired of you niggers running up doctors' bills nobody can collect. You never have more than the law allows; your wages never get big enough to garnishee." His voice grew querulous as he related his wrongs. "No, I 'm not going to see Ca'line Siner. If she wants me to visit her, let her send ten dollars to cover that and back debts, and I 'll—" The end of his sentence was lost in the closing of his door. The light he carried declined from a beam to a twinkling here and there, and then vanished in blackness. Dr. Jallup's house became dead again. The little porch light in its glass box might have been a candle burning before a tomb.

Peter Siner stood at the fence, licking his dry lips, with nerves vibrating like a struck bell. He pushed himself slowly away from the top plank and found his legs so weak that he could hardly walk. He moved slowly back down the unseen street. The dog he had disturbed gave a few last growls and settled into silence.

Peter moved along, wetting his dry lips, and stirring feebly among his dazed thoughts, hunting some other plan of action. There was a tiny burning spot on the left side of his occiput. It felt like a heated cambric needle which had been slipped into his scalp. Then he realized that he must go home, get ten dollars, and bring them back to Dr. Jallup. He started to run, but almost toppled over on his leaden legs.

He plodded through the darkness, retracing the endless trail to Niggertown. As he passed a dark mass of shrubbery and trees, he recalled his mother's advice to ask aid of Captain Renfrew. It was the old Renfrew place that Peter was passing.

The negro hesitated, then turned in at the gate in the bare hope of obtaining the ten dollars at once. Inside the gate Peter's feet encountered the scattered bricks of an old walk. The negro stood and called Captain Renfrew's name in a guarded voice. He was not at all sure of his action.

Peter had called twice and was just about to go when a lamp appeared around the side of the house on a long portico that extended clear around the building. Bathed in the light of the lamp which he held over his head, there appeared an old man wearing a worn dressing-gown.

"Who is it?" he asked in a wavery voice.

Peter told his name and mission.

The old Captain continued holding up his light. "Oh, Peter Siner; Caroline Siner 's sick? All right, I 'll have Jallup run over; I 'll 'phone him."

Peter was beginning his thanks preparatory to going, when the old man interrupted.

"No, just stay here until Jallup comes by in his car. He 'll pick us both up. It 'll save time. Come on inside. What 's the matter with old Caroline?"

The old dressing-gown led the way around the continuous piazza to a room that stood open and brightly lighted on the north face of the old house.

A great relief came to Peter at this unexpected succor. He followed around the piazza, trying to describe Caroline's symptoms. The room Peter entered was a library, a rather stately old room, lined with books all around the walls to about as high as a man could reach. Spaces for doors and windows were let in among the book-cases. The volumes themselves seemed composed mainly of histories and old-fashioned scientific books, if Peter could judge from a certain severity of their bindings. On a big library table burned a gasolene-lamp, which threw a brilliant whiteness all over the room. The table was piled with books and periodicals. Books and papers were heaped on every chair in the study except a deep Morris chair in which the old Captain had been sitting. A big meridional globe, about two and a half feet in diameter gleamed through a film of dust in the embrasure of a window. The whole room had the womanless look of a bachelor's quarters, and was flavored with tobacco and just a hint of whisky.

Old Captain Renfrew evidently had been reading when Peter called from the gate. Now the old man went to a telephone and rang long and briskly to awaken the boy who slept in the central office. Peter fidgeted as the old Captain stood with receiver to ear.

"Hard to wake." The old gentleman spoke into the transmitter, but was talking to Peter. "Don't be so uneasy, Peter. Human beings are harder to kill than you think."

There was a kindliness, even a fellowship, in Captain Renfrew's tones that spread like oil over Peter's raw nerves. It occurred to the negro that this was the first time he had been addressed as an authentic human being since his conversation with the two Northern men on the Pullman, up in Illinois. It surprised him. It was sufficient to take his mind momentarily from his mother. He looked a little closely at the old man at the telephone. The Captain wore few indices of kindness. Lines of settled sarcasm netted his eyes and drooped away from his old mouth. The very swell of his full temples and their crinkly veins marked a sardonic old man.

At last he roused central over the wire, and impressed upon him the necessity of creating a stridor in Dr. Jallup's dead house, and a moment later a continued buzzing in the receiver betokened the operator's efforts to do so.

The old gentleman turned around at last, holding the receiver a little distance from his ear.

"I understand you went to Harvard, Peter."

"Yes, sir." Peter took his eyes momentarily from the telephone. The old Southerner in the dressing-gown scrutinized the brown man. He cleared his throat.

"You know, Peter, it gives me a—a certain satisfaction to see a Harvard man in Hooker's Bend. I'm a Harvard man myself."

Peter stood in the brilliant light, astonished, not at Captain Renfrew's being a Harvard man,—he had known that,—but that this old gentleman was telling the fact to him, Peter Siner, a negro graduate of Harvard.

It was extraordinary; it was tantamount to an offer of friendship, not patronage. Such an offer in the South disturbed Peter's poise; it touched him queerly. And it seemed to explain why Captain Renfrew had received Peter so graciously and was now arranging for Dr. Jallup to visit Caroline.

Peter was moved to the conventional query, asking in what class the Captain had been graduated. But while his very voice was asking it, Peter thought what a strange thing it was that he, Peter Siner, a negro, and this lonely old gentleman, his benefactor, were spiritual

The old gentleman turned around at last

brothers, both sprung from the loins of Harvard, that ancient mother of souls.

From the darkness outside, Dr. Jallup's horn summoned the two men. Captain Renfrew got out of his gown and into his coat and turned off his gasolene light. They walked around the piazza to the front of the house. In the street the head-lights of the roadster shot divergent rays through the darkness. They went out. The old Captain took a seat in the car beside the physician, while Peter stood on the running-board. A moment later, the clutch snarled, and the machine puttered down the street. Peter clung to the standards of the auto top, peering ahead.

The men remained almost silent. Once Dr. Jallup, watching the dust that lay modeled in sharp lights and shadows under the head-lights, mentioned lack of rain. Their route did not lead over the Big Hill. They turned north at Hobbett's corner, drove around by River Street, and presently entered the northern end of the semicircle.

The speed of the car was reduced to a crawl in the bottomless dust of the crescent. The head-lights swept slowly around the cabins on the concave side of the street, bringing them one by one into stark brilliance and dropping them into obscurity. The smell of refuse, of uncleaned stables and sties and outhouses hung in the darkness. Peter bent down under the top of the motor and pointed out his place. A minute later the machine came to a noisy halt and was choked into silence. At that moment, in the sweep of the head-light, Peter saw Viny Berry, one of Nan's younger sisters, coming up from Niggertown's public well, carrying two buckets of water.

Viny was hurrying, plashing the water over the sides of her buckets. The importance of her mission was written in her black face.

"She's awful thirsty," she called to Peter in guarded tones. "Nan called me to fetch some fraish water fum de well."

Peter took the water that had been brought from the semi-cesspool at the end of the street. Viny hurried across the street to home and to bed. With the habitual twinge of his sanitary conscience, Peter considered the water in the buckets.

"We'll have to boil this," he said to the doctor.

"Boil it?" repeated Jallup, blankly. Then, he added: "Oh, yes—boil. Certainly."

A repellent odor of burned paper, breathed air, and smoky lights filled the close room. Nan had lighted another lamp and now the place was discernible in a dull yellow glow. In the corner lay a half-burned wisp of paper. Nan herself stood by the mound on the bed, putting straight the quilts that her patient had twisted awry.

"She sho am bad, Doctor," said the colored woman, with big eyes.

Seen in the light, Dr. Jallup was a little sandy-bearded man with a round, simple face, oddly overlaid with that inscrutability carefully cultivated by country doctors. With professional cheeriness, he approached the mound of bedclothes.

"A little under the weather, Aunt Ca'line?" He slipped his fingers alongside her throat to test her temperature, at the same time drawing a thermometer from his waistcoat pocket.

The old negress stirred, and looked up out of sick eyes.

"Doctor," she gasped, "I sho got a misery heah." She indicated her stomach.

"How do you feel?" he asked hopefully.

The woman panted, then whispered:

"Lak a knife was a-cuttin' an' a-tearin' out my innards." She rested, then added, "Not so bad now; feels mo' lak somp'n's tearin' in de nex' room."

"Like something tearing in the next room?" repeated Jallup, emptily.

"Yes, suh," she whispered. "I jes can feel hit—away off, lak."

The doctor attempted to take her temperature, but the thermometer in her mouth immediately nauseated her; so he slipped the instrument under her arm.

Old Caroline groaned at the slightest exertion, then, as she tossed her black head, she caught a glimpse of old Captain Renfrew.

She halted abruptly in her restlessness, stared at the

old gentleman, wet her dry lips with a queer brown-furred tongue.

"Is dat you, Mars' Milt?" she gasped in feeble astonishment. A moment later she guessed the truth. "I s'pose you had to bring de doctor. 'Fo' Gawd, Mars' Milt—" She lay staring, with the covers rising and falling as she gasped for breath. Her feverish eyes shifted back and forth between the grim old gentleman and the tall, broad-shouldered brown man at the foot of her bed. She drew a baggy black arm from under the cover.

"Da' 's Peter, Mars' Milt," she pointed. "Da' 's Peter, my son. He—he use' to be my son 'fo' he went off to school; but sence he come home, he been a-laughin' at me." Tears came to her eyes; she panted for a moment, then added: "Yeah, he done marked his mammy down fuh a nigger, Mars' Milt. Whut I thought wuz gwine be sweet lays bitter in my mouf." She worked her thick lips as if the rank taste of her sickness were the very flavor of her son's ingratitude.

A sudden gasp and twist of her body told Nan that the old woman was again seized with a spasm. The neighbor woman took swift control, and waved out Peter and old Mr. Renfrew, while she and the doctor aided the huge negress.

The two evicted men went into Peter's room and shut the door. Peter, unnerved, groped, and presently found and lighted a lamp. He put it down on his little table among his primary papers and examination papers. He indicated to Captain Renfrew the single chair in the room.

But the old gentleman stood motionless in the mean room, with its head-line streaked walls. Sounds of the heavy lifting of Peter's mother came through the thin door and partition with painful clearness. Peter opened his own small window, for the air in his room was foul.

Captain Renfrew stood in silence, with a remote sarcasm in his wrinkled eyes. What was in his heart, why he had subjected himself to the noisomeness of failing flesh, Peter had not the faintest idea. Once, out of studently habit, he glanced at Peter's philosophic books, but apparently he read the titles without really observing them. Once he looked at Peter.

"Peter," he said colorlessly, "I hope you'll be careful of Caroline's feelings if she ever gets up again. She has been very faithful to you, Peter."

Peter's eyes dampened. A great desire mounted in him to explain himself to this strange old gentleman, to show him how inevitable had been the breach. For some reason a veritable passion to reveal his heart to this his sole benefactor surged through the youth.

"Mr. Renfrew," he stammered, "Mr. Renfrew— I—I—" His throat abruptly ached and choked. He felt his face distort in a spasm of uncontrollable grief. He turned quickly from this strange old man with a remote sarcasm in his eyes and a remote affection in his tones. Peter clenched his jaws, his nostrils spread in his effort stoically to bottle up his grief and remorse, like a white man; in an effort to keep from howling his agony aloud, like a negro. He stood with aching throat and blurred eyes, trembling, swallowing, and silent.

Presently Nan Berry opened the door. She held a half-burned paper in her hand; Dr. Jallup stood near the bed, portioning out some calomel and quinine. The prevalent disease in Hooker's Bend is malaria; Dr. Jallup always physicked for malaria. On this occasion he diagnosed it must be a very severe attack of malaria indeed, so he measured out enormous doses.

He took a glass of the water that Viny had brought, held up old Caroline's head, and washed down two big capsules into the already poisoned stomach of the old negress. His simple face was quite inscrutable as he did this. He left other capsules for Nan to administer at regular intervals. Then he and Captain Renfrew motored out of Niggertown, out of its dust and filth and stench.

At four o'clock in the morning Caroline Siner died.

CHAPTER VI

WHEN Nan Berry saw that Caroline was dead, the black woman dropped a glass of water and a capsule of calomel and stared. A queer terror seized her. She began such a wailing that it aroused others in Niggertown. At the sound they got out of their beds and came to the Siner cabin, their eyes big with mystery and fear. At the sight of old Caroline's motionless body they lifted their voices through the night.

The lamentation carried far beyond the confines of Niggertown. The last gamblers in the cedar glade heard it, and it broke up their gaming and drinking. White persons living near the black crescent were waked out of their sleep and listened to the eerie sound. It rose and fell in the darkness like a melancholy organ chord. The wailing of the women quivered against the heavy grief of the men. The half-asleep listeners were moved by its weirdness to vague and sinister fancies. The dolor veered away from what the Anglo-Saxon knows as grief and was shot through with the uncanny and the terrible. White children crawled out of their small beds and groped their way to their parents. The women shivered and asked of the darkness, *"What* makes the negroes howl so?"

Nobody knew,—least of all, the negroes. Nobody suspected that the bedlam harked back to the jungle, to black folk in African kraals beating tom-toms and howling, not in grief, but in an ecstasy of terror lest the souls of their dead might come back in the form of tigers or pythons or devils and work woe to the tribe. Through the night the negroes wailed on, performing through custom an ancient rite of which they knew nothing. They supposed themselves heartbroken over the death of Caroline Siner.

Amid this din Peter Siner sat in his room, stunned by the sudden taking off of his mother. The reproaches that she had expressed to old Captain Renfrew clung in Peter's brain. The brown man had never before realized the faint amusement and condescension that had flavored all his relations with his mother since his return home. But he knew now that she had felt his disapproval of her lifelong habits; that she saw he never explained or attempted to explain his thoughts to her, assuming her to be too ignorant; as she put it, "a fool."

The pathos of his mother's last days, what she had expected, what she had received, came to Peter with the bitterness of what is finished and irrevocable. She had been dead only a few minutes, yet she could never know his grief and remorse; she could never forgive him. She was utterly removed in a few minutes, in a moment, in the failing of a breath. The finality of death overpowered him.

Into his room, through the thin wall, came the catch of numberless sobs, the long-drawn open wails, and the spasms of sobbing. Blurred voices called, "O Gawd! Gawd hab mercy! Hab mercy!" Now words were lost in the midst of confusion. The clamor boomed through the thin partition as if it would shake down his newspapered walls. With wet cheeks and an aching throat, Peter sat by his table, staring at his book-case in silence, like a white man.

The dim light of his lamp fell over his psychologies and philosophies. These were the books that had given him precedence over the old washwoman who kept him in college. It was reading these books that had made him so wise that the old negress could not even follow his thoughts. Now in the hour of his mother's death the backs of his metaphysics blinked at him emptily. What signified their endless pages about dualism and monism, about phenomenon and noumenon? His mother was dead. And she had died embittered against him because he had read and had been bewildered by these empty, wordy volumes.

A sense of profound defeat, of being ultimately fooled and cozened by the subtleties of white men, filled Peter Siner. He had eaten at their table, but their meat was not his meat. The uproar continued. Standing out of the din arose the burden of negro voices, "Hab mercy! Gawd hab mercy!"

In the morning the Ladies of Tabor came and washed and dressed Caroline Siner's body and made it ready for burial. For twenty years the old negress had paid ten cents a month to her society to insure her burial, and now the lodge made ready to fulfil its pledge. After many comings and goings, the black women called Peter to see their work, as if for his approval.

The huge dead woman lay on the four-poster with a sheet spread over the lower part of her body. The ministrants had clothed it in the old black-silk dress, with its spreading seams and panels of different materials. It reminded Peter of the new dress he had meant to get his mother, and of the modish suit which at that moment molded his own shoulders and waist. The pitifulness of her sacrifices trembled in Peter's throat. He pressed his lips together, and nodded silently to the black Ladies of Tabor.

Presently the white undertaker, a silent little man with a brisk yet sympathetic air, came and made some measurements. He talked to Peter in undertones about the finishing of the casket, how much the Knights of Tabor would pay, what Peter wanted. Then he spoke of the hour of burial, and mentioned a somewhat early hour because some of the negroes wanted to ship as roustabouts on the up-river packet, which was due at any moment.

These decisions, asked of Peter, kept pricking him and breaking through the stupefaction of this sudden tragedy. He kept nodding a mechanical agreement until the undertaker had arranged all the details. Then the little man moved softly out of the cabin and went stepping away through the dust of Niggertown with professional briskness. A little later two black grave-diggers set out with picks and shovels for the negro graveyard.

Numberless preparations for the funeral were going on all over Niggertown. The Knights of Tabor were putting on their regalia. Negro women were sending out hurry notices to white mistresses that they would be unable to cook the noonday meal. Dozens of negro girls flocked to the hair-dressing establishment of Miss Mallylou Speers. All were bent on having their wool straightened for the obsequies, and as only a few of them could be accommodated, the little room was packed. A smell of burning hair pervaded it. The girls sat around waiting their turn. Most of them already had their hair down,—or, rather loose, for it stood out in thick mats. The hair-dresser had a small oil stove on which lay heating half a dozen iron combs. With a hot comb she teased each strand of wool into perfect straightness and then plastered it down with a greasy pomade. The result was a stiff effect, something like the hair of the Japanese. It required about three hours to straighten the hair of one negress. The price was a dollar and a half.

By half-past nine o'clock a crowd of negro men, in lodge aprons and with spears, and negro women, with sashes of ribbon over their shoulders and across the breasts, assembled about the Siner cabin. In the dusty curving street were ranged half a dozen battered vehicles,—a hearse, a delivery wagon, some rickety buggies, and a hack. Presently the undertaker arrived with a dilapidated black hearse which he used especially for negroes. He jumped down, got out his straps and coffin stands, directed some negro men to bring in the coffin, then hurried into the cabin with his air of brisk precision.

He placed the coffin on the stands near the bed; then a number of men slipped the huge black body into it. The undertaker settled old Caroline's head against the cotton pillows, running his hand down beside her cheek and tipping her face just so. Then he put on the cover, which left a little oval opening just above her dead face. The sight of old Caroline's face seen through the little oval pane moved some of the women to renewed sobs. Eight black men took up the coffin and carried it out with the slow, wide-legged steps of roustabouts. Parson Ranson, in a rusty Prince Albert coat, took Peter's arm and led him to the first vehicle after the hearse. It was a delivery wagon, but it was the best vehicle in the procession.

As Peter followed the coffin out, he saw the Knights and Ladies of Tabor lined up in marching order behind the van. The men held their spears and swords at attention; the women carried flowers. Behind the marchers came other old vehicles, a sorry procession.

At fifteen minutes to ten the bell in the steeple of the colored church tolled a single stroke. The sound quivered through the sunshine over Niggertown. At its signal the poor procession moved away through the dust. At intervals the bell tolled after the vanishing train.

As the negroes passed through the white town the merchants, lolling in their doors, asked passers-by what negro had died. The idlers under the mulberry in front of the livery-stable nodded at the old negro preacher in his long greenish-black coat, and Dawson Bobbs remarked:

"Well, old Parson Ranson's going to tell 'em about it to-day," and he shifted his toothpick with a certain effect of humor.

Old Mr. Tomwit asked if his companions had ever heard how Newt Bodler, a wit famous in Wayne County, once broke up a negro funeral with a hornets' nest. The idlers nodded a smiling affirmative as they watched the cortège go past. They had all heard it. But Mr. Tomwit would not be denied. He sallied forth into humorous reminiscence. Another loafer contributed an anecdote of how he had tied ropes to a dead negro so as to make the corpse sit up in bed and frighten the mourners.

All their tales were of the vintage of the years immediately succeeding the Civil War,—pioneer humor, such as convulsed the readers of Peck's Bad Boy, Mr. Bowser, Sut Lovingood. The favorite dramatic properties of such writers were the hornets' nest, the falling ladder, the banana peel. They cultivated the humor of contusions, the wit of impact. This style still holds the stage of Hooker's Bend.

In telling these tales the white villagers meant no special disrespect to the negro funeral. It simply reminded them of humorous things; so they told their jokes, like the naïve children of the soil that they were.

At last the poor procession passed beyond the white church, around a bend in the road, and so vanished. Presently the bell in Niggertown ceased tolling.

Peter always remembered his mother's funeral in fragments of intolerable pathos,—the lifting of old Parson Ranson's hands toward heaven, the songs of the black folk, the murmur of the first shovelful of dirt as it was lowered to the coffin, and the final raw mound of earth littered with a few dying flowers. With that his mother—who had been so near to, and so disappointed in, her son—was blotted from his life. The other events of the funeral flowed by in a sort of dream: he moved about; the negroes were speaking to him in the queer overtones one uses to the bereaved; he was being driven back to Niggertown; he reëntered the Siner cabin. One or two of his friends stayed in the room with him for a while and said vague things, but there was nothing to say.

Later in the afternoon Cissie Dildine and her mother brought his dinner to him. Vannie Dildine, a thin yellow woman, uttered a few disjointed words about Sister Ca'line being a good woman, and stopped amid sentence. There was nothing to say. Death had cut a wound across Peter Siner's life. Not for days, nor weeks, nor months, would his existence knit solidly back together. The poison of his ingratitude to his faithful old black mother would for a long, long day prevent the healing.

CHAPTER VII

DURING a period following his mother's death Peter Siner's life drifted emptily and without purpose. He had the feeling of one convalescing in a hospital. His days passed unconnected by any thread of purpose; they were like cards scattered on a table, meaning nothing.

At times he struggled against his lethargy. When he awoke in the morning and found the sun shining on his dusty primers and examination papers, he would think that he ought to go back to his old task; but he never did. In his heart grew a conviction that he would never teach school at Hooker's Bend.

He would rise and dress slowly in the still cabin, thinking he must soon make new plans and take up some work. He never decided precisely what work; his thoughts trailed on in vague, idle designs.

In fact, during Peter's reaction to his shock there began to assert itself in him that capacity for profound indolence inherent in his negro blood. To a white man time is a cumulative excitant. Continuous and absolute idleness is impossible; he must work, hunt, fish, play, gamble, or dissipate,—do something to burn up the accumulating sugar in his muscles. But to a negro idleness is an increasing balm; it is a stretching of his legs in the sunshine, a cat-like purring of his nerves; while his thoughts spread here and there in inconsequences, like water without a channel, making little humorous eddies, winding this way and that into oddities and fantasies without ever feeling that constraint of sequence which continually operates in a white brain. And it is this quality that makes negroes the entertainers of children *par excellence.*

Peter Siner's mental slackening made him understandable, and gave him a certain popularity in Niggertown. Black men fell into the habit of dropping in at the Siner cabin, where they would sit outdoors, with chairs propped against the wall, and philosophize on the desultory life of the crescent. Sometimes they would relate their adventures on the river packets and around the docks at Paducah, Cairo, St. Joe, and St. Louis; usually a recountal of drunkenness, gaming, fighting, venery, arrests, jail sentences, petty peculations, and escapes. Through these Iliads of vagabondage ran an irresponsible gaiety, a non-morality, and a kind of unbrave zest for adventure. They told of their defeats and flights with as much relish and humor as of their charges and victories. And while the spirit was thoroughly pagan, these accounts were full of the clichés of religion. A roustabout whom every one called the Persimmon confided to Peter that he meant to cut loose some logs in a raft up the river, float them down a little way, tie them up again, and claim the prize-money for salvaging them, God willing.

The Persimmon was so called from a scar on his long slanting head. A steamboat mate had once found him asleep in the passageway of a lumber pile which the boat was lading, and he waked the negro by hitting him in the head with a persimmon bolt. In this there was nothing unusual or worthy of a nickname. The point was, the mate had been mistaken: the Persimmon was not working on his boat at all. In time this became one of the stock anecdotes which pilots and captains told to passengers traveling up and down the river.

The Persimmon was a queer-looking negro; his head was a long diagonal from its peak down to his pendent lower lip, for he had no chin. The salient points on this black slope were the Persimmon's sad, protruding yellow eyeballs, over which the lids always drooped about half closed. An habitual tipping of this melancholy head to one side gave the Persimmon the look of one pondering and deploring the amount of sin there was in the world. This saintly impression the Persimmon's conduct and language never bore out.

At the time of the Persimmon's remarks about the raft two of Peter's callers, Jim Pink Staggs and Parson Ranson, took the roustabout to task. Jim Pink based his objection on the grounds of glutting the labor market.

"Ef us niggers keeps turnin' too many raf's loose fuh de prize-money," he warned, "somebody 's goin' to git 'spicious, an' you 'll ruin a good thing."

The Persimmon absorbed this with a far-away look in his half-closed eyes.

"It 's a ticklish job," argued Parson Ranson, "an' I would n't want to wuck at de debbil's task aroun' de ribber, ca'se you mout fall in, Persimmon, an' git drownded."

"I would n't do sich a thing a-tall," admitted the Persimmon, "but I jes' natchelly got to git ten dollars to he'p pay on my divo'ce."

"I kain't see whut you want wid a divo'ce," said Jim Pink, yawning, "when you been ma'ied three times widout any."

"It's fuh a Christmas present," explained the Persimmon, carelessly, "fuh th' woman I'm libin' wid now. Mahaly 's a great woman fuh style. I 'm goin' to divo'ce my other wives, one at a time lak my lawyer say."

"On what grounds?" asked Peter, curiously.

"Desuhtion."

"Desertion?"

"Uh huh; I desuhted 'em."

Jim Pink shook his head, picked up a pebble, and began idly juggling it, making it appear double, single, treble, then single again.

"Too many divo'ces in dis country now, Persimmon," he moralized.

"Well, whut's de cause uv 'em?" asked the Persimmon, suddenly bringing his protruding yellow eyes around on the sleight-of-hand performer.

Jim Pink was slightly taken aback; then he said:

"'Spicion; nothin' but 'spicion."

"Yeah, 'spicion," growled the Persimmon; "'spicion an' de husban' leadin' a irreg'lar life."

Jim Pink looked at his companion, curiously.

"The husban'—leadin' a irreg'lar life?"

"Yeah,"—the Persimmon nodded grimly,—"the husban' comin' home at onexpected hours. You know whut I means, Jim Pink."

Jim Pink let his pebble fall and lowered the fore legs of his chair softly to the ground.

"Now, look heah, Persimmon, you don' want to be draggin' no foreign disco'se into yo' talk heah befo' Mr. Siner an' Parson Ranson."

The Persimmon rose deliberately.

"All I want to say is, I drapped off'n de matrimonial tree three times a'ready, Jim Pink, an' I think I feels somebody shakin' de limb ag'in."

The old negro preacher rose, too, a little behind Jim Pink.

"Now, boys! boys!" he placated. "You jes think dat, Persimmon."

"Yeah," admitted Persimmon, "I jes think it; but ef I b'lieve ever'thing is so whut I think is so, I 'd part Jim Pink's wool wid a brickbat."

Parson Ranson tried to make peace, but the Persimmon spread his hands in a gesture that included the three men. "Now, I ain't sayin' nothin'," he stated solemnly, "an' I ain't makin' no threats; but ef anything happens, you-all kain't say that nobody did n' tell nobody about nothin'."

With this the Persimmon walked to the gate, let himself out, still looking back at Jim Pink, and then started down the dusty street.

Mr. Staggs seemed uncomfortable under the Persimmon's protruding yellow stare, but finally, when the roustabout was gone, he shrugged, regained his aplomb, and remarked that some niggers spent their time in studyin' 'bout things they had n't no info'mation on whatever. Then he strolled off up the crescent in the other direction.

All this would have made fair minstrel patter if Peter Siner had shared the white conviction that every emotion expressed in a negro's patois is humorous. Unfortunately, Peter was too close to the negroes to hold such a tenet. He knew this quarrel was none the less rancorous for having been couched in the queer circumlocution of black folk. And behind it all shone the background of racial promiscuity out of which it sprang. It was like looking at an open sore that touched all of Niggertown, men and boys, young girls and women. It caused tragedies, murders, fights, and desertions in the black village as regularly as the rota-

tion of the calendar; yet there was no public sentiment against it. Peter wondered how this attitude
of his whole people could possibly be.

With the query the memory of Ida May came back
to him, with its sense of dim pathos. It seemed to
Peter now as if their young and uninstructed hands
had destroyed a safety-vault to filch a penny.

The reflex of a thought of Ida May always brought
Peter to Cissie; it always stirred up in him a desire
to make this young girl's path gentle and smooth.
There was a fineness, a delicacy about Cissie, that, it
seemed to Peter, Ida May had never possessed. Then,
too, Cissie was moved by a passion for self-betterment.
She deserved a cleaner field than the Niggertown of
Hooker's Bend.

Peter took Parson Ranson's arm, and the two moved
to the gate by common consent. It was no longer
pleasant to sit here. The quarrel they had heard somehow had flavored their surroundings.

Peter turned his steps mechanically northward up the
crescent toward the Dildine cabin. Nothing now restrained him from calling on Cissie; he would keep
no dinner waiting; he would not be warned and berated
on his return home. The nagging, jealous love of his
mother had ended.

As the two men walked along, it was borne in upon
Peter that his mother's death definitely ended one
period of his life. There was no reason why he should
continue his present unsettled existence. It seemed

best to marry Cissie at once and go North. Further time in this place would not be good for the girl. Even if he could not lift all Niggertown, he could at least help Cissie. He had had no idea, when he first planned his work, what a tremendous task he was essaying. The white village had looked upon the negroes so long as non-moral and non-human that the negroes, with the flexibility of their race, had assimilated that point of view. The whites tried to regulate the negroes by endless laws. The negroes had come to accept this, and it seemed that they verily believed that anything not discovered by the constable was permissible. Mr. Dawson Bobbs was Niggertown's conscience. It was best for Peter to take from this atmosphere what was dearest to him, and go at once.

The brown man's thoughts came trailing back to the old negro parson hobbling at his side. He looked at the old man, hesitated a moment, then told him what was in his mind.

Parson Ranson's face wrinkled into a grin.

"You's gwine to git ma'ied?"

"And I thought I'd have you perform the ceremony."

This suggestion threw the old negro into excitement.

"Me, Mr. Peter?"

"Yes. Why not?"

"Why, Mr. Peter, I kain't jine you an' Miss Cissie Dildine."

Peter looked at him, astonished.

"Why can't you?"

"Why n't you git a white preacher?"

"Well," deliberated Peter, gravely, "it's a matter of principle with me, Parson Ranson. I think we colored people ought to be more self-reliant, more self-serving. We ought to lead our own lives instead of being mere echoes of white thought." He made a swift gesture, moved by this passion of his life. "I don't mean racial equality. To my mind racial equality is an empty term. One might as well ask whether pink and violet are equal. But what I do insist on is autonomous development."

The old preacher nodded, staring into the dust. "Sho! 'tonomous 'velopment."

Peter saw that his language, if not his thought, was far beyond his old companion's grasp, and he lacked the patience to simplify himself.

"Why don't you want to marry us, Parson?"

Parson Ranson lifted his brows and filled his forehead with wrinkles.

"Well, I dunno. You an' Miss Cissie acts too much lak white folks fuh a nigger lak me to jine you, Mr. Peter."

Peter made a sincere effort to be irritated, but he was not.

"That's no way to feel. It's exactly what I was talking about,—racial self-reliance. You've married hundreds of colored couples."

"Ya-as, suh,"—the old fellow scratched his black

jaw,—"I kin yoke up a pair uv ordina'y niggers all right. Sometimes dey sticks, sometimes dey don't." The old man shook his white, kinky head. "I 'll bust in an' try to hitch up you-all. I—I dunno whedder de cer'mony will hol' away up North or not."

"It 'll be all right anywhere, Parson," said Peter, seriously. "Your name on the marriage-certificate will—can you write?"

"N-no, suh."

After a brief hesitation Peter repeated determinedly:

"It 'll be all right. And, by the way, of course, this will be a very quiet wedding."

"Yas-suh." The old man bobbed importantly.

"I would n't mention it to any one."

"No, suh; no, suh. I don' blame you a-tall, Mr. Peter, wid dat Tump Pack gallivantin' roun' wid a forty-fo'. Hit would keep 'mos' anybody's weddin' ve'y quiet onless he wuz lookin' fuh a short cut to heab'n."

As the two negroes passed the Berry cabin, Nan Berry thrust out her spiked head and called to Peter that Captain Renfrew wanted to see him.

Peter paused, with quickened interest in this strange old man who had come to his mother's death-bed with a doctor. Peter asked Nan what the Captain wanted.

Nan did not know. Wince Washington had told Nan that the Captain wanted to see Peter. Bluegum Frakes had told Wince; Jerry Dillihay had told Bluegum; but any further meanderings of the message, when it started, or what its details might be, Nan could not state.

It was a typical message from a resident of the white town to a denizen of Niggertown. Such messages are delivered to any black man for any other black man, not only in the village, but anywhere in the outlying country. It may be passed on by a dozen or a score of mouths before it reaches its objective. It may be a day or a week in transit, but eventually it will be delivered verbatim. This queer system of communication is a relic of slavery, when the master would send out word for some special negro out of two or three hundred slaves to report at the big house.

However, as Peter approached the Dildine cabin, thoughts of his approaching marriage drove from his mind even old Captain Renfrew's message. His heart beat fast from having made his first formal step toward wedlock. The thought of having Cissie all to himself, swept his nerves in a gust.

He opened the gate, and ran up between the dusty lines of dwarf box, eager to tell her what he had done. He thumped on the cracked, unpainted door, and impatiently waited the skirmish of observation along the edge of the window-blinds. This was unduly drawn out. Presently he heard women's voices whispering to each other inside. They seemed urgent, almost angry voices. Now and then he caught a sentence:

"What difference will it make?" "I could n't." "Why could n't you?" "Because—" "That's because you've been to Nashville." "Oh, well—" A chair was moved over a bare floor. A little later footsteps came to the entrance, the door opened, and Cissie's withered yellow mother stood before him.

Vannie offered her hand and inquired after Peter's health, with a stopped voice that instantly recalled his mother's death. After the necessary moment of talk, the mulatto inquired for Cissie.

The yellow woman seemed slightly ill at ease.

"Cissie ain't so well, Peter."

"She's not ill?"

"N-no; but the excitement an' ever'thing—" answered Vannie, vaguely.

In the flush of his plans, Peter was keenly disappointed.

"It's very important, Mrs. Dildine."

Vannie's dried yellow face framed the ghost of a smile.

"Ever'thing a young man's got to say to a gal is ve'y important, Peter."

It seemed to Peter a poor time for a jest; his face warmed faintly.

"It—it's about some of the details of our—our wedding."

"If you'll excuse her to-day, Peter, an' come after supper—"

Peter hesitated, and was about to go away when Cissie's voice came from an inner room, telling her mother to admit him.

The yellow woman glanced at the door on the left side of the hall, crossed over and opened it, stood to one side while Peter entered, and closed it after him, leaving the two alone.

The room into which Peter stepped was dark, after the fashion of negro houses. Only after a moment's survey did he see Cissie sitting near a big fireplace made of rough stone. The girl started to rise as Peter advanced toward her, but he solicitously forbade it and hurried over to her. When he leaned over her and put his arms about her, his ardor was slightly dampened when she gave him her cheek instead of her lips to kiss.

"Surely, you 're not too ill to be kissed?" he rallied faintly.

"You kissed me. I thought we had agreed, Peter, you were not to come in the daytime any more."

"Oh, is that it?" Peter patted her shoulder, cheerfully. "Don't worry; I have just removed any reason why I should n't come any time I want to."

Cissie looked at him, her dark eyes large in the gloom.

"What have you done?"

"Got a preacher to marry us; on my way now for a license. Dropped in to ask if you 'll be ready by tomorrow or next day."

The girl gasped.

"But, Peter—"

Peter drew a chair beside her in a serious argumentative mood.

"Yes, I think we ought to get married at once. No reason why we should n't get it over with— Why, what 's the matter?"

"So soon after your mother's death, Peter?"

"It 's to get away from Hooker's Bend, Cissie—to get you away. I don't like for you to stay here. It 's all so—" he broke off, not caring to open the disagreeable subject.

The girl sat staring down at some fagots smoldering on the hearth. At that moment they broke into flame and illuminated her sad face.

"You 'll go, won't you?" asked Peter at last, with a faint uncertainty.

The girl looked up.

"Oh—I—I 'd be glad to, Peter,"—she gave a little shiver. "Ugh! this Niggertown is a—a terrible place!"

Peter leaned over, took one of her hands, and patted it.

"Then we 'll go," he said soothingly. "It 's decided —to-morrow. And we 'll have a perfectly lovely wedding trip," he planned cheerfully, to draw her mind from her mood. "On the car going North I 'll get a whole drawing-room. I 've always wanted a drawing-room, and you 'll be my excuse. We 'll sit and watch the fields and woods and cities slip past us, and know, when we get off, we can walk on the streets as freely as anybody. We'll be a genuine man and wife."

His recital somehow stirred him. He took her in his arms, pressed her cheek to his, and after a moment kissed her lips with the trembling ardor of a bridegroom.

Cissie remained passive a moment, then put up her hands, turned his face away, and slowly released herself.

Peter was taken aback.

"What *is* the matter, Cissie?"

"I can't go, Peter."

Peter looked at her with a feeling of strangeness.

"Can't go?"

The girl shook her head.

"You mean—you want us to live here?"

Cissie sat exceedingly still and barely shook her head.

The mulatto had a sensation as if the portals which disclosed a new and delicious life were slowly closing against him. He stared into her oval face.

"You don't mean, Cissie—you don't mean you don't want to marry me?"

The fagots on the hearth burned now with a cheerful flame. Cissie stared at it, breathing rapidly from the top of her lungs. She seemed about to faint. As Peter watched her the jealousy of the male crept over him.

"Look here, Cissie," he said in a queer voice, "you— you don't mean, after all, that Tump Pack is—"

"Oh, no! No!" Her face showed her repulsion. Then she drew a long breath and apparently made up her mind to some sort of ordeal.

"Peter," she asked in a low tone, "did you ever think what we colored people are trying to reach?" She stared into his uncomprehending eyes. "I mean what is our aim, our goal, whom are we trying to be like?"

"We aren't trying to be like any one." Peter was entirely at a loss.

"Oh, yes, we are," Cissie hurried on. "Why do colored girls straighten their hair, bleach their skins, pinch their feet? Aren't they trying to look like white girls?"

Peter agreed, wondering at her excitement.

"And you went North to college, Peter, so you could think and act like a white man—"

Peter resisted this at once; he was copying nobody. The whole object of college was to develop one's personality, to bring out—

The girl stopped his objections almost piteously.

"Oh, don't argue! You know arguing throws me off. I—now I've forgotten how I meant to say it!" Tears of frustration welled up in her eyes.

Her mood was alarming, almost hysterical. Peter began comforting her.

"There, there, dear, dear Cissie, what is the matter? Don't say it at all." Then, inconsistently, he added: "You said I copied white men. Well, what of it?"

Cissie breathed her relief at having been given the

thread of her discourse. She sat silent for a moment, with the air of one screwing up her courage.

"It's this," she said in an uncertain voice: "sometimes we—we—girls—here in Niggertown copy the wrong thing first."

Peter looked blankly at her.

"The wrong thing first, Cissie?"

"Oh, yes; we—we begin on clothes and—and hair, and—and that isn't the real matter."

"Why, no-o-o, that is n't the real matter," said Peter, puzzled.

Cissie looked at his face and became hopeless.

"Oh, *don't* you understand! Lots of us—lots of us make that mistake! I—I did; so—so, Peter, I can't go with you!" She flung out the last phrase, and suddenly collapsed on the arm of her chair, sobbing.

Peter was amazed. He got up, sat on the arm of his own chair next to hers and put his arms about her, bending over her, mothering her. Her distress was so great that he said as earnestly as his ignorance permitted:

"Yes, Cissie, I understand now." But his tone belied his words, and the girl shook her head. "Yes, I do, Cissie," he repeated emptily. But she only shook her head as she leaned over him, and her tears slowly formed and trickled down on his hand. Then all at once old Caroline's accusation against Cissie flashed on Peter's mind. She had stolen that dinner in the turkey roaster, after all. It so startled him that he sat up straight. Cissie also sat up. She stopped crying, and sat looking into the fire.

"You mean—morals?" said Peter in a low tone.

Cissie barely nodded, her wet eyes fixed on the fire.

"I see. I was stupid."

The girl sat a moment, drawing deep breaths. At last she rose slowly.

"Well—I'm glad it's over. I'm glad you know." She stood looking at him almost composedly except for her breathing and her tear-stained face. "You see, Peter, if you had been like Tump Pack or Wince or any of the boys around here, it—it would n't have made much difference; but—but you went off and—and learned to think and feel like a white man. You—you changed your code, Peter." She gave a little shaken sound, something between a sob and a laugh. "I—I don't think th-that's very fair, Peter, to—to go away an'—an' change an' come back an' judge us with yo' n-new code." Cissie's precise English broke down.

Just then Peter's logic caught at a point.

"If you did n't know anything about my code, how do you know what I feel now?" he asked.

She looked at him with a queer expression.

"I found out when you kissed me under the arbor. It was too late then."

She stood erect, with dismissal very clearly written in her attitude. Peter walked out of the room.

CHAPTER VIII

WITH a certain feeling of clumsiness Peter groped in the dark hall for his hat, then, as quietly as he could, let himself out at the door. Outside he was surprised to find that daylight still lingered in the sky. He thought night had fallen. The sun lay behind the Big Hill, but its red rays pouring down through the boles of the cedars tinted long delicate avenues in the dusty atmosphere above his head. A sharp chill in the air presaged frost for the night. Somewhere in the crescent a boy yodeled for his dog at about half-minute intervals, with the persistence of children.

Peter walked a little distance, but finally came to a stand in the dust, looking at the negro cabins, not knowing where to go or what to do. Cissie's confession had destroyed all his plans. It had left him as adynamic as had his mother's death. It seemed to Peter that there was a certain similarity between the two events; both were sudden and desolating. And just as his mother had vanished utterly from his reach, so now it seemed Cissie was no more. Cissie the clear-eyed, Cissie the ambitious, Cissie the refined, had vanished away, and in her place stood a thief.

The thing was grotesque. Peter began a sudden shuddering in the cold. Then he began moving toward the empty cabin where he slept and kept his things. He moved along, talking to himself in the dusty emptiness of the crescent. He decided that he would go home, pack his clothes, and vanish. A St. Louis boat would be down that night, and he would just have time to pack his clothes and catch it. He would not take his books, his philosophies. He would let them remain, in the newspapered room, until all crumbled into uniform philosophic dust, and the teachings of Aristotle blew about Niggertown.

Then, as he thought of traveling North, the vision of the honeymoon he had just planned revived his numb brain into a dismal aching. He looked back through the dusk at the Dildine roof. It stood black against an opalescent sky. Out of the foreground, bending over it, arose a clump of tall sunflowers, in whose silhouette hung a suggestion of yellow and green. The whole scene quivered slightly at every throb of his heart. He thought what a fool he was to allow a picaresque past to keep him away from such a woman, how easy it would be to go back to the soft luxury of Cissie, to tell her it made no difference; and somehow, just at that moment it seemed not to.

Then the point of view which Peter had been four years acquiring swept away the impulse, and it left him moving toward his cabin again, empty, cold, and planless.

He was drawn out of his reverie by the soft voice of a little negro boy asking him apprehensively whom he was talking to.

Peter stopped, drew forth a handkerchief, and dabbed the moisture from his cold face in the meticulous fashion of college men.

With the boy came a dog which was cautiously smelling Peter's shoes and trousers. Both boy and dog were investigating the phenomenon of Peter. Peter, in turn, looked down at them with a feeling that they had materialized out of nothing.

"What did you say?" he asked vaguely.

The boy was suddenly overcome with the excessive shyness of negro children, and barely managed to whisper:

"I—I ast wh-who you wuz a-talkin' to."

"Was I talking?"

The little negro nodded, undecided whether to stand his ground or flee. Peter touched the child's crisp hair.

"I was talking to myself," he said, and moved forward again.

The child instantly gained confidence at the slight caress, took a fold of Peter's trousers in his hand for friendliness, and the two trudged on together.

"Wh-whut you talkin' to yo' se'f for?'

Peter glanced down at the little black head that promised to think up a thousand questions.

"I was wondering where to go."

"Lawsy! is you los' yo' way?"

He stroked the little head with a rush of self-pity.

"Yes, I have, son; I 've completely lost my way."

The child twisted his head around and peered up alongside Peter's arm. Presently he asked:

"Ain't you Mr. Peter Siner?"

"Yes."

"Ain't you de man whut 's gwine to ma'y Miss Cissie Dildine?"

Peter looked down at his small companion with a certain concern that his marriage was already gossip known to babes.

"I 'm Peter Siner," he repeated.

"Den I knows which way you wants to go," piped the youngster in sudden helpfulness. "You wants to go over to Cap'n Renfrew's place acrost de Big Hill. He done sont fuh you. Mr. Wince Washington tol' me, ef I seed you, to tell you dat Cap'n Renfrew wants to see you. I dunno whut hit 's about. I ast Wince, an' he did n' know."

Peter recalled the message Nan Berry had given him some hours before. Now the same summons had seeped around to him from another direction.

"I—I 'll show you de way to Cap'n Renfrew's ef— ef you 'll come back wid me th'ugh de cedar glade," proposed the child. "I—I ain't skeered in de cedar glade, b-b-but hit 's so dark I kain't see my way back home. I—I—"

Peter thanked him and declined his services. After

all, he might as well go to see Captain Renfrew.   He
owed the old gentleman some thanks—and ten dollars.

The only thing of which Peter Siner was aware
during his walk over the Big Hill and through the village was his last scene with Cissie.   He went over it
again and again, repeating their conversation, inventing new replies, framing new action, questioning more
fully into the octoroon's vague confession and his be-
numbed acceptance of it.   The moment his mind completed the little drama it started again from the very
beginning.

At Captain Renfrew's gate this mental mummery
paused long enough for him to vacillate between walking in or going around and shouting from the back
gate.   It is a point of etiquette in Hooker's Bend that
negroes shall enter a white house from the back stoop.
Peter had no desire to transgress this custom.   On the
other hand, if Captain Renfrew was receiving him as
a fellow of Harvard, the back door, in its way, would
prove equally embarrassing.

After a certain indecision he compromised by entering the front gate and calling the Captain's name
from among the scattered bricks of the old walk.

The house lay silent, half smothered in a dark
tangle of shrubbery.   Peter called twice before he
heard the shuffle of house slippers, and then saw the
Captain's dressing-gown at the piazza steps.

"Is that you, Peter?" came a querulous voice.

"Yes, Captain.   I was told you wanted to see me."

"You've been deliberate in coming," criticized the old gentleman, testily. "I sent you word by some black rascal three days ago."

"I just received the message to-day." Peter remained discreetly at the gate.

"Yes; well, come in, come in. See if you can do anything with this damnable lamp."

The old man turned with a dignified drawing-together of his dressing-gown and moved back. Apparently, the renovation of a cranky lamp was the whole content of the Captain's summons to Peter.

There was something so characteristic in this incident that Peter was moved to a vague sense of mirth. It was just like the old régime to call in a negro, a special negro, from ten miles away to move a jar of ferns across the lawn or trim a box hedge or fix a lamp.

Peter followed the old gentleman around to the back piazza facing his study. There, laid out on the floor, were all the parts of a gasolene lamp, together with a pipe-wrench, a hammer, a little old-fashioned vise, a bar of iron, and an envelop containing the mantels and the more delicate parts of the lamp.

"It's extraordinary to me," criticized the Captain, "why they can't make a gasolene lamp that will go, and remain in a going condition."

"Has it been out of fix for three days?" asked Peter, sorry that the old gentleman should have lacked a light for so long.

"No," growled the Captain; "it started gasping at

four o'clock last night; so I put it out and went to bed.
I 've been working at it this evening.   There 's a little
hole in the tip,—if I could see it,—a hair-sized hole,
painfully small.   Why any man wants to make gasolene lamps with microscopic holes that ordinary intel-
ligence must inform him will become clogged I cannot
conceive."

Peter ventured no opinion on this trait of lamp-
makers, but said that if the Captain knew where he
could get an oil hand-lamp for a little more light, he
thought he could unstop the hole.

The Captain looked at his helper and shook his head.

"I am surprised at you, Peter.   When I was your
age, I could see an aperture like that hole under the
last quarter of the moon.   In this strong light I could
have—er—lunged the cleaner through it, sir.   You
must have strained your eyes in college."   He paused,
then added: "You 'll find hand-lamps in any of the
rooms fronting this porch.   I don't know whether
they have oil in them or not—the shiftless niggers that
come around to take care of this building—no depend-
ence to be put in them.   When I try it myself, I do
even worse."

The old gentleman's tone showed that he was thaw-
ing out of his irritable mood, and Peter sensed that he
meant to be amusing in an austere, unsmiling fashion.
The Captain rubbed his delicate wrinkled hands together in a pleased fashion and sat down in a big porch
chair to await Peter's assembling of the lamp.   The

brown man started down the long piazza in search of a
hand-light.

He found a lamp in the first room he entered, returned to the piazza, sat down on the edge of it, and began his tinkering. The old Captain apparently
watched him with profound satisfaction. Presently,
after the fashion of the senile, he began endless and
minute instructions as to how the lamp should be
cleaned.

"Take the wire in your left hand, Peter,—that's
right,—now hold the tip a little closer to the light—no,
place the mantels on the right side—that's the way I
do it. System. . . ." the old man's monologue ran on
and on, and became a murmur in Peter's ears. It was
rather soothing than otherwise. Now and then it held
tremulous vibrations that might have been from age or
that might have been from some deep satisfaction
mounting even to joy. But to Peter that seemed
hardly probable. No doubt it was senility. The Captain was a tottery old man, past the age for any fundamental joy.

Night had fallen now, and a darkness, musky with
autumn weeds, hemmed in the sphere of yellow light
on the old piazza. A black-and-white cat materialized
out of the gloom, purring, and arching against a pillar.
The whole place was filled with a sense of endless leisure. The old man, the cat, the perfume of the weeds,
soothed in Peter even the rawness of his hurt at Cissie.

Indeed, in a way, the old manor became a sort of

apology for the octoroon girl. The height and the reach of the piazza, exaggerated by the darkness, suggested a time when retinues of negroes passed through its dignified colonnades. Those black folk were a part of the place. They came and went, picked up and used what they could, and that was all life held for them. They were without wage, without rights, even to the possession of their own bodies; so by necessity they took what they could. That was only fifty-odd years ago. Thus, in a way, Peter's surroundings began a subtle explanation of and apology for Cissie, the whole racial training of black folk in petty thievery. And that this should have touched Cissie—the meanness, the pathos of her fate moved Peter.

The negro was aroused from his reverie by the old Captain's getting out of his chair and saying, "Very good," and then Peter saw that he had finished the lamp. The two men rose and carried it into the study, where Peter pumped and lighted it; a bit later its brilliant white light flooded the room.

"Quite good." The old Captain stood rubbing his hands with his odd air of continued delight. "How do you like this place, anyway, Peter?" He wrapped his gown around him, sat down in the old Morris chair beside the book-piled table, and indicated another seat for Peter.

The mulatto took it, aware of a certain flexing of Hooker's Bend custom, where negroes, unless old or infirm, are not supposed to sit in the presence of whites.

"Do you mean the study, Captain?"

"Yes, the study, the whole place."

"It's very pleasant," replied Peter; "it has the atmosphere of age."

Captain Renfrew nodded.

"These old places," pursued Peter, "always give me an impression of statesmanship, somehow. I always think of grave old gentlemen busy with the cares of public policy."

The old man seemed gratified.

"You are sensitive to atmosphere. If I may say it, every Southron of the old régime was a statesman by nature and training. The complete care of two or three hundred negroes, a regard for their bodily, moral, and spiritual welfare, inevitably led the master into the impersonal attitude of statecraft. It was a training, sir, in leadership, in social thinking, in, if you please, altruism." The old gentleman thumped the arm of his chair with a translucent palm. "Yes, sir, negro slavery was God's great lesson to the South in altruism and loving-kindness, sir! My boy, I do believe with all my heart that the institution of slavery was placed here in God's country to rear up giants of political leadership, that our nation might weather the revolutions of the world. Oh, the Yankees are necessary! I know that!" The old Captain held up a palm at Peter as if repressing an imminent retort. "I know the Yankees are the Marthas of the nation. They furnish food and fuel to the ship of state, but, my boy, the reservoir of our country's spiritual and mental strength, the Mary of our nation, must always be the South. Virginia is the mother of Presidents!"

The Captain's oration left him rather breathless. He paused a moment, then asked:

"Peter, have you ever thought that we men of the leisure class owe a debt to the world?"

Peter smiled.

"I know the theory of the leisure class, but I 've had very little practical experience with leisure."

"Well, that 's a subject close to my heart. As a scholar and a thinker, I feel that I should give the fruits of my leisure to the world. Er—in fact, Peter, that is why I sent for you to come and see me."

"Why you sent for me?" Peter was surprised at this turn.

"Precisely. You."

Here the old gentleman got himself out of his chair, walked across to one of a series of drawers in his bookcases, opened it, and took out a sheaf of papers and a quart bottle. He brought the papers and the bottle back to the table, made room for them, put the papers in a neat pile, and set the bottle at a certain distance from the heap.

"Now, Peter, please hand me one of those wineglasses in the religious section of my library—I always keep two or three glasses among my religious works, in memory of the fact that our Lord and Master wrought a miracle at the feast of Cana, especially to bless the cup. Indeed, Peter, thinking of that miracle at the wedding-feast, I wonder, sir, how the prohibitionists can defend their conduct even to their own consciences, because logically, sir, logically, the miracle of our gracious Lord completely cuts away the ground from beneath their feet!

"No wonder, when the Mikado sent a Japanese envoy to America to make a tentative examination of Christianity as a proper creed for the state religion of Japan—no wonder, with this miracle flouted by the prohibitionists, the embassy carried back the report that Americans really have no faith in the religion they profess. Shameful! Shameful! Place the glass there on the left of the bottle. A little farther away from the bottle, please, just a trifle more. Thank you."

The Captain poured himself a tiny glassful, and its bouquet immediately filled the room. There was no guessing how old that whisky was.

"I will not break the laws of my country, Peter, no matter how godless and sacrilegious those laws may be; therefore I cannot offer you a drink, but you will observe a second glass among the religious works, and the bottle sits in plain view on the table—er—em." He watched Peter avail himself of his opportunity, and then added, "Now, you may just drink to me, standing, as you are, like that."

They drank, Peter standing, the old gentleman seated.

"It is just as necessary," pursued the old connoisseur, when Peter was reseated, "it is just as necessary for a gentleman to have a delicate palate for the tints of the vine as it is for him to have a delicate eye for the tints of the palette. Nature bestowed a taste both in art and wine on man, which he should strive to improve at every opportunity. It is a gift from God. Perhaps you would like another glass. No? Then accommodate me."

He drained this one, with Peter standing, worked his withered lips back and forth to experience its full taste, then swallowed, and smacked.

"Now, Peter," he said, "the reason I asked you to come to see me is that I need a man about this house. That will be one phase of your work. The more important part is that you shall serve as a sort of secretary. I have here a manuscript." He patted the pile of papers. "My handwriting is rather difficult. I want you to copy this matter out and get it ready for the printer."

Peter became more and more astonished.

"Are you offering me a permanent place, Captain Renfrew?" he asked.

The old man nodded.

"I need a man with a certain liberality of culture. I will no doubt have you run through books and periodicals and make note of any points germane to my thesis."

Peter looked at the pile of script on the table.

"That is very flattering, Captain; but the fact is, I

came by your place at this hour because I am just in
the act of leaving here on the steamboat to-night."

The Captain looked at Peter with concern on his
face. "Leaving Hooker's Bend?"

"Yes, sir."

"Why?"

Peter hesitated.

"Well, my mother is dead—"

"Yes, but your—your—your work is still here,
Peter." The Captain fell into a certain confusion.
"A man's work, Peter; a man's work."

"Do you mean my school-teaching?"

Then came a pause. The conversation somehow
had managed to leave them both somewhat at sea.
The Captain began again, in a different tone:

"Peter, I wish you to remain here with me for another reason. I am an old man, Peter. Anything
could happen to me here in this big house, and nobody
would know it. I don't like to think of it." The old
man's tone quite painted his fears. "I am not afraid
of death, Peter. I have walked before God all my life
save in one or two points, which, I believe, in His
mercy, He has forgiven me; but I cannot endure the
idea of being found here some day in some unconsid-
ered posture, fallen out of a chair, or a-sprawl on
the floor. I wish to die with dignity, Peter, as I have
lived."

"Then you mean that you want me to stay here with
you until—until the end, Captain?"

The old man nodded.

"That is my desire, Peter, for an honorarium which you yourself shall designate. At my death, you will receive some proper portion of my estate; in fact, the bulk of my estate, because I leave no other heirs. I am the last Renfrew of my race, Peter."

Peter grew more and more amazed as the old gentleman unfolded this strange proposal. What queerer, pleasanter berth could he find than that offered him here in the quietude of the old manor, among books, tending the feeble flame of this old aristocrat's life? An air of scholasticism hung about the library. In some corner of this dark oaken library his philosophies would rest comfortably.

Then it occurred to Peter that he would have to continue his sleeping and eating in Niggertown, and since his mother had died and his rupture with Cissie, the squalor and smells of the crescent had become impossible. He told the old Captain his objections as diplomatically as possible. The old man made short work of them. He wanted Peter to sleep in the manor within calling distance, and he might begin this very night and stay on for a week or so as a sort of test whether he liked the position or not. The Captain waited with some concern until Peter agreed to a trial.

After that the old gentleman talked on interminably of the South, of the suffrage movement, the destructive influence it would have on the home, the Irish question, the Indian question, whether the mound-builders

did not spring from the two lost tribes of Israel—an
endless outpouring of curious facts, quaint reasoning,
and extraordinary conclusions, all delivered with the
great dignity and in the flowing periods of an orator.

It was fully two o'clock in the morning when it occurred to the Captain that his new secretary might like
to go to bed. The old man took the hand-lamp which
was still burning and led the way out to the back piazza past a number of doors to a corner bedroom. He
shuffled along in his carpet slippers, followed by the
black-and-white cat, which ran along, making futile
efforts to rub itself against his lean shanks. Peter
followed in a sort of stupor from the flood of words,
ideas, and strange fancies that had been poured into
his ears.

The Captain turned off the piazza into one of those
old-fashioned Southern rooms with full-length windows, which were really glazed doors, a ceiling so high
that Peter could make out only vague concentric rings
of stucco-work among the shadows overhead, and a
floor space of ball-room proportions. In one corner
was a huge canopy bed, across from it a clothes-press
of dark wood, and in another corner a large screen
hiding the bathing arrangements.

Peter's bedroom was a sleeping apartment, in the
old sense of the word before the term "apartment" had
lost its dignity.

The Captain placed the lamp on the great table and
indicated Peter's possession with a wave of the hand.

"If you stay here, Peter, I will put in a call-bell, so I can awaken you if I need you during the night. Now I wish you healthful slumbers and pleasant dreams." With that the old gentleman withdrew ceremoniously.

When the Captain was gone, the mulatto remained standing in the vast expanse, marveling over this queer turn of fortune. Why Captain Renfrew had selected him as a secretary and companion Peter could not fancy.

The magnificence of his surroundings revived his late dream of a honeymoon with Cissie. Certainly, in his fancy, he had visioned a honeymoon in Pullman parlor cars and suburban bungalows. He had been mistaken. This great chamber rose about him like a corrected proof of his desire.

Into just such a room he would like to lead Cissie; into this great room that breathed pride and dignity. What a glowing heart the girl would have made for its somber magnificence!

He walked over to the full-length windows and opened them; then he unbolted the jalousies outside and swung them back. The musk of autumn weeds breathed in out of the darkness. Peter drew a long breath, with a sort of wistful melting in his chest.

CHAPTER IX

A TURMOIL aroused Peter Siner the next morning, and when he discovered where he was, in the big canopy bed in the great room, he listened curiously and heard a continuous chattering and quarreling After a minute or two he recognized the voice of old Rose Hobbett. Rose was cooking the Captain's breakfast, and she performed this function in a kind of solitary rage. She banged the vessels, slammed the stove-eyes on and off, flung the stove-wood about, and kept up a snarling animadversion upon every topic that drifted through her kinky head. She called the kitchen a rat-hole, stated the Captain must be as mean as the devil to live as long as he did, complained that no one ever paid any attention to her, that she might as well be a stray cat, and so on.

As Peter grew wider awake, the monotony of the old negress's rancor faded into an unobserved noise. He sat up on the edge of his bed between the parted curtains and divined there was a bath behind the screen in the corner of his room. Sure enough, he found two frayed but clean towels, a pan, a pitcher, and a small tub all made of tin. Peter assembled his find and began splashing his heavily molded chest with a feeling of well-being. As he splashed on the water, he amused himself by listening again to old Rose. She was now complaining that some white young 'uns had called her "raving Rose." She hoped "God'lmighty would send down two she bears and eat 'em up." Peter was amazed by the old crone's ability to maintain an unending flow of concentrated and aimless virulence.

The kitchen of the Renfrew manor was a separate building, and presently Peter saw old Rose carrying great platters across the weed-grown compound into the dining-room. She bore plate after plate piled high with cookery,—enough for a company of men. A little later came a clangor on a rusty triangle, as if she were summoning a house party. Old Rose did things in a wholesale spirit.

Peter started for his door, but when he had opened the shutter, he stood hesitating. Breakfast introduced another delicate problem. He decided not to go to the dining-room at once, but to wait and allow Captain Renfrew to indicate whether he, Peter, should break his fast with the master in the dining-room or with old Rose in the kitchen.

A moment later he saw the Captain coming down the long back piazza. Peter almost addressed his host, but the old Southerner proceeded into the dining-room apparently without seeing Peter at all.

The guest was gathering his breath to call good morning, but took the cue with a negro's sensitiveness, and let his eyes run along the weeds in the compound. The drying stalks were woven with endless spider-webs, all white with frost. Peter stood regarding their delicate geometrics a moment longer and then reëntered his room, not knowing precisely what to do. He could hear Rose walking across the piazza to and from the dining-room, and the clink of tableware. A few minutes later a knock came at his door, and the old woman entered with a huge salver covered with steaming dishes.

The negress came into the room scowling, and seemed doubtful for a moment just how to shut the door and still hold the tray with both hands. She solved the problem by backing against the door tremendously. Then she saw Peter. She straightened and stared at him with outraged dignity.

"Well, 'fo' Gawd! Is I bringin' dish-here breakfus' to a nigger?"

"I suppose it 's mine," agreed Peter, amused.

"But whuffo, whuffo, nigger, is it dat you ain't come to de kitchen an' eat off'n de shelf? Is you sick?"

Peter admitted fair bodily vigor.

"Den whut de debbil is I got into!" cried Rose, angrily. "I ain't gwine wuck at no sich place, ca'yin' breakfus' to a big beef uv a nigger, stout as a mule. Say, nigger, wha-chu doin' in heah, anyway? Hoccum dis?"

Peter tried to explain that he was there to do a little writing for the Captain.

"Well, 'fo' Gawd, when niggers gits to writin' fuh

white folks, ants 'll be jumpin' fuh bullfrogs,—an havin' other niggers bring dey breakfusses. You jes as much a nigger as I is, Peter Siner, de brightes' day you ever seen!"

Peter began a conciliatory phrase.

Old Rose banged the platter on the table and then threatened:

"Dis is de las' time I fetches a moufful to you, Peter Siner, or any other nigger. You ain't no black Jesus, even ef you is a woods calf."

Peter paused in drawing a chair to the table.

"What did you say, Rose?" he asked sharply.

"You heared whut I say."

A wave of anger went over Peter.

"Yes, I did. You ought to be ashamed to speak ill of the dead."

The crone tossed her malicious head, a little abashed, perhaps, yet very glad she had succeeded in hurting Peter. She turned and went out the door, mumbling something which might have been apology or renewed invectives.

Peter watched the old virago close the door and then sat down to his breakfast. His anger presently died away, and he sat wondering what could have happened to Rose Hobbett that had corroded her whole existence. Did she enjoy her vituperation, her continual malice? He tried to imagine how she felt.

The breakfast Rose had brought him was delicious: hot biscuits of feathery lightness, three wide slices of ham, a bowl of scrambled eggs, a pot of coffee, some preserved raspberries, and a tiny glass of whisky.

The plate which Captain Renfrew had set before his guest was a delicate dawn pink ringed with a wreath of holly. It was old Worcester porcelain of about the decade of 1760. The coffee-pot was really an old Whieldon teapot in broad cauliflower design. Age and careless heating had given the surface a fine reticulation. His cup and saucer, on the contrary, were thick pieces of ware such as the cabin-boys toss about on steamboats. The whole ceramic mélange told of the fortuities of English colonial and early American life, of the migration of families westward. No doubt, once upon a time, that dawn-pink Worcester had married into a Whieldon cauliflower family. A queer sort of genealogy might be traced among Southern families through their mixtures of tableware.

As Peter mused over these implications of long ancestral lines, it reminded him that he had none. Over his own past, over the lineage of nearly every negro in the South, hung a curtain. Even the names of the colored folk meant nothing, and gave no hint of their kin and clan. At the end of the war between the States, Peter's people had selected names for themselves, casually, as children pick up a pretty stone. They meant nothing. It occurred to Peter for the first time, as he sat looking at the chinaware, that he knew nothing about himself; whether his kinsmen were valiant or recreant he did not know. Even his own father he knew little about except that his mother had said his name was Peter, like his own, and that he had gone down the river on a tie boat and was drowned.

A faint sound attracted Peter's attention. He looked out at his open window and saw old Rose making off the back way with something concealed under her petticoat. Peter knew it was the unused ham and biscuits that she had cooked. For once the old negress hurried along without railing at the world. She moved with a silent, but, in a way, self-respecting, flight. Peter could see by the tilt of her head and the set of her shoulders that not only did her spoil gratify her enmity to mankind in general and the Captain in particular, but she was well within her rights in her acquisition. She disappeared around a syringa bush, and was heard no more until she reappeared to cook the noon meal, as vitriolic as ever.

When Peter entered the library, old Captain Renfrew greeted him with morning wishes, thus sustaining the fiction that they had not seen each other before, that morning.

The old gentleman seemed pleased but somewhat excited over his new secretary. He moved some of his books aimlessly from one table to another, placed them in exact piles as if he were just about to plunge into heroic labor, and could not give time to such details once he had begun.

As he arranged his books just so, he cleared his throat.

"Now, Peter, we want to get down to this," he announced dynamically; "do this thing, shove this work out!" He started with tottery briskness around to his manuscript drawer, but veered off to the left to aline some magazines. "System, Peter, system. Without system one may well be hopeless of performing any great literary labor; but with system, the constant piling up of brick on brick, stone on stone—it 's the way Rome was built, my boy."

Peter made a murmur supposed to acknowledge the correctness of this view.

Eventually the old Captain drew out his drawer of manuscript, stood fumbling with it uncertainly. Now and then he glanced at Peter, a genuine secretary who stood ready to help him in his undertaking. The old gentleman picked up some sheets of his manuscript, seemed about to read them aloud, but after a moment shook his head, and said, "No, we 'll do that to-night," and restored them to their places. Finally he turned to his helper.

"Now, Peter," he explained, "in doing this work, I always write at night. It 's quieter then,—less distraction. My mornings I spend downtown in conversation with my friends. If you should need me, Peter, you can walk down and find me in front of the livery-stable. I sit there for a while each morning."

The gravity with which he gave this schedule of his personal habits amused Peter, who bowed with a serious, "Very well, Captain."

"And in the meantime," pursued the old man, looking vaguely about the room, "you will do well to familiarize yourself with my library in order that you may be properly qualified for your secretarial labors."

Peter agreed again.

"And now if you will get my hat and coat, I will be off and let you go to work," concluded the Captain, with an air of continued urgency.

Peter became thoroughly amused at such an outcome of the old gentleman's headlong attack on his work,—a stroll down to the village to hold conversation with friends. The mulatto walked unsmilingly to a little closet where the Captain hung his things. He took down the old gentleman's tall hat, a gray greatcoat worn shiny about the shoulders and tail, and a finely carved walnut cane. Some reminiscence of the manners of butlers which Peter had seen in theaters caused him to swing the overcoat across his left arm and polish the thin nap of the old hat with his right sleeve. He presented it to his employer with a certain duplication of a butler's obsequiousness. He offered the overcoat to the old gentleman's arms with the same air. Then he held up the collar of the greatcoat with one hand and with the other reached under its skirts, and drew down the Captain's long day coat with little jerks, as if he were going through a ritual.

Peter grew more and more hilarious over his barber's manners. It was his contribution to the old gentleman's literary labors, and he was doing it beautifully, so he thought. He was just making some minute adjustments of the collar when, to his amazement, Captain Renfrew turned on him.

"Damn it, sir!" he flared out. "What do you think you are? I did n't engage you for a kowtowing valet in waiting, sir! I asked you, sir, to come under my roof as an intellectual co-worker, as one gentleman asks another, and here you are making these niggery motions! They are disgusting! They are defiling! They are beneath the dignity of one gentleman to another, sir! What makes it more degrading, I perceive by your mannerism that you assume a specious servility, sir, as if you would flatter me by it!"

The old lawyer's face was white. His angry old eyes jerked Peter out of his slight mummery. The negro felt oddly like a grammar-school boy caught making faces behind his master's back. It shocked him into sincerer manners.

"Captain," he said with a certain stiffness, "I apologize for my mistake; but may I ask how you desire me to act?"

"Simply, naturally, sir," thundered the Captain, "as one alumnus of Harvard to another! It is quite proper for a young man, sir, to assist an old gentleman with his hat and coat, but without fripperies and genuflections and absurdities!"

The old man's hauteur touched some spring of resentment in Peter. He shook his head.

"No, Captain; our lack of sympathy goes deeper than manners. My position here is anomalous. For instance, I can talk to you sitting, I can drink with you standing, but I can't breakfast with you at all. I do that *in camera*, like a disgraceful divorce proceeding. It's precisely as I was treated coming down here South again; it's as I've been treated ever since I've been back; it's—" He paused abruptly and swallowed down the rancor that filled him. "No," he repeated in a different tone, "there is no earthly excuse for me to remain here, Captain, or to let you go on measuring out your indulgences to me. There is no way for us to get together or to work together—not this far South. Let me thank you for a night's entertainment and go."

Peter turned about, meaning to make an end of this queer adventure.

The old Captain watched him, and his pallor increased. He lifted an unsteady hand.

"No, no, Peter," he objected, "not so soon. This has been no trial, no fair trial. The little—little—er—details of our domestic life here, they will—er—arrange themselves, Peter. Gossip—talk, you know, we must avoid that." The old lawyer stood staring with strange eyes at his protégé. "I—I'm interested in you, Peter. My actions may seem—odd, but—er—a negro boy going off and doing what you have done—extraordinary. I—I have spoken to your mother,

Caroline, about you often. In fact, Peter, I—I made some little advances in order that you might complete your studies. Now, now, don't thank me! It was purely impersonal. You seemed bright. I have often thought we gentle people of the South ought to do more to encourage our black folk—not—not as social equals—" Here the old gentleman made a wry mouth as if he had tasted salt.

"Stay here and look over the library," he broke off abruptly. "We can arrange some ground of—of common action, some—"

He settled the lapels of his great-coat with precision, addressed his palm to the knob of his stick, and marched stiffly out of the library, around the piazza, and along the dismantled walk to the front gate.

Peter stood utterly astonished at this strange information. Suddenly he ran after the old lawyer, and rounded the turn of the piazza in time to see him walk stiffly down the shaded street with tremulous dignity. The old gentleman was much the same as usual, a little shakier, perhaps, his tall hat a little more polished, his shiny gray overcoat set a little more snugly at the collar.

CHAPTER X

THE village of Hooker's Bend amuses itself mainly with questionable jests that range all the way from the slightly brackish to the hopelessly obscene. Now, in using this type of anecdote, the Hooker's-Benders must not be thought to design an attack upon the decencies of life; on the contrary, they are relying on the fact that their hearers have, in the depths of their beings, a profound reverence for the object of their sallies. And so, by taking advantage of the moral shock they produce and linking it to the idea of an absurdity, they convert the whole psychical reaction into an explosion of humor. Thus the ring of raconteurs telling blackguardly stories around the stoves in Hooker's Bend stores, are, in reality, exercising one another in the more delicate sentiments of life, and may very well be classed as a round table of Sir Galahads, *sans peur et sans reproche.*

However, the best men weary in well doing, and for the last few days Hooker's Bend had switched from its intellectual staple of conversation to consider the comedy of Tump Pack's undoing. The incident held undeniably comic elements. For Tump to start out carrying a forty-four, meaning to blow a rival out of his path, and to wind up hard at work, picking cotton

174

at nothing a day for a man whose offer of three dollars a day he had just refused, certainly held the makings of a farce.

On the heels of this came the news that Peter Siner meant to take advantage of Tump's arrest and marry Cissie Dildine. Old Parson Ranson was responsible for the spread of this last rumor. He had fumbled badly in his effort to hold Peter's secret. Not once, but many times, always guarded by a pledge of secrecy, had he revealed the approaching wedding. When pressed for a date, the old negro said he was "not at lib'ty to tell."

Up to this point white criticism viewed the stage-setting of the black comedy with the impersonal interest of a box party. Some of the round table said they believed there would be a dead coon or so before the scrape was over.

Dawson Bobbs, the ponderous constable, went to the trouble to telephone Mr. Cicero Throgmartin, for whom Tump was working, cautioning Throgmartin to make sure that Tump Pack was in the sleeping-shack every night, as he might get wind of the wedding and take a notion to bolt and stop it. "You know, you can't tell what a fool nigger 'll do," finished Bobbs.

Throgmartin was mildly amused, promised the necessary precautions, and said:

"It looks like Peter has put one over on Tump, and maybe a college education does help a nigger some, after all."

The constable thought it was just luck.

"Well, I dunno," said Throgmartin, who was a philosopher, and inclined to view every matter from various angles. "Peter may of worked this out somehow."

"Have you heard what Henry Hooker done to Siner in the land deal?"

Throgmartin said he had.

"No, I don't mean *that*. I mean Henry's last wrinkle in garnisheeing old Ca'line's estate in his bank for the rest of the purchase money on the Dilihay place."

There was a pause.

"You don't mean it!"

"Damn 'f I don't."

The constable's sentence shook with suppressed mirth, and the next moment roars of laughter came over the telephone wire.

"Say, ain't he the bird!"

"He's the original early bird. I'd like to get a snap-shot of the worm that gets away from him."

Both men laughed heartily again.

"But, say," objected Throgmartin, who was something of a lawyer himself,—as, indeed, all Southern men are,—"I thought the Sons and Daughters of Benevolence owed Hooker, not Peter Siner, nor Ca'line's estate."

"Well, it *is* the Sons and Daughters, but Ca'line was one of 'em, and they ain't no limited li'bility 'sociation. Henry can jump on anything any of 'em 's got. Henry got the Persimmon to bring him a copy of their by-laws."

"Well, I swear! Say, if Henry was n't kind of held back by his religion, he 'd use a gun, would n't he?"

"I dunno. I can say this for Henry's religion: It 's jest like Henry's wife,—it 's the dearest thing to his heart; he 'd give his life for it, but it don't do nobody a damn bit of good except jest Henry."

The constable's little eyes twinkled as he heard Throgmartin roaring with laughter and sputtering appreciative oaths.

At that moment a ringing of the bell jarred the ears of both telephonists. A voice asked for Dr. Jallup. It was an ill time to interrupt two gentlemen. The flair of a jest is lost in a pause. The officer stated sharply that he was the constable of Wayne County and was talking business about the county's prisoners. His tone was so charged with consequence that the voice that wanted a doctor apologized hastily and ceased.

Came a pause in which neither man found anything to say. Laughter is like that,—a gay bubble that a touch will destroy. Presently Bobbs continued, gravely enough:

"Talking about Siner, he 's stayin' up at old man Renfrew's now."

" 'At so?"

"Old Rose Hobbett swears he 's doin' some sort of

writin' up there and livin' in one of the old man's best rooms."

"Hell he is!"

"Yeah?" the constable's voice questioned Throg-· martin's opinion about such heresy and expressed his own.

"D' recken it's so? Old Rose is such a thief and a liar."

"Nope," declared the constable, "the old nigger never would of made up a lie like that,—never would of thought of it. Old Cap'n Renfrew's gettin' childish; this nigger's takin' advantage of it. Down at the liver'-stable the boys were talkin' about Siner goin' to git married, an' dern if old man Renfrew did n't git cut up about it!"

"Well," opined Throgmartin, charitably, "the old man livin' there all by himself—I reckon even a nigger is some comp'ny. They're funny damn things, niggers is; never know a care nor trouble. Lord! I wish I was as care-free as they are!"

"Don't you, though!" agreed the constable, with the weight of the white man's burden on his shoulders. For this is a part of the Southern credo,—that all negroes are gay, care-free, and happy, and that if one could only be like the negroes, gay, care-free, and happy— Ah, if one could only be like the negroes!

None of this gossip reached Peter directly, but a sort of back-wash did catch him keenly through young

Sam Arkwright and serve as a conundrum for several days.

One morning Peter was bringing an armful of groceries up the street to the old manor, and he met the boy coming in the opposite direction. The negro's mind was centered on a peculiar problem he had found in the Renfrew library, so, according to a habit he had acquired in Boston, he took the right-hand side of the pavement, which chanced to be the inner side. This violated a Hooker's-Bend convention, which decrees that when a white and a black meet on the sidewalk, the black man invariably shall take the outer side.

For this *faux pas* the gangling youth stopped Peter, fell to abusing and cursing him for his impudence, his egotism, his attempt at social equality,—all of which charges, no doubt, were echoes from the round table. Such wrath over such an offense was unusual. Ordinarily, a white villager would have thought several uncomplimentary things about Peter, but would have said nothing.

Peter stopped with a shock of surprise, then listened to the whole diatribe with a rising sense of irritation and irony. Finally, without a word, he corrected his mistake by retracing his steps and passing Sam again, this time on the outside.

Peter walked on up the street, outwardly calm, but his ears burned, and the queer indignity stuck in his mind. As he went along he invented all sorts of ironical remarks he might have made to Arkwright, which would have been unwise; then he thought of sober reasoning he could have used, which would perhaps have been just as ill-advised. Still later he wondered why Arkwright had fallen into such a rage over such a trifle. Peter felt sure there was some contributing rancor in the youth's mind. Perhaps he had received a scolding at home or a whipping at school, or perhaps he was in the midst of one of those queer attacks of megalomania from which adolescents are chronic sufferers. Peter fancied this and that, but he never came within hail of the actual reason.

When the brown man reached the old manor, the quietude of the library, with its blackened mahogany table, its faded green Axminster, the meridional globe with its dusty twinkle, banished the incident from his mind. He returned to his work of card-indexing the Captain's books. He took half a dozen at a time from the shelves, dusted them on the piazza, then carried them to the embrasure of the window, which offered a pleasant light for reading and for writing the cards.

He went through volume after volume,—speeches by Clay, Calhoun, Yancy, Prentiss, Breckenridge; an old life of General Taylor, Foxe's "Book of Martyrs"; a collection of the old middle-English dramatists, such as Lillo, Garrick, Arthur Murphy, Charles Macklin, George Colman, Charles Coffey, men whose plays have long since declined from the boards and disappeared from the reading-table.

The Captain's collection of books was strongly
colored by a religious cast,—John Wesley's sermons,
Charles Wesley's hymns; a treatise presenting a bibli-
cal proof that negroes have no souls; a little book called
"Flowers Gathered," which purported to be a compilation of the sayings of ultra-pious children, all of whom
died young; an old book called "Elements of Criticism,"
by Henry Home of Kames; another tome entitled
"Studies of Nature," by St. Pierre. This last was a
long argument for the miraculous creation of the world
as set forth in Genesis. The proof offered was a
résumé of the vegetable, animal, and mineral kingdoms,
showing their perfect fitness for man's use, and the
immediate induction was that they were designed for
man's use. Still another work calculated the exact
age of the earth by the naïve method of counting the
generations from Adam to Christ, to the total adding
eighteen hundred and eighty-five years (for the book
was written in 1885), and the original six days it
required the Lord to build the earth. By referring to
Genesis and finding out precisely what the Creator did
on the morning of the first day, the writer contrived
to bring his calculation of the age of the earth and
everything in the world to a precision of six hours,
give or take,—a somewhat closer schedule than that
made by the Tennessee river boats coming up from
St. Louis.

These and similar volumes formed the scientific
section of Captain Renfrew's library, and it was this

paucity of the natural sciences that formed the problem which Peter tried to solve. All scientific additions came to an abrupt stop about the decade of 1880-90. That was the date when Charles Darwin's great fructifying theory, enunciated in 1859, began to seep into the South.

In the Captain's library the only notice of evolution was a book called "Darwinism Dethroned." As for the elaborations of the Darwinian hypothesis by Spencer, Fiske, DeVries, Weismann, Haeckel, Kidd, Bergson, and every subsequent philosophic or biologic writer, all these men might never have written a line so far as Captain Renfrew's library was informed.

Now, why such extraordinary occlusions? Why should Captain Renfrew deny himself the very commonplaces of thought, theories familiarly held by the rest of America, and, indeed, by all the rest of the civilized world?

Musing by the window, Peter succeeded in stating his problem more broadly: Why was Captain Renfrew an intellectual reactionist? The old gentleman was the reverse of stupid. Why should he confine his selection of books to a few old oddities that had lost their battle against a theory which had captured the intellectual world fifty years before?

Nor was it Captain Renfrew alone. Now and then Peter saw editorials appearing in leading Southern journals, seriously attacking the evolutionary hypothesis. Ministers in respectable churches still fulminated against it. Peter knew that the whole South still clings, in a way, to the miraculous and special creation of the earth as described in Genesis. It clings with an intransigentism and bitterness far exceeding any other part of America. Why? To Peter the problem appeared insoluble.

He sat by the window lost in his reverie. Just outside on the ledge half a dozen English sparrows abused one another with chirps that came faintly through the small diamond panes. Their quick movements held Peter's eyes, and their endless quarreling presently recalled his episode with young Arkwright. It occurred to him, casually, that when Arkwright grew up he would subscribe to every reactionary doctrine set forth in the library Peter was indexing.

With that thought came a sort of mental flare, as if he were about to find the answer to the whole question through the concrete attack made on him by Sam.

It is an extraordinary feeling,—the sudden, joyful dawn of a new idea. Peter sat up sharply and leaned forward with a sense of being right on the fringe of a new and a great perception. Young Arkwright, the old Captain, the whole South, were unfolding themselves in a vast answer, when a movement outside the window caught the negro's introspective eyes.

A girl was passing; a girl in a yellow dress was passing the Renfrew gate. Even then Peter would not have wavered in his synthesis had not the girl paused slightly and given a swift side glance at the old manor. Then the man in the window recognized Cissie Dildine.

A slight shock traveled through Siner's body at the sight of Cissie's colorless face and darkened eyes. He stood up abruptly, with a feeling that he had some urgent thing to say to the young woman. His sharp movement toppled over the big globe.

The crash caused the girl to stop and look. For a moment they stood thus, the girl in the chill street, the man in the pleasant window, looking at each other. Next moment Cissie hurried on up the village street toward the Arkwright house. No doubt she was on her way to cook the noon meal.

Peter remained standing at the window, with a heavily beating heart. He watched her until she vanished behind a wing of the shrubbery in the Renfrew yard.

When she had gone, he looked at his books and cards, sat down, and tried to resume his indexing. But his mind played away from it like a restive horse. It had been two weeks since he last saw Cissie. Two weeks. . . . His nerves vibrated like the strings of a pianoforte. He had scarcely thought of her during the fortnight; but now, having seen her, he found himself powerless to go on with his work. He pottered a while longer among the books and cards, but they were meaningless. They appeared an utter futility. Why index a lot of nonsense? Somehow this recalled his flare, his adumbration of some great idea connected with young Arkwright and the old Captain, and the South.

He put his trembling nerves to work, trying to recapture his line of thought. He sat for ten minutes, following this mental train, then that, losing one, groping for another. His thoughts were jumpy. They played about Arkwright, the Captain, Cissie, his mother's death, Tump Pack in prison, the quarrel between the Persimmon and Jim Pink Staggs. The whole of Niggertown came rushing down upon him, seizing him in its passion and dustiness and greasiness, putting to flight all his cultivated white-man ideas.

After half an hour's searching he gave it up. Before he left the room he stooped, and tried to set up again the globe that the passing of the girl had caused him to throw down; but its pivot was out of plumb, and he had to lean it against the window-seat.

The sight of Captain Renfrew coming in at the gate sent Peter to his room. The hour was near twelve, and it had become a little point of household etiquette for the mulatto and the white man not to be together when old Rose jangled the triangle. By this means they forestalled the mute discourtesy of the old Captain's walking away from his secretary to eat. The subject of their separate meals had never been mentioned since their first acrimonious morning. The matter had dropped into the abeyance of custom, just as the old gentleman had predicted.

Peter had left open his jalousies, but his windows

were closed, and now as he entered he found his apartment flooded with sunshine and filled with that equable warmth that comes of straining sunbeams through glass.

He prepared for dinner with his mind still hovering about Cissie. He removed a book and a lamp from the lion-footed table, and drew up an old chair with which the Captain had furnished his room. It was a delicate old Heppelwhite of rosewood. It had lost a finial from one of its back standards, and a round was gone from the left side. Peter never moved the chair that vague plans sometime to repair it did not occur to him.

When he had cleared his table and placed his chair beside it, he wandered over to his tall west window and stood looking up the street through the brilliant sunshine, toward the Arkwright home. No one was in sight. In Hooker's Bend every one dines precisely at twelve, and at that hour the streets are empty. It would be some time before Cissie came back down the street on her way to Niggertown. She first would have to wash and put away the Arkwright dishes. It would be somewhere about one o'clock. Nevertheless, he kept staring out through the radiance of the autumn sunlight with an irrational feeling that she might appear at any moment. He was afraid she would slip past and he not see her at all. The thought disturbed him somewhat. It kept him sufficiently on the alert to stand tapping the balls of his fingers against the glass and looking steadily toward the Arkwright house.

Presently the watcher perceived that a myriad spider-webs filled the sunshine with a delicate dancing glister. It was the month of voyaging spiders. Invisible to Peter, the tiny spinners climbed to the tipmost twigs of the dead weeds, listed their abdomens, and lassoed the wind with gossamer lariats; then they let go and sailed away to a hazard of new fortunes. The air was full of the tiny adventurers. As he stared up the street, Peter caught the glint of these invisible airships whisking away to whatever chance might hold for them. There was something epic in it. It recalled to the mulatto's mind some of Fabre's lovely descriptions. It reminded him of two or three books on entomology which he had left in his mother's cabin. He felt he ought to go after them while the spiders were migrating. He suddenly made up his mind he would go at once, as soon as he had had dinner; somewhere about one o'clock.

He looked again at the Arkwright house. The thought of walking down the street with Cissie, to get his books, quickened his heart.

He was still at the window when his door opened and old Rose entered with his dinner. She growled under her breath all the way from the door to the table on which she placed the tray. Only a single phrase detached itself and stood out clearly amid her mutterings, "Hope it chokes you."

Peter arranged his chair and table with reference to the window, so he could look up the street while he was eating his dinner.

The ill-wishing Rose had again furnished a gourmet's meal, but Peter's preoccupation prevented its careful and appreciative gustation. An irrational feeling of the octoroon's imminence spurred him to fast eating. He had hardly begun his soup before he found himself drinking swiftly, looking up the street over his spoon, as if he meant to rush out and swing aboard a passing train.

Siner checked his precipitation, annoyed at himself. He began again, deliberately, with an attempt to keep his mind on the savor of his food. He even thought of abandoning his little design of going for the books; or he would go at a different hour, or to-morrow, or not at all. He told himself he would far better allow Cissie Dildine to pass and repass unspoken to, instead of trying to arrange an accidental meeting. But the brown man's nerves would n't hear to it. That automatic portion of his brain and spinal column which, physiologists assert, performs three fourths of a man's actions and conditions nine tenths of his volitions—that part of Peter would n't consider it. It began to get jumpy and scatter havoc in Peter's thoughts at the mere suggestion of not seeing Cissie. Imperceptibly this radical left wing of his emotions speeded up his meal again. He caught himself, stopped his knife and fork in the act of rending apart a broiled chicken.

"Confound it! I'll start when she comes in sight, no matter whether I've finished this meal or not," he promised himself.

And suddenly he felt unhurried, in the midst of a large leisure, with a savory broiled chicken dinner before him,—not exactly before him, either; most of it had been stuffed away. Only the fag-end remained on his plate. A perfectly good meal had been ruined by an ill-timed resistance to temptation.

The glint of a yellow dress far up the street had just prompted him to swift action when the door opened and old Rose put her head in to say that Captain Renfrew wanted to see Peter in the library.

The brown man came to a shocked standstill.

"What! Right now?" he asked.

"Yeah, right now," carped Rose. "Ever'thing he wants, he wants right now. He's been res'less as a cat in a bulldog's den ever sence he come home fuh dinner. Dunno whut's come into he ole bones, runnin' th'ugh his dinner lak a razo'-back." She withdrew in a continued mumble of censure.

Peter cast a glance up the street, timed Cissie's arrival at the front gate, picked up his hat, and walked briskly to the library in the hope of finishing any business the Captain might have, in time to encounter the octoroon. He even began making some little conversational plans with which he could meet Cissie in a simple, unstudied manner. He recalled with a certain satisfaction that he had not said a word of con-

demnation the night of Cissie's confession.   He would
make a point of that, and was prepared to argue that,
since he had said nothing, he meant nothing.   In fact,
he was prepared to throw away the truth completely
and enter the conversation as an out-and-out opportu-
nist, alleging whatever appeared to fit the occasion, as
all men talk to all women.

The old Captain was just getting into his chair as
Peter entered.   He paused in the midst of lowering
himself by the chair-arms and got erect again.   He
began speaking a little uncertainly:

"Ah—by the way, Peter—I sent for you—"

"Yes, sir."   Peter looked out at the window.

The old gentleman scrutinized Peter a moment; then
his faded eyes wandered about the library.

"Still working at the books, cross-indexing them—"

"Yes, sir."   Peter could divine by the crinkle of his
nerves the very loci of the girl as she passed down the
thoroughfare.

"Very good," said the old lawyer, absently.   He was
obviously preoccupied with some other topic.   "Very
good," he repeated with racking deliberation; "quite
good.   How did that globe get bent?"

Peter, looking at it, did not remember either knocking it over or setting it up.

"I don't know," he said rapidly.   "I had n't noticed
it."

"Old Rose did it," meditated the Captain aloud,

"but it's no use to accuse her of it; she'd deny it. And yet, on the other hand, Peter, she'll be nervous until I do accuse her of it. She'll be dropping things, breaking up my china. I dare say I'd best accuse her at once, storm at her some to quiet her nerves, and get it over."

This monologue spurred Peter's impatience into an agony.

"I believe you were wanting me, Captain?" he suggested, with a certain urge for action.

The Captain's little pleasantry faded. He looked at Peter and became uncomfortable again.

"Well, yes, Peter. Downtown I heard—well, a rumor connected with you—"

Such an extraordinary turn caught the attention of even the fidgety Peter. He looked at his employer and wondered blankly what he had heard.

"I don't want to intrude on your private affairs, Peter, not at all—not—not in the least—"

"No-o-o," agreed Peter, completely at a loss.

The old gentleman rubbed his thin hands together, lifted his eyebrows up and down nervously. "Are—are you about to—to leave me, Peter?"

Peter was greatly surprised at the slightness and simplicity of this question and at the evidence of emotion it carried.

"Why, no," he cried; "not at all! Who told you I was? It is a deep gratification to me—"

"To be exact," proceeded the old man, with a vague fear still in his eyes, "I heard you were going to marry."

"Marry!" This flaw took Peter's sails even more unexpectedly than the other. "Captain, who in the world—who could have told—"

"Are you?"

"No."

"You are n't?"

"Indeed, no!"

"I heard you were going to marry a negress here in town called Cissie Dildine." A question was audible in the silence that followed this statement. The obscure emotion that charged all the old man's queries affected Peter.

"I am not, Captain," he declared earnestly; "that's settled."

"Oh—you say it's settled," picked up the old lawyer, delicately.

"Yes."

"Then you had thought of it?" Immediately, however, he corrected this breach of courtesy into which his old legal habit of cross-questioning had led him. "Well, at any rate," he said in quite another voice, "that eases my mind, Peter. It eases my mind. It was not only, Peter, the thought of losing you, but this girl you were thinking of marrying—let me warn you, Peter—she's a negress."

The mulatto stared at the strange objection.

"A negress!"

The old man paused and made that queer movement with his wrinkled lips as if he tasted some salty flavor.

"I—I don't mean exactly a—a negress," stammered the old gentleman; "I mean she's not a—a good girl, Peter; she's a—a thief, in fact—she's a thief—a thief, Peter. I couldn't endure for you to marry a thief, Peter."

It seemed to Peter Siner that some horrible compulsion kept the old Captain repeating over and over the fact that Cissie Dildine was a thief, a thief, a thief. The word cut the very viscera in the brown man. At last, when it seemed the old gentleman would never cease, Peter lifted a hand.

"Yes, yes," he gasped, with a sickly face, "I—I've heard that before."

He drew a shaken breath and moistened his lips. The two stood looking at each other, each profoundly at a loss as to what the other meant. Old Captain Renfrew collected himself first.

"That is all, Peter." He tried to lighten his tones. "I think I'll get to work. Let me see, where do I keep my manuscript?"

Peter pointed mechanically at a drawer as he walked out at the library door. Once outside, he ran to the front piazza, then to the front gate, and with a racing heart stood looking up and down the sleepy thoroughfare. The street was quite empty.

CHAPTER XI

OLD Captain Renfrew was a trustful, credulous soul, as, indeed, most gentleman who lead a bachelor's life are. Such men lack that moral hardening and whetting which is obtained only amid the vicissitudes of a home; they are not actively and continuously engaged in the employment and detection of chicane; want of intimate association with a woman and some children begets in them a soft and simple way of believing what is said to them. And their faith, easily raised, is just as easily shattered. Their judgment lacks training.

Peter Siner's simple assertion to the old Captain that he was not going to marry Cissie Dildine completely allayed the old gentleman's uneasiness. Even the further information that Peter had had such a marriage under advisement, but had rejected it, did not put him on his guard.

From long non-intimacy with any human creature, the old legislator had forgotten that human life is one long succession of doing the things one is not going to do; he had forgotten, if he ever knew, that the human brain is primarily not a master, but a servant; its function is not to direct, but to devise schemes and apologies to gratify impulses. It is the ways and means committee to the great legislature of the body.

For several days after his fear that Peter Siner would marry Cissie Dildine old Captain Renfrew was as felicitous as a lover newly reconciled to his mistress. He ambled between the manor and the livery-stable with an abiding sense of well-being. When he approached his home in the radiance of high noon and saw the roof of the old mansion lying a bluish gray in the shadows of the trees, it filled his heart with joy to feel that it was not an old and empty house that awaited his coming, but that in it worked a busy youth who would be glad to see him enter the gate.

The fear of some unattended and undignified death which had beset the old gentleman during the last eight or ten years of his life vanished under Peter's presence. When he thought of it at all now, he always previsioned himself being lifted in Peter's athletic arms and laid properly on his big four-poster.

At times, when Peter sat working over the books in the library, the Captain felt a prodigious urge to lay a hand on the young man's broad and capable shoulder. But he never did. Again, the old lawyer would sit for minutes at a time watching his secretary's regular features as the brown man pursued his work with a trained intentness. The old gentleman derived a deep pleasure from such long scrutinies. It pleased him to imagine that, when he was young, he had possessed the same vigor, the same masculinity, the same capacity for persistent labor. Indeed, all old gentlemen are prone to choose the most personable and virile young man they can find for themselves to have been like.

The two men had little to say to each other. Their thoughts beat to such different tempos that any attempt at continued speech discovered unequal measures. As a matter of fact, in all comfortable human conversation, words are used as mere buoys dropped here and there to mark well-known channels of thought and feeling. Similarity of mental topography is necessary to mutual understanding. Between any two generations the landscape is so changed as to be unrecognizable. Our fathers are monarchists; our sons, bolsheviki.

Old Rose Hobbett was more of an age with the Captain, and these two talked very comfortably as the old virago came and went with food at meal-time. For instance, the Captain always asked his servant if she had fed his cat, and old Rose invariably would sulk and poke out her lips and put off answering to the last possible moment of insolence, then would grumble out that she was jes 'bout to feed the varmint, an' 't wuz funny nobody could n't give a hard-wuckin' colored woman breathin'-space to turn roun' in.

This reply was satisfactory to the Captain, because he knew what it meant,—that Rose had half forgotten the cat, and had meant wholly to forget it, but since she had been snapped up, so to speak, in the very act of forgetting, she would dole it out a piece or two of the meat that she had meant to abscond with as soon as the dishes were done.

While Rose was fulminating, the old gentleman recalled his bent globe and decided the moment had come for a lecture on that point. It always vaguely embarrassed the Captain to correct Rose, and this increased his dignity. Now he cleared his throat in a certain way that brought the old negress to attention, so well they knew each other.

"By the way, Rose, in the future I must request you to use extraordinary precautions in cleansing and dusting articles of my household furniture, or, in case of damage, I shall be forced to withold an indemnification out of your pay."

Eight or ten years ago, when the Captain first repeated this formula to his servant, the roll and swing of his rhetoric, and the last word, "pay," had built up lively hopes in Rose that the old gentleman was announcing an increase in her regular wage of a dollar a week. Experience, however, had long since corrected this faulty interpretation.

She came to a stand in the doorway, with her kinky gray head swung around, half puzzled, wholly rebellious.

"Whut is I bruk now?"

"My globe."

The old woman turned about with more than usual angry innocence.

"Why, I ain't tech yo' globe!"

"I foresaw that," agreed the Captain, with patient irony, "but in the future don't touch it more carefully. You bent its pivot the last time you refrained from handling it."

"But I tell you I ain't tech yo' globe!" cried the negress, with the anger of an illiterate person who feels, but cannot understand, the satire leveled at her.

"I agree with you," said the Captain, glad the affair was over.

This verbal ducking into the cellar out of the path of her storm stirred up a tempest.

"But I tell you I ain't bruk it!"

"That's what I said."

"Yeah, yeah, yeah," she flared; "you says I ain't, but when you says I ain't, you means I is, an' when you says I is, you means I ain't. Dat's de sort o' flapjack I's wuckin' fur!"

The woman flirted out of the dining-room, and the old gentleman drew another long breath, glad it was over. He really had little reason to quarrel about the globe, bent or unbent; he never used it. It sat in his study year in and year out, its dusty twinkle brightened at long intervals by old Rose's spiteful rag.

The Captain ate on placidly. There had been a time when he was dubious about such scenes with Rose. Once he felt it beneath his dignity as a Southern gentleman to allow any negro to speak to him disrespectfully. He used to feel that he should discharge her instantly, and during the first years of their entente had done so a number of times. But he could get no one else who suited him so well; her biscuits, her corn-light-bread, her lye-hominy, which only the old darkies know how to make. And, to tell the truth, he missed the old creature herself, her understanding of him and his ideas, her contemporaneity; and no one else would work for a dollar a week.

Presently in the course of his eating the old gentleman required another biscuit, and he wanted a hot one. Three mildly heated disks lay on a plate before him, but they had been out of the oven for five minutes and had been reduced to an unappetizing tepidity.

A little hand-bell sat beside the Captain's plate whose special use was to summon hot biscuits. Now, the old lawyer looked at its worn handle speculatively. He was not at all sure Rose would answer the bell. She would say she had n't heard it. He felt faintly disgruntled at not foreseeing this exigency and buttering two biscuits while they were hot, or even three.

He considered momentarily a project of going after a hot biscuit for himself, but eventually put it by. South of the Mason-Dixon Line, self-help is half-scandal. At last, quite dubiously, he did pick up the bell and gave it a gentle ring, so if old Rose chose not to hear it, she probably would n't; thus he could believe her and not lose his temper and so widen an already uncomfortable breach.

To the Captain's surprise, the old creature not only

brought the biscuits, but she did it promptly. No sooner had she served them, however, than the Captain saw she really had returned with a new line of defense.

She mumbled it out as usual, so that her employer was forced to guess at a number of words: "Dat nigger, Peter, mus' 'a' busted yo' gl—"

"No, he did n't."

"Mus' uv."

"No, he did n't. I asked him, and he said he did n't."

The old harridan stared, and her speech suddenly became clear-cut:

"Well, 'fo' Gawd, I says I did n't, too!"

At this point the Captain made an unintelligible sound and spread the butter on his hot biscuit.

"He 's jes a nigger, lak I is," stated the cook, warmly.

The Captain buttered a second hot biscuit.

"We 's jes two niggers."

The Captain hoped she would presently sputter herself out.

"Now look heah," cried the crone, growing angrier and angrier as the reaches of the insult spread itself before her, "is you gwine to put one o' us niggers befo' de udder? 'Ca'se ef you is, I mus' say, it 's Kady-lock-a-do' wid me."

The Captain looked up satirically.

"What do you mean by Katie-lock-the-door with you?" he asked, though he had an uneasy feeling that he knew.

"You know whut I means. I means I's gwine to leab dis place."

"Now look here, Rose," protested the lawyer, with dignity, "Peter Siner occupies almost a fiduciary relation to me."

The old negress stared with a slack jaw. "A relation o' yo's!"

The lawyer hesitated some seconds, looking at the hag. His high-bred old face was quite inscrutable, but presently he said in a serious voice:

"Peter occupies a position of trust with me, Rose."

"Yeah," mumbled Rose; "I see you trus' him."

"One day he is going to do me a service, a very great service, Rose."

The hag continued looking at him with a stubborn expression.

"You know better than any one else, Rose, my dread of some—some unmannerly death—"

The old woman made a sound that might have meant anything.

"And Peter has promised to stay with me until—until the end."

The old negress considered this solemn speech, and then grunted out:

"Which en'?"

"Which end?" The Captain was irritated.

"Yeah; yo' en' or Peter's en'?"

"By every law of probability, Peter will outlive me."

"Yeah, but Peter 'll come to a en' wid you when he

ma'ies dat stuck-up yellow fly-by-night, Cissie Dildine."

"He's not going to marry her," said the Captain, comfortably.

"Huh!"

"Peter told me he did n't intend to marry Cissie Dildine."

"Shu! Then whut fur dey go roun' peepin' at each other lak a couple o' niggers roun' a haystack?"

The old lawyer was annoyed.

"Peeping where?"

"Why, right in front o' dis house, dat 's wha; ever' day when dat hussy passes up to de Arkwrights', wha she wucks. She pokes along an' walls her eyes roun' at dis house lak a calf wid de splivins."

"That going on now?"

"Ever' day."

A deep uneasiness went through the old man. He moistened his lips.

"But Peter said—"

"Good Gawd! Mars' Renfrew, whut diff'ence do it make whut Peter say? Ain't you foun' out yit when a he-nigger an' a she-nigger gits to peepin' at each rudder, whut dey says don't lib in de same neighbo'hood wid whut dey does?"

This was delivered with such energy that it completely undermined the Captain's faith in Peter, and the fact angered the old gentleman.

"That 'll do, Rose; that 'll do. That 's all I need of you."

The old crone puffed up again at this unexpected flare, and went out of the room, plopping her feet on the floor and mumbling. Among these ungracious sounds the Captain caught, "Blin' ole fool!" But there was no need becoming offended and demanding what she meant. Her explanation would have been vague and unsatisfactory.

The verjuice which old Rose had sprinkled over Peter and Cissie by calling them "he-nigger" and "she-nigger" somehow minimized them, animalized them in the old lawyer's imagination. Rose's speech was charged with such contempt for her own color that it placed the mulatto and the octoroon down with apes and rabbits.

The lawyer fought against his feeling, for the sake of his secretary, who had come to occupy so wide a sector of his comfort and affection. Yet the old virago evidently spoke from a broad background of experience. She was at least half convincing. While the Captain repelled her charge against his quiet, hard-working brown helper, he admitted it against Cissie Dildine, whom he did not know. She was an animal, a female centaur, a wanton and a strumpet, as all negresses are wantons and strumpets. All white men in the South firmly believe that. They believe it with a peculiar detestation; and since they used these persons very profitably for a hundred and fifty years as breeding animals, one might say they believe it a trifle ungratefully.

CHAPTER XII

THE semi-daily passings of Cissie Dildine before the old Renfrew manor on her way to and from the Arkwright home upset Peter Siner's working schedule to an extraordinary degree.

After watching for two or three days, Peter worked out a sort of time-table for Cissie. She passed up early in the morning, at about five forty-five. He could barely see her then, and somehow she looked very pathetic hurrying along in the cold, dim light of dawn. After she had cooked the Arkwright breakfast, swept the Arkwright floors, dusted the Arkwright furniture, she passed back toward 'Niggertown, somewhere near nine. About eleven o'clock she went up to cook dinner, and returned at one or two in the afternoon. Occasionally, she made a third trip to get supper.

This was as exactly as Peter could predict the arrivals and departures of Cissie, and the schedule involved a large margin of uncertainty. For half an hour before Cissie passed she kept Peter watching the clock at nervous intervals, wondering if, after all, she had gone by unobserved. Invariably, he would move his work to a window where he had the whole street under his observation. Then he would proceed with

his indexing with more and more difficulty. At first
the paragraphs would lose connection, and he would be
forced to reread them. Then the sentences would drop
apart. Immediately before the girl arrived, the words
themselves grew anarchic. They stared him in the
eye, each a complete entity, self-sufficient, individual,
bearing no relation to any other words except that of
mere proximity,—like a spelling lesson. Only by an
effort could Peter enforce a temporary cohesion among
them, and they dropped apart at the first slackening of
the strain.

Strange to say, when the octoroon actually was walking past, Peter did not look at her steadily. On the
contrary, he would think to himself: "How little I
care for such a woman! My ideal is thus and so—"
He would look at her until she glanced across the yard
and saw him sitting in the window; then immediately
he bent over his books, as if his stray glance had lighted
on her purely by chance, as if she were nothing more
to him than a passing dray or a fluttering leaf. Indeed, he told himself during these crises that he had
no earthly interest in the girl, that she was not the
sort of woman he desired,—while his heart hammered,
and the lines of print under his eyes blurred into gray
streaks across the page.

One afternoon Peter saw Cissie pass his gate, hurrying, almost running, apparently in flight from something. It sent a queer shock through him. He stared
after her, then up and down the street. He wondered

why she ran. Even when he went to bed that night, the strangeness of Cissie's flight kept him awake, inventing explanations.

None of Peter's preoccupations was lost upon Captain Renfrew. None is so suspicious as a credulous man aroused. After Rose had struck her blow at the secretary, the old gentleman noted all of Peter's permutations and misconstrued a dozen quite innocent actions on Peter's part into signs of bad faith.

By a little observation he identified Cissie Dildine, and what he saw did not reëstablish his peace of mind. On the contrary, it became more than probable that the cream-colored negress would lure Peter away. This possibility aroused in the old lawyer a grim, voiceless rancor against Cissie. In his thoughts he linked the girl with every manner of evil design against Peter. She was an adventuress, a Cyprian, a seductress attempting to snare Peter in the brazen web of her comeliness. For to the old gentleman's eyes there was an abiding impudicity about Cissie's very charms. The passionate repose of her face was immodest; the possession of a torso such as a sculptor might have carved was brazen. The girl was shamefully well appointed.

One morning as Captain Renfrew came home from town, he chanced to walk just behind the octoroon, and quite unconsciously the girl delivered an added fillip to the old gentleman's uneasiness.

Just before Cissie passed in front of the Renfrew manor, womanlike, she paused to make some slight improvements in her appearance before walking under the eyes of her lover. She adjusted some strands of hair which had blown loose in the autumn wind, looked at herself in a purse mirror, retouched her nose with her greenish powder; then she picked a little sprig of sumac leaves that burned in the corner of a lawn and pinned its flame on the unashamed loveliness of her bosom.

This negro instinct for brilliant color is the theme of many jests in the South, but it is entirely justified esthetically, although the constant sarcasm of the whites has checked its satisfaction, if it has not corrupted the taste.

The bit of sumac out of which the octoroon had improvised a nosegay lighted up her skin and eyes, and created an ensemble as closely resembling a Henri painting as anything the streets of Hooker's Bend were destined to see.

But old Captain Renfrew was far from appreciating any such bravura in scarlet and gold. At first he put it down to mere niggerish taste, and his dislike for the girl edged his stricture; then, on second thought, the oddness of sumac for a nosegay caught his attention. Nobody used sumac for a buttonhole. He had never heard of any woman, white or black, using sumac for a bouquet. Why should this Cissie Dildine trig herself out in sumac?

The Captain's suspicions came to a point like a

setter. He began sniffing about for Cissie's motives
in choosing so queer an ornament. He wondered if
it had anything to do with Peter Siner.

All his life, Captain Renfrew's brain had been deliberate. He moved mentally, as he did physically,
with dignity. To tell the truth, the Captain's thoughts
had a way of absolutely stopping now and then, and
for a space he would view the world as a simple collection of colored surfaces without depth or meaning.
During these intervals, by a sort of irony of the gods,
the old gentleman's face wore a look of philosophic
concentration, so that his mental hiatuses had given
him a reputation for profundity, which was county
wide. It had been this, years before, that had carried
him by a powerful majority into the Tennessee legislature. The voters agreed, almost to a man, that they
preferred depth to a shallow facility. The rival candi-
date had been shallow and facile. The polls returned
the Captain, and the young gentleman—for the Captain
was a young gentleman in those days—was launched
on a typical politician's career. But some Republican
member from east Tennessee had impugned the rising
statesman's honor with some sort of improper liaison.
In those days there seemed to be proper and improper
liaisons. There had been a duel on the banks of the
Cumberland River in which the Captain succeeded in
wounding his traducer in the arm, and was thus vindi-
cated by the gods. But the incident ended a career that

might very well have wound up in the governor's chair, or even in the United States Senate, considering how very deliberate the Captain was mentally.

To-day, as the Captain walked up the street following Cissie Dildine, one of these vacant moods fell upon him, and it was not until they had reached his own gate that it suddenly occurred to the old gentleman just what Cissie's sumac did mean. It was a signal to Peter. The simplicity of the solution stirred the old man. Its meaning was equally easy to fathom. When a woman signals any man it conveys consent. Denials receive no signals; they are inferred. In this particular case Captain Renfrew found every reason to believe that this flaring bit of sumac was the prelude to an elopement.

In the window of his library the Captain saw his secretary staring at his cards and books with an intentness plainly assumed. Peter's fixed stare had none of those small movements of the head that mark genuine intellectual labor. So Peter was posing, pretending he did not see the girl, to disarm his employer's suspicions, —pretending not to see a girl rigged out like that!

Such duplicity sent a queer spasm of anguish through the old lawyer. Peter's action held half a dozen barbs for the Captain. A fellow-alumnus of Harvard staying in his house merely for his wage and keep! Peter bore not the slightest affection for him; the mulatto lacked even the chivalry to notify the Captain of his intentions, because he knew the Captain objected. And yet all these self-centered objections were nothing to what old Captain Renfrew felt for Peter's own sake. For Peter to marry a nigger and a strumpet, for him to elope with a wanton and a thief! For such an upstanding lad, the very picture of his own virility and mental alertness when he was of that age, for such a boy to fling himself away, to drop out of existence— oh, it was loathly!

The old man entered the library feeling sick. It was empty. Peter had gone to his room, according to his custom. But in this particular instance it seemed to Captain Renfrew his withdrawal was flavored with a tang of guilt. If he were innocent, why should not such a big, strong youth have stayed and helped an old gentleman off with his overcoat?

The old Captain blew out a windy breath as he helped himself out of his coat in the empty library. The bent globe still leaned against the window-seat. The room had never looked so somber or so lonely.

At dinner the old man ate so little that Rose Hobbett ceased her monotonous grumbling to ask if he felt well. He said he had had a hard day, a difficult day. He felt so weak and thin that he foretold the gray days when he could no longer creep to the village and sit with his cronies at the livery-stable, when he would be house-fast, through endless days, creeping from room to room like a weak old rat in a huge empty house, finally to die in some disgusting fashion. And

now Peter was going to leave him, was going to throw
himself away on a lascivious wench. A faint moisture
dampened the old man's withered eyes. He drank an
extra thimbleful of whisky to try to hearten himself.
Its bouquet filled the time-worn stateliness of the
dining-room.

During the weeks of Peter's stay at the manor it had
grown to be the Captain's habit really to write for two
or three hours in the afternoon, and his pile of manuscript had thickened under his application.

The old man was writing a book called "Reminiscences of Peace and War." His book would form
another unit of that extraordinary crop of personal
reminiscences of the old South which flooded the
presses of America during the decade of 1908–18.
During just that decade it seemed as if the aged men
and women of the South suddenly realized that the
generation who had lived through the picturesqueness
and stateliness of the old slave régime was almost gone,
and over their hearts swept a common impulse to com-
memorate, in the sunset of their own lives, its fading
splendor and its vanished deeds.

On this particular afternoon the Captain settled
himself to work, but his reminiscences did not get on.
He pinched a bit of floss from the nib of his pen and
tried to swing into the period of which he was writing.
He read over a few pages of his copy as mental prim-
ing, but his thoughts remained flat and dull. Indeed,

his whole life, as he reviewed it in the waning afternoon, appeared empty and futile. It seemed hardly
worth while to go on.

The Captain had come to that point in his memoirs
where the Republican representative from Knox
County had set going the petard which had wrecked
his political career.

From the very beginnings of his labors the old lawyer had looked forward to writing just this period
of his life. He meant to clear up his name once for
all. He meant to use invective, argument, testimony,
and a powerful emotional appeal, such as a country
lawyer invariably attempts with a jury.

But now that he had arrived at the actual composition of his defense, he sat biting his penholder,
with all the arguments he meant to advance slipped
from his mind. He could not recall the points of the
proof. He could not recall them with Peter Siner
moving restlessly about the room, glancing through
the window, unsettled, nervous, on the verge of eloping
with a negress.

His secretary's tragedy smote the old man. The
necessity of doing something for Peter put his thoughts
to rout. A wild idea occurred to the Captain that if
he should write the exact truth, perhaps his memoirs
might serve Peter as a signal against a futile, empty
journey.

But the thought no sooner appeared than it was rejected. In the Anglo-Saxon, especially the Anglo-

Saxon of the Southern United States, abides no such Gallic frankness as moved a Jean-Jacques. Southern memoirs always sound like the conversation between two maiden ladies,—nothing intimate, simply a few general remarks designed to show from what nice families they came.

So the Captain wrote nothing. During all the afternoon he sat at his desk with a leaden heart, watching Peter move about the room. The old man maintained more or less the posture of writing, but his thoughts were occupied in pitying himself and pitying Peter. Half a dozen times he looked up, on the verge of making some plea, some remonstrance, against the madness of this brown man. But the sight of Peter sitting in the window-seat staring out into the street silenced him. He was a weak old man, and Peter's nerves were strung with the desire of youth.

At last the two men heard old Rose clashing in the kitchen. A few minutes later the secretary excused himself from the library, to go to his own room. As Peter was about to pass through the door, the Captain was suddenly galvanized into action by the thought that this perhaps was the last time he would ever see him. He got up from his chair and called shakenly to Peter. The negro paused. The Captain moistened his lips and controlled his voice.

"I want to have a word with you, Peter, about a—a little matter. I—I've mentioned it before."

"Yes, sir." The negro's tone and attitude reminded

the Captain that the supper gong would soon sound
and they would best separate at once.

"It—it's about Cissie Dildine," the old lawyer
hurried on.

Peter nodded slightly.

"Yes, you mentioned that before."

The old man lifted a thin hand as if to touch Peter's
arm, but he did not. A sort of desperation seized him.

"But listen, Peter, you don't want to do—what's
in your mind!"

"What is in my mind, Captain?"

"I mean marry a negress. You don't want to marry
a negress!"

The brown man stared, utterly blank.

"Not marry a negress!"

"No, Peter; no," quavered the old man. "For yourself it may make no difference, but your children—think
of your children, your son growing up under a brown
veil! You can't tear it off. God himself can't tear
it off! You can never reach him through it. Your
children, your children's children, a terrible procession
that stretches out and out, marching under a black
shroud, unknowing, unknown! All you can see are
their sad forms beneath the shroud, marching away—
marching away. God knows where! And yet—it's
your own flesh and blood!"

Suddenly the old lawyer's face broke into the hard,
tearless contortions of the aged. His terrible emotion
communicated itself to the sensitive brown man.

"But, Captain, I myself am a negro. Whom should I marry?"

"No one; no one! Let your seed wither in your loins! It's better to do that; it's better—" At that moment the clashing of the supper gong fell on the old man's naked nerves. He straightened up by some reflex mechanism, turned away from what he thought was his last interview with his secretary, and proceeded down the piazza into the great empty dining-room.

CHAPTER XIII

WITH overwrought nerves Peter Siner entered his room. At five o'clock that afternoon he had seen Cissie Dildine go up the street to the Arkwright home to cook one of those occasional suppers. He had been watching for her return, and in the midst of it the Captain's extraordinary outburst had stirred him up.

Once in his room, the negro placed the broken Hepplewhite in such a position that he could rake the street with a glance. Then he tried to compose himself and await the coming of his supper and the passage of Cissie. There was something almost pathetic in Peter's endless watching, all for a mere glimpse or two of the girl in yellow. He himself had no idea how his nerves and thoughts had woven themselves around the young woman. He had no idea what a passion this continual doling out of glimpses had begotten. He did not dream how much he was, as folk naïvely put it, in love with her.

His love was strong enough to make him forget for a while the old lawyer's outbreak. However, as the dusk thickened in the shrubbery and under the trees, certain of the old gentleman's phrases revisited the mulatto's mind: "A terrible procession . . . march-

ing under a black shroud. . . . Your children, your
children's children, a terrible procession, . . . marching away, God knows where. . . . And yet—it's your
own flesh and blood!" They were terrific sentences,
as if the old man had been trying to tear from his vision
some sport of nature, some deformity. As the implications spread before Peter, he became more and
more astonished at its content. Even to Captain Renfrew black men were dehumanized,—shrouded, un-
touchable creatures.

It delivered to Peter a slow but a profound shock.
He glanced about at the faded magnificence of the
room with a queer feeling that he had been introduced
into it under a sort of misrepresentation. He had
taken up his abode with the Captain, at least on the
basis of belonging to the human family, but this passionate outbreak, this puzzling explosion, cut that
ground from under his feet.

The more Peter thought about it, the stranger grew
his sensation. Not even to be classed as a human being
by this old gentleman who in a weak, helpless fashion
had crept somewhat into Peter's affections,—not to be
considered a man! The mulatto drew a long, troubled
breath, and by the mere mechanics of his desire kept
staring through the gloom for Cissie.

Peter Siner had known all along that the unread
whites of Hooker's Bend—and that included nearly
every white person in the village—considered black
men as simple animals; but he had supposed that the

more thoughtful men, of whom Captain Renfrew was
a type, at least admitted the Afro-American to the common brotherhood of humanity.   But they did not.

As Peter sat staring into the darkness the whole
effect of the dehumanizing of the black folk of the
South began to unfold itself before his imagination.
It explained to him the tragedies of his race, their
sufferings at the hand of mob violence; the casualness,
even the levity with which black men were murdered;
the chronic dishonesty with which negroes were treated;
the constant enactment of adverse legislation against
them; the cynical use of negro women.   They were
all vermin, animals; they were one with the sheep and
the swine; a little nearer the human in form, perhaps,
and, oddly enough, one that could be bred to a human
being, as testified a multitude of brown and yellow and
cream-colored folk, but all marching away, as the Captain had so passionately said, marching away, their
forms hidden from human intercourse under a shroud
of black, an endless procession marching away, God
knew whither!   And yet they were the South's own
flesh and blood.

The horror of such a complex swelled in Peter's mind
to monstrous proportions.   As night thickened at his
window, the negro sat dazed and wondering at the
mightiness of his vision.   His thoughts went groping,
trying to solve some obscure problem it posed.   He
thought of the Arkwright boy; he thought of the white
men smiling as his mother's funeral went past the

livery-stable; he thought of Captain Renfrew's manuscript that he was transcribing. Through all the old man's memoirs ran a certain lack of sincerity. Peter always felt amid his labors that the old Captain was making an attorney's plea rather than a candid exposition. At this point in his thoughts there gradually limned itself in the brown man's mind the answer to that enigma which he almost had unraveled on the day he first saw Cissie Dildine pass his window. With it came the answer to the puzzle contained in the old Captain's library. The library was not an ordinary compilation of the world's thought; it, too, was an attorney's special pleading against the equality of man. Any book or theory that upheld the equality of man was carefully excluded from the shelves. Darwin's great hypothesis, and every development springing from it, had been banned, because the moment that a theory was propounded of the great biologic relationship of all flesh, from worms to vertebrates, there instantly followed a corollary of the brotherhood of man.

What Christ did for theology, Darwin did for biology,—he democratized it. The One descended to man's brotherhood from the Trinity; the other climbed up to it from the worms.

The old Captain's library lacked sincerity. Southern orthodoxy, which persists in pouring its religious thought into the outworn molds of special creation, lacks sincerity. Scarcely a department of Southern life escapes this fundamental attitude of special pleader and disingenuousness. It explains the Southern fondness for legal subtleties. All attempts at Southern poetry, belles-lettres, painting, novels, bear the stamp of the special plea, of authors whose exposition is careful.

Peter perceived what every one must perceive, that when letters turn into a sort of glorified prospectus of a country, all value as literature ceases. The very breath of art and interpretation is an eager and sincere searching of the heart. This sincerity the South lacks. Her single talent will always be forensic, because she is a lawyer with a cause to defend. And such is the curse that arises from lynchings and venery and extortions and dehumanizings,—sterility; a dumbness of soul.

Peter Siner's thoughts lifted him with the tremendous buoyancy of inspiration. He swung out of his chair and began tramping his dark room. The skin of his scalp tickled as if a ghost had risen before him. The nerves in his thighs and back vibrated. He felt light, and tingled with energy.

Unaware of what he was doing, he set about lighting the gasolene-lamp. He worked with nervous quickness, as if he were in a great hurry. Presently a brilliant light flooded the room. It turned the gray illumination of the windows to blackness.

Joy enveloped Peter. His own future developed under his eyes with the same swift clairvoyance that marked his vision of the ills of his country. He saw himself remedying those ills. He would go about showing white men and black men the simple truth, the spiritual necessity for justice and fairness. It was not a question of social equality; it was a question of clearing a road for the development of Southern life. He would show white men that to weaken, to debase, to dehumanize the negro, inflicted a more terrible wound on the South than would any strength the black man might develop. He would show black men that to hate the whites, constantly to suspect, constantly to pilfer from them, only riveted heavier shackles on their limbs.

It was all so clear and so simple! The white South must humanize the black not for the sake of the negro, but for the sake of itself. 'No one could resist logic so fundamental.

Peter's heart sang with the solemn joy of a man who had found his work. All through his youth he had felt blind yearnings and gropings for he knew not what. It had driven him with endless travail out of Niggertown, through school and college, and back to Niggertown,—this untiring Hound of Heaven. But at last he had reached his work. He, Peter Siner, a mulatto, with the blood of both white and black in his veins, would come as an evangel of liberty to both white and black. The brown man's eyes grew moist from joy. His body seemed possessed of tremendous energy.

As he paced his room there came into the glory of

Peter's thoughts the memory of the Arkwright boy as
he sat in the cedar glade brooding on the fallen needles.
Peter recalled the hobbledehoy's disjointed words as he
wrestled with the moral and physical problems of
adolescence. Peter recalled his impulse to sit down by
young Sam Arkwright, and, as best he might, give him
some clue to the critical and feverish period through
which he was passing.

He had not done so, but Peter remembered the instance down to the very desperation in the ·face of the
brooding youngster. And it seemed to Peter that this
rejected impulse had been a sign that he was destined
to be an evangel to the whites as well as to the blacks.

The joy of Peter's mission bore him aloft on vast
wings. His room seemed to fall away from him, and
he was moving about his country, releasing the two
races from their bonds of suspicion and cruelty.

Slowly the old manor formed about Peter again,
and he perceived that a tapping on the door had summoned him back. He walked to the door with his
heart full of kindness for old Rose. She was bringing him his supper. He felt as if he could take the
old woman in his arms, and out of the mere hugeness
of his love sweeten her bitter life. The mulatto
opened the door as eagerly as if he were admitting
some long-desired friend; but when the shutter swung
back, the old crone and her salver were not there. All
he could discern in the darkness were the white pillars

marking the night into panels. There was no light in the outer kitchen. The whole manor was silent.

As he stood listening, the knocking was repeated, this time more faintly. He fixed the sound at the window. He closed the door, walked across the brilliant room, and opened the shutters.

For several moments he saw nothing more than the tall quadrangle of blackness which the window framed; then a star or two pierced it; then something moved. He saw a woman's figure standing close to the casement, and out of 'the darkness Cissie Dildine's voice asked in its careful English:

"Peter, may I come in?"

CHAPTER XIV

FOR a full thirty seconds Peter Siner stared at the girl at the window before, even with her prompting, he thought of the amenity of asking her to come inside. As a further delayed courtesy, he drew the Heppelwhite chair toward her.

Cissie's face looked bloodless in the blanched light of the gasolene-lamp. She forced a faint, doubtful smile.

"You don't seem very glad to see me, Peter."

"I am," he assured her, mechanically, but he really felt nothing but astonishment and dismay. They filled his voice. He was afraid some one would see Cissie in his room. His thoughts went flitting about the premises, calculating the positions of the various trees and shrubs in relation to the windows, trying to determine whether, and just where, in his brilliantly lighted chamber the girl could be seen from the street.

The octoroon made no further comment on his confusion. Her eyes wandered from him over the stately furniture and up to the stuccoed ceiling.

"They told me you lived in a wonderful room," she remarked absently.

"Yes, it's very nice," agreed Peter in the same tone, wondering what might be the object of her hazardous visit. A flicker of suspicion suggested that she was trying to compromise him out of revenge for his renouncement of her, but the next instant he rejected this.

The girl accepted the chair Peter offered and continued to look about.

"I hope you don't mind my staring, Peter," she said.

"I stared when I first came here to stay," assisted Peter, who was getting a little more like himself, even if a little uneasier at the consequences of this visit.

"Is that a highboy?" She nodded nervously at the piece of furniture. "I've seen pictures of them."

"Uh huh. Revolutionary, I believe. The night wind is a little raw." He moved across the room and closed the jalousies, and thus cut off the night wind and also the west view from the street. He glanced at the heavy curtains parted over his front windows, with a keen desire to swing them together. Some fragment of his mind continued the surface conversation with Cissie.

"Is it post-Revolutionary or pre-Revolutionary?" she asked with a preoccupied air.

"Post, I believe. No, pre. I always meant to examine closely."

"To have such things would almost teach one history," Cissie said.

"Yeah; very nice." Peter had decided that the girl was in direct line with the left front window and an opening between the trees to the street,

The girl's eyes followed his.

"Are those curtains velour, Peter?"

"I—I believe so," agreed the man, unhappily.

"I—I wonder how they look spread."

Peter seized on this flimsy excuse with a wave of relief and thankfulness to Cissie. He had to restrain himself as he strode across the room and swung together the two halves of the somber curtains in order to preserve an appearance of an exhibit. His fingers were so nervous that he bungled a moment at the heavy cords, but finally the two draperies swung together, loosing a little cloud of dust. He drew together a small aperture where the hangings stood apart, and then turned away in sincere relief.

Cissie's own interest in historic furniture and textiles came to an abrupt conclusion. She gave a deep sigh and settled back into her chair. She sat looking at Peter seriously, almost distressfully, as he came toward her.

With the closing of the curtains and the establishment of a real privacy Peter became aware once again of the sweetness and charm Cissie always held for him. He still wondered what had brought her, but he was no longer uneasy.

"Perhaps I'd better build a fire," he suggested, quite willing now to make her visit seem not unusual.

"Oh, no,"—she spoke with polite haste,—"I'm just going to stay a minute. I don't know what you'll think of me." She looked intently at him.

"I think it lovely of you to come." He was disgusted with the triteness of this remark, but he could think of nothing else.

"I don't know," demurred the octoroon, with her faint, doubtful smile. "Persons don't welcome beggars very cordially."

"If all beggars were so charming—" Apparently he could n't escape banalities.

But Cissie interrupted whatever speech he meant to make, with a return of her almost painful seriousness.

"I really came to ask you to help me, Peter."

"Then your need has brought me a pleasure, at least." Some impulse kept the secretary making those foolish complimentary speeches which keep a conversation empty and insincere.

"Oh, Peter, I did n't come here for you to talk like that! Will you do what I want?"

"What do you want, Cissie?" he asked, sobered by her voice and manner.

"I want you to help me, Peter."

"All right, I will." He spaced his words with his speculations about the nature of her request. "What do you want me to do?"

"I want you to help me go away."

Peter looked at her in surprise. He hardly knew what he had been expecting, but it was not this.

Some repressed emotion crept into the girl's voice.

"Peter, I—I can't stay here in Hooker's Bend any longer. I want to go away. I—I've got to go away."

Peter stood regarding her curiously and at the same time sympathetically.

"Where do you want to go, Cissie?"

The girl drew a long breath; her bosom lifted and dropped abruptly.

"I don't know; that was one of the things I wanted to ask you about."

"You don't know where you want to go?" He smiled faintly. "How do you know you want to go at all?"

"Oh, Peter, all I know is I must leave Hooker's Bend!" She gave a little shiver. "I'm tired of it, sick of it—sick." She exhaled a breath, as if she were indeed physically ill. Her face suggested it; her eyes were shadowed. "Some Northern city, I suppose," she added.

"And you want me to help you?" inquired Peter, puzzled.

She nodded silently, with a woman's instinct to make a man guess the favor she is seeking.

Then it occurred to Peter just what sort of assistance the girl did want. It gave him a faint shock that a girl could come to a man to beg or to borrow money. It was a white man's shock, a notion he had picked up in Boston, because it happens frequently among village negroes, and among them it holds as little significance as children begging one another for bites of apples.

Peter thought over his bank balance, then started

toward a chest of drawers where he kept his check-book.

"Cissie, if I can be of any service to you in a substantial way, I'll be more than glad to—"

She put out a hand and stopped him; then talked straight on in justification of her determination to go away.

"I just can't endure it any longer, Peter." She shuddered again. "I can't stand Niggertown, or this side of town—any of it. They—they have no *feeling* for a colored girl, Peter, not—not a speck!" She gave a gasp, and after a moment plunged on into her wrongs: "When—when one of us even walks past on the street, they—they whistle and say a-all kinds of things out loud, j-just as if w-we were n't there at all. Th-they don't c-care; we 're just n-nigger w-women." Cissie suddenly began sobbing with a faint catching noise, her full bosom shaken by the spasms; her tears slowly welling over. She drew out a handkerchief with a part of its lace edge gone, and wiped her eyes and cheeks, holding the bit of cambric in a ball in her palm, like a negress, instead of in her fingers, like a white woman, as she had been taught. Then she drew a deep breath, swallowed, and became more composed.

Peter stood looking in helpless anger at this representative of all women of his race.

"Cissie, that's street-corner scum—the dirty sewage—"

"They make you feel naked," went on Cissie in the

monotone that succeeds a fit of weeping, "and ashamed —and afraid." She blinked her eyes to press out the undue moisture, and looked at Peter as if asking what else she could do about it than to go away from the village.

"Will it be any better away from here?" suggested Peter, doubtfully.

Cissie shook her head.

"I—I suppose not, if—if I go alone."

"I should n't think so," agreed Peter, somberly. He started to hearten her by saying white women also underwent such trials, if that would be a consolation; but he knew very well that a white woman's hardships were as nothing compared to those of a colored woman who was endowed with any grace whatever.

"And besides, Cissie," went on Peter, who somehow found himself arguing against the notion of her going, "I hardly see how a decent colored woman gets around at all. Colored boarding-houses are wretched places. I ate and slept in one or two, coming home. Rotten." The possibility of Cissie finding herself in such a place moved Peter.

The girl nodded submissively to his judgment, and said in a queer voice: "That 's why I—I did n't want to travel alone, Peter."

"No, it 's a bad idea—" and then Peter perceived that a queer quality was creeping into the tête-à-tête.

She returned his look unsteadily, but with a curious persistence.

"You-you mean you want m-me—to go with you, Cissie?" he
stammered

"I—I d-don't want to travel a-alone, Peter," she gasped.

Her look, her voice suddenly brought home to the man the amazing connotation of her words. He stared at her, felt his face grow warm with a sharp, peculiar embarrassment. He hardly knew what to say or do before her intent and piteous eyes.

"You—you mean you want m-me—to go with you, Cissie?" he stammered.

The girl suddenly began trembling, now that her last reserve of indirection had been torn away.

"Listen, Peter," she began breathlessly. "I'm not the sort of woman you think. If I hadn't accused myself, we'd be married now. I—I wanted you more than anything in the world, Peter, but I did tell you. Surely, surely, Peter, that shows I am a good woman —th-the real I. Dear, dear Peter, there is a difference between a woman and her acts. Peter, you're the first man in all my life, in a-all my life who ever came to me k-kindly and gently; so I had to l-love you and t-tell you, Peter."

The girl's wavering voice broke down completely; her face twisted with grief. She groped for her chair, sat down, buried her face in her arms on the table, and broke into a chattering outbreak of sobs that sounded like some sort of laughter.

Her shoulders shook; the light gleamed on her soft, black Caucasian hair. There was a little rent in one of the seams in her cheap jacket, at one of the curves where her side molded into her shoulder. The custom-made garment had found Cissie's body of richer mold than it had been designed to shield. And yet in Peter's distress and tenderness and embarrassment, this little rent held his attention and somehow misprized the wearer.

It seemed symbolic in the searching white light. He could see the very break in the thread and the widened stitches at the ends of the rip. Her coat had given way because she was modeled more nearly like the Venus de Milo than the run of womankind. He felt the little irony of the thing, and yet was quite unable to resist the comparison.

And then, too, she had referred again to her sin of peculation. A woman enjoys confessions from a man. A man's sins are mostly vague, indefinite things to a woman, a shadowy background which brings out the man in a beautiful attitude of repentance; but when a woman confesses, the man sees all her past as a close-up with full lighting. He has an intimate acquaintance with just what she's talking about, and the woman herself grows shadowy and unreal. Men have too many blots not to demand whiteness in women. By striking some such average, nature keeps the race a going moral concern.

So Peter, as he stood looking down on the woman who was asking him to marry her, was filled with as unhappy and as impersonal a tenderness as a born brother. He recalled the thoughts which had come to him when he saw Cissie passing his window. She was not the sort of woman he wanted to marry; she was not his ideal. He cast about in his head for some gentle way of putting her off, so that he would not hurt her any further, if such an easement were possible.

As he stood thinking, he found not a pretext, but a reality. He stooped over, and put a hand lightly on each of her arms.

"Cissie," he said in a serious, even voice, "if I should ever marry any one, it would be you."

The girl paused in her sobbing at his even, passionless voice.

"Then you—you won't?" she whispered in her arms.

"I can't, Cissie." Now that he was saying it, he uttered the words very evenly and smoothly. "I can't, dear Cissie, because a great work has just come into my life." He paused, expecting her to ask some question, but she lay silent, with her face in her arms, evidently listening.

"Cissie, I think, in fact I know, I can demonstrate to all the South, both white and black, the need of a better and more sincere understanding between our two races."

Peter did not feel the absurdity of such a speech in such a place. He patted her arm, but there was something in the warmth of her flesh that disturbed his austerity and caused him to lift his hand to the more impersonal axis of her shoulder. He proceeded to develop his idea.

"Cissie, just a moment ago you were complaining of the insults you meet everywhere. I believe, if I can spread my ideas, Cissie, that even a pretty colored girl like you may walk the streets without being subjected to obscenity on every corner." His tone unconsciously patronized Cissie's prettiness with the patronage of the male for the less significant thing, as though her ripeness for love and passion and children were, after all, not comparable with what he, a male, could do in the way of significantly molding life.

Cissie lifted her head and dried her eyes.

"So you aren't going to marry me, Peter?" Woman-like, now that she was well into the subject, she was far less embarrassed than Peter. She had had her cry.

"Why—er—considering this work, Cissie—"

"Aren't you going to marry anybody, Peter?"

The artist in Peter, the thing the girl loved in him, caught again that Messianic vision of himself.

"Why, no, Cissie," he said, with a return of his inspiration of an hour ago; "I'll be going here and there all over the South preaching this gospel of kindliness and tolerance, of forgiveness of the faults of others." Cissie looked at him with a queer expression. "I'll show the white people that they should treat the negro with consideration not for the sake of the negro, but for the sake of themselves. It's so simple, Cissie, it's so logical and clear—"

The girl shook her head sadly.

"And you don't want me to go with you, Peter?"

"Why, n-no, Cissie; a girl like you could n't go. Perhaps I 'll be misunderstood in places, perhaps I may have to leave a town hurriedly, or be swung over the walls, like Paul, in a basket." He attempted to treat it lightly.

But the girl looked at him with a horror dawning in her melancholy face.

"Peter, do you really mean that?" she whispered.

"Why, truly. You don't imagine—"

The octoroon opened her dark eyes until she might have been some weird.

"Oh, Peter, please, please put such a mad idea away from you! Peter, you 've been living here alone in this old house until you don't see things clearly. Dear Peter, don't you *know?* You can't go out and talk like that to white folks and—and not have some terrible thing happen to you! Oh, Peter, if you would only marry me, it would cure you of such wildness!" Involuntarily she got up, holding out her arms to him, offering herself to his needs, with her frightened eyes fixed on his.

It made him exquisitely uncomfortable again. He made a little sound designed to comfort and reassure her. He would do very well. He was something of a diplomat in his way. He had got along with the boys in Harvard very well indeed. In fact, he was rather a man of the world. No need to worry about him, though it was awfully sweet of her.

Cissie picked up her handkerchief with its torn edge, which she had laid on the table. Evidently she was about to go.

"I surely don't know what will become of me," she said, looking at it.

In a reversal of feeling Peter did not want her to go away quite then. He cast about for some excuse to detain her a moment longer.

"Now, Cissie," he began, "if you are really going to leave Hooker's Bend—"

"I'm not going," she said, with a long exhalation. "I—" she swallowed—"I just thought that up to— ask you to—to— You see," she explained, a little breathless, "I thought you still loved me and had forgiven me by the way you watched for me every day at the window."

This speech touched Peter more keenly than any of the little drama the girl had invented. It hit him so shrewdly he could think of nothing more to say.

Cissie moved toward the window and undid the latch.

"Good night, Peter." She paused a moment, with her hand on the catch. "Peter," she said, "I'd almost rather see you marry some other girl than try so terrible a thing."

The big, full-blooded athlete smiled faintly.

"You seem perfectly sure marriage would cure me of my mission."

Cissie's face reddened faintly.

"I think so," she said briefly. "Good night," and she disappeared in the dark space she had opened, and closed the jalousies softly after her.

CHAPTER XV

CISSIE DILDINE'S conviction that marriage would cure Peter of his mission persisted in the mulatto's mind long after the glamour of the girl had faded and his room had regained the bleak emptiness of a bachelor's bedchamber.

Cissie had been so brief and positive in her statement that Peter, who had not thought on the point at all, grew more than half convinced she was right.

Now that he pondered over it, it seemed there was a difference between the outlook of a bachelor and that of a married man. The former considered humanity as a balloonist surveys a throng,—immediately and without perspective,—but the latter always sees mankind through the frame of his family. A single man tends naturally to philosophy and reform; a married man to administration and statesmanship. There have been no great unmarried statesmen; there have been no great married philosophers or reformers.

Now that Cissie had pointed out this universal rule, Peter saw it very clearly. And Peter suspected that beneath this rough classification, and conditioning it, lay a plexus of obscure mental and physical reactions set up by the relations between husband and wife. It might very well be there was a difference between the

238

actual cerebral and nervous structure of a married man
and that of a single man.

At any rate, after these reflections, Peter now felt
sure that marriage would cure him of his mission; but
how had Cissie known it? How had she struck out
so involved a theory, one might say, in the toss of a
head? The more Peter thought it over the more extraordinary it became. It was another one of those
explosive ideas which Cissie, apparently, had the faculty
of creating out of a pure mental vacuum.

All this philosophy aside, Cissie's appearance just in
the nick of his inspiration, her surprising proposal of
marriage, and his refusal, had accomplished one thing:
it had committed Peter to the program he had outlined
to the girl.

Indeed, there seemed something fatalistic in such a
concatenation of events. Siner wondered whether or
not he would have obeyed his vision without this added
impulse from Cissie. He did not know; but now, since
it had all come about just as it had, he suspected he
would have been neglectful. He felt as if a dangerous
but splendid channel had been opened before his eyes,
and almost at the same instant a hand had reached down
and directed his life into it. This fancy moved the
mulatto. As he got himself ready for bed, he kept
thinking:

"Well, my life is settled at last. There is nothing
else for me to do. Even if this should end terribly for
me, as Cissie imagines, my life won't be wasted."

Next morning Peter Siner was awakened by old Rose Hobbett thrusting her head in at his door, staring around, and finally, seeing Peter in bed, grumbling:

"Why is you still heah, black man?"

The secretary opened his eyes in astonishment.

"Why should n't I be here?"

"Nobody wuz 'speckin' you to be heah." The crone withdrew her head and vanished.

Peter wondered at this unaccustomed interest of Rose, then hurried out of bed, supposing himself late for breakfast.

A dense fog had come up from the river, and the moisture floating into his open windows had dampened his whole room. Peter stepped briskly to the screen and began splashing himself. It was only in the midst of his ablutions that he remembered his inspiration and resolve of the previous evening. As he squeezed the water over his powerfully molded body, he recalled it almost impersonally. It might have happened to some third person. He did not even recall distinctly the threads of the logic which had lifted him to such a Pisgah, and showed him the whole South as a new and promised land. However, he knew that he could start his train of thought again, and again ascend the mountain.

Floating through the fog into his open window came the noises of the village as it set about living another day, precisely as it had lived innumerable days in the past. The blast of the six-o'clock whistle from the

planing-mill made the loose sashes of his windows
rattle. Came a lowing of cows and a clucking of hens,
a woman's calling. The voices of men in conversation
came so distinctly through the pall that it seemed a
number of persons must be moving about their morning work, talking and shouting, right in the Renfrew
yard.

But the thing that impressed Peter most was the
solidity and stability of this Southern village that he
could hear moving around him, and its certainty to go
on in the future precisely as it had gone on in the past.
It was a tremendous force. The very old manor about
him seemed huge and intrenched in long traditions,
while he, Peter Siner, was just a brown man, naked
behind a screen and rather cold from the fog and damp
of the morning.

He listened to old Rose clashing the kitchen utensils.
As he drew on his damp underwear, he wondered what
he could say to old Rose that would persuade her into
a little kindliness and tolerance for the white people.
As he listened he felt hopeless; he could never explain
to the old creature that her own happiness depended
upon the charity she extended to others. She could
never understand it. She would live and die precisely
the same bitter old beldam that she was, and nothing
could ever assuage her.

While Peter was thinking of the old creature, she
came shuffling along the back piazza with his breakfast.
She let herself in by lifting one knee to a horizontal,

balancing the tray on it, then opening the door with her freed hand.

When the shutter swung open, it displayed the old crone standing on one foot, wearing a man's grimy sock, which had fallen down over a broken, run-down shoe.

In Peter's mood the thought of this wretched old woman putting on such garments morning after morning was unspeakably pathetic. He thought of his own mother, who had lived and died only a shade or two removed from the old crone's condition.

Rose put down her foot, and entered the room with her lips poked out, ready to make instant attack if Peter mentioned his lack of supper the night before.

"Aunt Rose," asked the secretary, with his friendly intent in his tones, "how came you to look in this morning and say you did n't expect to find me in my room?"

She gave an unintelligible grunt, pushed the lamp to one side, and eased her tray to the table.

Peter finished touching his tie before one of those old-fashioned mirrors, not of cut-glass, yet perfectly true. He came from the mirror and moved his chair, out of force of habit, so he could look up the street toward the Arkwrights'.

"Aunt Rose," said the young man, wistfully, "why are you always angry?"

She bridled at this extraordinary inquiry.

"Me?"

"Yes, you."

She hesitated a moment, thinking how she could make her reply a personal assault on Peter.

"'Cause you come heah, 'sputin' my rights, da' 's' why."

"No," demurred Peter, "you were quarreling in the kitchen the first morning I came here, and you did n't know I was on the place."

"Well—I got my tribulations," she snapped, staring suspiciously at these unusual questions.

There was a pause; then Peter said placatingly:

"I was just thinking, Aunt Rose, you might forget your tribulations if you did n't ride them all the time."

"Hoccum! What you mean, ridin' my tribulations?"

"Thinking about them. The old Captain, for instance; you are no happier always abusing the old Captain."

The old virago gave a sniff, tossed her head, but kept her eyes rolled suspiciously on Peter.

"Very often the way we think and act makes us happy or unhappy," moralized Peter, broadly.

"Look heah, nigger, you ain't no preacher sont out by de Lawd to me!"

"Anyway, I am sure you would feel more friendly toward the Captain if you acted openly with him; for instance, if you did n't take off all his cold victuals, and handkerchiefs and socks, soap, kitchenware—"

The cook snorted.

"I'd feel dat much mo' nekked an' hongry, dat's how I'd feel."

"Perhaps, if you'd start over, he might give you a better wage."

"Huh!" she snorted in an access of irony. "I see dat skinflint gib'n' me a better wage. Puuh!" Then suddenly she realized where the conversation had wandered, and stared at the secretary with widening eyes. "Good Lawd! Did dat fool Cap'n set up a nigger in dis bedroom winder jes to ketch ole Rose packin' off a few ole lef'-overs?" Peter began a hurried denial, but she rushed on: "'Fo' Gawd, I hopes his viddles chokes him! I hope his ole smoke-house falls down on his ole haid. I hope to Jesus—"

Peter pleaded with her not to think the Captain was behind his observations, but the hag rushed out of the bedroom, swinging her head from side to side, uttering the most terrible maledictions. She would show him! She wouldn't put another foot in his old kitchen. Wild horses couldn't drag her into his smoke-house again.

Peter ran to the door and called after her down the piazza, trying to exonerate the Captain; but she either did not or would not hear, and vanished into the kitchen, still furious.

Old Rose made Peter so uneasy that he deserted his breakfast midway and hurried to the library. In the solemn old room he found the Captain alone and in rather a pleased mood. The old gentleman stood patting and alining a pile of manuscript. As the mulatto entered he exclaimed:

"Well, here 's Peter again!" as if his secretary had been off on a long journey. Immediately afterward he added, "Peter, guess what I did last night." His voice was full of triumph.

Peter was thinking about Aunt Rose, and stood looking at the Captain without the slightest idea.

"I wrote all of this,"—he indicated his manuscript,— "over a hundred pages."

Peter considered the work without much enthusiasm.

"You must have worked all night."

The old attorney rubbed his hands.

"I think I may claim a touch of inspiration last night, Peter. Reminiscences rippled from under my pen, propitious words, prosperous sentences. Er—the fact is, Peter, you will see, when you begin copying, I had come to a matter—a—a matter of some moment in my life. Every life contains such moments, Peter. I had meant to write something in the nature of a defen—an explanation, Peter. But after you left the library last night it suddenly occurred to me just to give each fact as it took place, quite frankly. So I did that—not— not what I meant to write, at all—ah. As you copy it, you may find it not entirely without some interest to yourself, Peter."

"To me?" repeated Peter, after the fashion of the inattentative.

"Yes, to yourself." The Captain was oddly moved. He took his hands off the script, walked a little away from the table, came back to it. "It—ah—may explain a good many things that—er—may have puzzled you." He cleared his throat and shifted his subject briskly. "We ought to be thinking about a publisher. What publisher shall we have publish these reminiscences? Make some stir in Tennessee's political circles, Peter; tremendous sales; clear up questions everybody is interested in. H-m—well, I 'll walk down town and you"—he motioned to the script—"begin copying—"

"By the way, Captain," said Peter as the old gentleman turned for the door, "has Rose said anything to you yet?"

The old man detached his mind from his script with an obvious effort.

"What about?"

"About leaving your service."

"No-o, not especially; she 's always leaving my service."

"But in this case it was my fault; at least I brought it about. I remonstrated with her about taking your left-over victuals and socks and handkerchiefs and things. She was quite offended."

"Yes, it always offends her," agreed the old man, impatiently. "I never mention it myself unless I catch her red-handed; then I storm a little to keep her in bounds."

Naturally, Peter knew of this extraordinary system of service in the South; nevertheless he was shocked at its implications.

"Captain," suggested Peter, "would n't you find it to your own interest to give old Rose a full cash payment for her services and allow her to buy her own things?"

The Captain dismissed the subject with a wave of his hand. "She 's a nigger, Peter; you can't hire a nigger not to steal. Born in 'em. Then I 'm not sure but what it would be compounding a felony, hiring a person not to steal; might be so construed. Well, now, there 's the script. Read it carefully, my boy, and remember that in order to gain a certain *status quo* certain antecedents are—are absolutely necessary, Peter. Without them my—my life would have been quite empty, Peter. It 's—it 's very strange—amazing. You will understand as you read. I 'll be back to dinner, so good-by." In the strangest agitation the old Captain walked out of the library. The last glimpse Peter had of him was his meager old figure silhouetted against the cold gray fog that filled the compound.

Neither the Captain's agitation nor his obvious desire that Peter should at once read the new manuscript really got past the threshold of the mulatto's consciousness. Peter's thoughts still hovered about old Rose, and from that point spread to the whole system of colored service in the South. For Rose's case was typical. The wage of cooks in small Southern villages is a pittance—and what they can steal. The tragedy of the mothers of a whole race working for their board and thievings came over Peter with a rising grimness. And there was no public sentiment against such practice. It was accepted everywhere as natural and inevitable. The negresses were never prosecuted; no effort was made to regain the stolen goods. The employers realized that what they paid would not keep soul and body together; that it was steal or perish.

It was a fantastic truth that for any colored girl to hire into domestic service in Hooker's Bend was more or less entering an apprenticeship in peculation. What she could steal was the major portion of her wage, if two such anomalous terms may be used in conjunction.

Yet, strange to say, the negro women of the village were quite honest in other matters. They paid their small debts. They took their mistresses' pocket-books to market and brought back the correct change. And if a mistress grew too indignant about something they had stolen, they would bring it back and say: "Here is a new one. I'd rather buy you a new one than have you think I would take anything."

The whole system was the lees of slavery, and was surely the most demoralizing, the most grotesque method of hiring service in the whole civilized world. It was so absurd that its mere relation lapses into humor, that bane of black folk.

Such painful thoughts filled the gloomy library and harassed Peter in his copying. He took his work to the

window and tried to concentrate upon it, but his mind
kept playing away.

Indeed, it seemed to Peter that to sit in this old
room and rewrite the wordy meanderings of the old
gentleman's book was the very height of emptiness.
How utterly futile, when all around him, on every
hand, girls like Cissie Dildine were being indentured
to corruption! And, as far as Peter knew, he was
the only person in the South who saw it or felt it or
cared anything at all about it.

When Cissie Dildine came to the surface of Peter's
mind she remained there, whirling around and around
in his chaotic thoughts. He began talking to her
image, after a certain dramatic trick of his mind, and
she began offering her environment as an excuse for
what had come between them and estranged them.
She stole, but she had been trained to steal. She was
a thief, the victim of an immense immorality. The
charm of Cissie, her queer, swift-working intuition, the
candor of her confession, her voluptuousness—all came
rushing down on Peter, harassing him with anger and
love and desire. To copy any more script became impossible. He lost his place; he hardly knew what he
was writing.

He flung aside the whole work, got to his feet with
the imperative need of an athlete for the open. He
started out of the room, but as an afterthought scrib-
bled a nervous line, telling the Captain he might not
be back for dinner. Then he found his hat and coat

and walked briskly around the piazza to the front gate.

The trees and shrubs were dripping, but the fog had almost cleared away, leaving only a haze in the air. A pale, level line of it cut across the scarp of the Big Hill. The sun shone with a peculiar soft light through the vapors.

As Peter passed out at the gate, the fancy came to him that he might very well be starting on his mission. It came with a sort of surprise. He wondered how other men had set about reforms. With unpremeditation? He wondered to whom Jesus of Nazareth preached his first sermon. The thought of that young Galilean, sensitive, compassionate, inexperienced, speaking to his first hearer, filled Peter with a strange trembling tenderness. He looked about the familiar street of Hooker's Bend, the old trees over the pavement, the shabby village houses, and it all held a strangeness when thus juxtaposed to the thought of Nazareth nineteen hundred years before.

The mulatto started down the street with his footsteps quickened by a sense of spiritual adventure.

CHAPTER XVI

O N the corner, against the blank south wall of
Hobbett's store, Peter Siner saw the usual crowd
of negroes warming themselves in the soft sunshine.
They were slapping one another, scuffling, making
feints with knives or stones, all to an accompaniment
of bragging, profanity, and loud laughter. Their behavior was precisely that of adolescent white boys of
fifteen or sixteen years of age.

Jim Pink Staggs was furnishing much amusement
with an impromptu sleight-of-hand exhibition. The
black audience clustered around Jim Pink in his pin-
stripe trousers and blue-serge coat. They exhibited
not the least curiosity as to the mechanics of the tricks,
but asked for more and still more, with the naïve
delight of children in the mysterious.

Peter Siner walked down the street with his Messianic impulse strong upon him. He was in that stage
of feeling toward his people where a man's emotions
take the color of religion. Now, as he approached the
crowd of negroes, he wondered what he could say, how
he could transfer to them the ideas and the emotion
that lifted up his own heart.

As he drew nearer, his concern mounted to anxiety.
Indeed, what could he say? How could he present

251

so grave a message? He was right among them now. One of the negroes jostled him by striking around his body at another negro. Peter stopped. His heart beat, and he had a queer sensation of being operated by some power outside himself. Next moment he heard himself saying in fairly normal tones:

"Fellows, do you think we ought to be idling on the street corners like this? We ought to be at work, don't you think?"

The horse-play stopped at this amazing sentiment.

"Whuffo, Peter?" asked a voice.

"Because the whole object of our race nowadays is to gain the respect of other races, and more particularly our own self-respect. We have n't it now. The only way to get it is to work, work, work."

"Ef you feel lak you 'd ought to go to wuck," suggested one astonished hearer, "you done got my p'mission, black boy, to hit yo' natchel gait to de fust job in sight."

Peter was hardly less surprised than his hearers at what he was saying. He paid no attention to the interruption.

"Fellows, it 's the only way our colored people can get on and make the most out of life. Persistent labor is the very breath of the soul, men; it—it is." Here Peter caught an intimation of the whole flow of energy through the universe, focusing in man and being transformed into mental and moral values. And it suddenly occurred to him that the real worth of any people

was their efficiency in giving this flow of force moral
and spiritual forms. That is the end of man; that
is what is prefigured when a baby's hand reaches for the
sun. But Peter considered his audience, and his
thought stammered on his tongue. The Persimmon,
with his protruding, half-asleep eyes, was saying:

"I don' know, Peter, as I 's so partic'lar 'bout makin'
de mos' out'n dis worl'. You know de Bible say—hit
say,"—here the Persimmon's voice dropped a tone
lower, in unconscious imitation of negro preachers,—
"la-ay not up yo' treasure on uth, wha moss do corrup',
an' thieves break th'ugh *an'* steal."

Came a general nodding and agreement of soft,
blurry voices.

"'At sho whut it say, black man!"

"Sho do!"

"Lawd God loves a nigger on a street corner same as
He do a millionaire in a six-cylinder, Peter."

"Sho do, black man; but He 's jes about de onlies'
thing on uth 'at do."

"Well, I don' know," came a troubled rejoinder.
"Thaiuh 's de debbil, ketchin' mo' niggers nowadays
dan he do white men, I 'fo' Gawd b'liebes."

"Well, dat 's because dey *is* so many mo' niggers
dan dey is white folks," put in a philosopher.

"Whut you say 'bout dat, Brudder Peter?" inquired
the Persimmon, seriously. None of this discussion
was either derision or burlesque. None of the crowd
had the slightest feeling that these questions were not

just as practical and important as the suggestion that they all go to work.

When Peter realized how their ignorant and undisciplined thoughts flowed off into absurdities, and that they were entirely unaware of it, it brought a great depression to his heart. He held up a hand with an earnestness that caught their vagrant attention.

"Listen!" he pleaded. "Can't you see how much there is for us black folks to do, and what little we have done?"

"Sho is a lot to do; we admits dat," said Bluegum Frakes. "But whut's de use doin' hit ef we kin manage to shy roun' some o' dat wuck an' keep on libin' anyhow, specially wid wages so high?"

The question stopped Peter. Neither his own thoughts, nor any book that he had ever read nor any lecture that he had heard ever attempted to explain the enormous creative urge which is felt by every noble mind, and which, indeed, is shared to some extent by every human creature. Put to it like that, Siner concocted a sort of allegory, telling of a negro who was shiftless in the summer and suffered want in the winter, and applied it to the present high wage and to the low wage that was coming; but in his heart Peter knew such utilitarianism was not the true reason at all. Men do not weave tapestries to warm themselves, or build temples to keep the rain away.

The brown man passed on around the corner, out of the faint warmth of the sunshine and away from the empty and endless arguments which his coming had provoked among the negroes.

The futile ending of his first adventure surprised Peter. He walked uncertainly up the business street of the village, hardly knowing where to turn next.

Cold weather had driven the merchants indoors, and the thoroughfare was quite deserted except for a few hogs rooting among the refuse heaps piled in front of the stores. It was not a pleasant sight, and it repelled Peter all the more because he was accustomed to the antiseptic look of a Northern city. He walked up to the third door from the corner, when a buzz of voices brought him to a standstill and finally persuaded him inside.

At the back end of a badly lighted store a circle of white men and boys had formed around an old-fashioned, egg-shaped stove. Near by, on some meal-bags, sat two negroes, one of whom wore a broad grin, the other, a funny, sheepish look.

The white men were teasing the latter negro about having gone to jail for selling a mortgaged cow. The men went about their fun-making leisurely, knowing quite well the negro could not get angry or make any retort or leave the store, all of these methods of self-defense being ruled out by custom.

"You must have forgot your cow was mortgaged, Bob."

"No-o-o, suh; I—I—I did n't fuhgit," drawling his vowels to a prodigious length.

"Did n't you know you 'd get into trouble?"

"No-o-o, suh."

"Know it now, don't you?"

"Ya-a-s, suh."

"Have a good time in jail, Bob?"

"Ya-a-s, suh. Shot cra-a-aps nearly all de time tull de jailer broke hit up."

"Would n't he let you shoot any more?"

"No-o-o, suh; not after he won all our money." Here Bob flung up his head, poked out his lips like a bugle, and broke into a grotesque, "Hoo! hoo! hoo!" It was such an absurd laugh, and Bob's tale had come to such an absurd dénouement, that the white men roared, and shuffled their feet on the flared base of the stove. Some spat in or near a box filled with sawdust, and betrayed other nervous signs of satisfaction. When a man so spat, he stopped laughing abruptly, straightened his face, and stared emptily at the rusty stove until further inquisition developed some other preposterous escapade in Bob's jail career.

The merchant, looking up at one of these intermissions, saw Peter standing at his counter. He came out of the circle and asked Peter what he wanted. The mulatto bought a package of soda and went out.

The chill north wind smelled clean after the odors of the store. Peter stood with his package of soda, breathing deeply, looking up and down the street, wondering what to do next. Without much precision of purpose, he walked diagonally across the street, northward, toward a large faded sign that read, "Killibrew's Grocery." A little later Peter entered a big, rather clean store which smelled of spices, coffee, and a faint dash of decayed potatoes. Mr. Killibrew himself, a big, rotund man, with a round head of prematurely white hair, was visible in a little glass office at the end of his store. Even through the glazed partition Peter could see Mr. Killibrew smiling as he sat comfortably at his desk. Indeed, the grocer's chief assets were a really expansive friendliness and a pleasant, easily provoked laughter.

He was fifty-two years old, and had been in the grocery business since he was fifteen. He had never been to school at all, but had learned bookkeeping, business mathematics, salesmanship, and the wisdom of the market-place from his store, from other merchants, and from the drummers who came every week with their samples and their worldly wisdom. These drummers were, almost to a man, very sincere friends of Mr. Killibrew, and not infrequently they would write the grocer from the city, or send him telegrams, advising him to buy this or to unload that, according to the exigencies of the market. As a result of this he was very well off indeed, and all because he was a friendly, agreeable sort of man.

The grocer heard Peter enter and started to come out of his office, when Peter stopped him and asked if he might speak with him alone.

The white-haired man with the pink, good-natured

face stood looking at Peter with rather a questioning but pleasant expression.

"Why, certainly, certainly." He turned back to the swivel-chair at his desk, seated himself, and twisted about on Peter as he entered. Mr. Killibrew did not offer Peter a seat,—that would have been an infraction of Hooker's Bend custom,—but he sat leaning back, evidently making up his mind to refuse Peter credit, which he fancied the mulatto would ask for, and yet do it pleasantly.

"I was wondering, Mr. Killibrew," began Peter, feeling his way along, "I was wondering if you would mind talking over a little matter with me. It's considered a delicate subject, I believe, but I thought a frank talk would help."

During the natural pauses of Peter's explanation Mr. Killibrew kept up a genial series of nods and ejaculations.

"Certainly, Peter. I don't see why, Peter. I'm sure it will help, Peter."

"I'd like to talk frankly about the relations of our two races in the South, in Hooker's Bend."

The grocer stopped his running accompaniment of affirmations and looked steadfastly at Peter. Presently he seemed to solve some question and broke into a pleasant laugh.

"Now, Peter, if this is some political shenanigan, I must tell you I'm a Democrat. Besides that, I don't care a straw about politics. I vote, and that's all."

Peter put down the suspicion that he was on a political errand.

"Not that at all, Mr. Killibrew. It's a question of the white race and the black race. The particular feature I am working on is the wages paid to cooks."

"I did n't know you were a cook," interjected the grocer in surprise.

"I am not."

Mr. Killibrew looked at Peter, thought intensely for a few moments, and came to an unescapable conclusion.

"You don't mean you've formed a cook's union here in Hooker's Bend, Peter!" he cried, immensely amazed.

"Not at all. It's this," clarified Peter. "It may seem trivial, but it illustrates the principle I'm trying to get at. Does n't your cook carry away cold food?"

It required perhaps four seconds for the merchant to stop his speculations on what Peter had come for and adjust his mind to the question.

"Why, yes, I suppose so," he agreed, very much at sea. "I—I never caught up with her." He laughed a pleasant, puzzled laugh. "Of course she does n't come around and show me what she's making off with. Why?"

"Well, it's this. Would n't you prefer to give your cook a certain cash payment instead of having her taking uncertain amounts of your foodstuffs and wearing apparel?"

The merchant leaned forward in his chair.

"Did old Becky Davis send you to me with any such proposition as that, Peter?"

"No, not at all. But, Mr. Killibrew, would n't you like better and more trustworthy servants as cooks, as farm-hands, chauffeurs, stable-boys? You see, you and your children and your children's children are going to have to depend on negro labor, as far as we can see, to the end of time."

"We-e-ell, yes," admitted Mr. Killibrew, who was not accustomed to considering the end of time.

"Would n't it be better to have honest, self-respecting help than dishonest help?"

"Certainly."

"Then let's think about cooks. How can one hope to rear an honest, self-respecting citizenry as long as the mothers of the race are compelled to resort to thievery to patch out an insufficient wage?"

"Why, I don't suppose niggers ever will be honest," admitted the grocer, very frankly. "You naturally don't trust a nigger. If you credit one for a dime, the next time he has any money he 'll go trade somewhere else." The grocer broke into his contagious laugh. "Do you know how I 've built up my business here, Peter? By never trusting a nigger." Mr. Killibrew continued his pleased chuckle. "Yes, I get the whole cash trade of the niggers in Hooker's Bend by never cheating one and never trusting one."

The grocer leaned back in his squeaking chair and

looked out through the glass partition, over the brightly
colored packages that lined his shelves from floor to
ceiling. All that prosperity had come about through
a policy of honesty and distrust. It was something to
be proud of.

"Now, let me see," he proceeded, recurring pleasantly to what he recalled of Peter's original proposition: "Aunt Becky sent you here to tell me if I'd
raise her pay, she'd stop stealin' and—and raise some
honest children." Mr. Killibrew threw back his head
and broke into loud, jelly-like laughter. "Why, don't
you know, Peter, she's an old liar. If I gave her a
hundred a week, she'd steal. And children! Why,
the old humbug! She's too old; she's had her crop.
And, besides all that, I don't mind what the old
woman takes. It isn't much. She's a good old
darky, faithful as a dog." He arose from his swivel-
chair briskly and floated Peter out before him.

"Tell her, if she wants a raise," he concluded heartily, "and can't pinch enough out of my kitchen and
the two dollars I pay her—tell her to come to me,
straight out, and I'll give her more, and she can pinch
more."

Mr. Killibrew moved down the aisle of his store
between fragrant barrels and boxes, laughing mellowly
at old Aunt Becky's ruse, as he saw it. As he turned
Peter out, he invited him to come again when he needed
anything in the grocery line.

And he was so pleasant, hearty, and sincere in his

friendliness toward both Peter and old Aunt Becky
that Peter, even amid the complete side-tracking and
derailing of his mission, decided that if ever he did
have occasion to purchase any groceries, he would do
his trading at this market ruled by an absolute honesty
with, and a complete distrust in, his race.

At the conclusion of the Killibrew interview Peter
instinctively felt that he had just about touched the
norm of Hooker's Bend. The village might contain
men who would dive a little deeper into the race question with Peter; assuredly, there would be hundreds
who would not dive so deep. Mr. Killibrew's attitude
on the race question turned on how to hold the negro
patronage of the village to his grocery. It was not
an abstract question at all, but a concrete fact, which
he had worked out to his own satisfaction. With Mr.
Killibrew, with all Hooker's Bend, there was no negro
question.

CHAPTER XVII

WHEN Peter Siner started on his indefinite errand among the village stores he believed it would require much tact and diplomacy to discuss the race question without offense. To his surprise, no precaution was necessary. Everybody agreed at once that the South would be benefited by a more trustworthy labor, that if the negroes were trustworthy they could be paid more; but nobody agreed that if negroes were paid more they would become more trustworthy. The prevailing dictum was, A nigger's a nigger.

As Peter came out into the shabby little street of Hooker's Bend discouragement settled upon him. He felt as if he had come squarely against some blank stone wall that no amount of talking could budge. The black man would have to change his psychology or remain where he was, a creature of poverty, hovels, and dirt; but amid such surroundings he could not change his psychology.

The point of these unhappy conclusions somehow turned against Cissie Dildine. The mulatto became aware that his whole crusade had been undertaken in behalf of the octoroon. Everything the merchants said against negroes became accusations against Cissie in a sharp personal way. "A nigger is a nigger"; "A thief is a thief"; "She would n't quit stealing if I paid her a hundred a week." Every stroke had fallen squarely on Cissie's shoulders. A nigger, a thief; and she would never be otherwise.

It was all so hopeless, so unchangeable, that Peter walked down the bleak street unutterably depressed. There was nothing he could do. The situation was static. It seemed best that he should go away North and save his own skin. It was impossible to take Cissie with him. Perhaps in time he would come to forget her, and in so doing he would forget the pauperism and pettinesses of all the black folk of the South. Because through Cissie Peter saw the whole negro race. She was flexuous and passionate, kindly and loving, childish and naïvely wise; on occasion she could falsify and steal, and in the depth of her Peter sensed a profound capacity for fury and violence. For all her precise English, she was untamed, perhaps untamable.

Cissie was a far cry from the sort of woman Peter imagined he wanted for a mate; yet he knew that if he stayed on in Hooker's Bend, seeing her, desiring her, with her luxury mocking the loneliness of the old Renfrew manor, presently he would marry her. Already he had had his little irrational moments when it seemed to him that Cissie herself was quite fine and worthy and that her peculations were something foreign and did not pertain to her at all.

He would better go North. It would be safer up there. No doubt he could find another colored girl in the North. The thought of fondling any other woman filled Peter with a sudden, sharp repulsion. However, Peter was wise. He knew he would get over that in time.

With this plan in mind, Peter set out down the street, intending to cross the Big Hill at the church, walk over to his mother's shack, and pack his few belongings preparatory to going away.

It was not a heroic retreat. The conversation which he had had with his college friend Farquhar recurred to Peter. Farquhar had tried to persuade Peter to remain North and take a position in a system of garages out of Chicago.

"You can do nothing in the South, Siner," assured Farquhar; "your countrymen must stand on their own feet, just as you are doing."

Peter had argued the vast majority of the negroes had no chance, but Farquhar pressed the point that Peter himself disproved his own statement. At the time Peter felt there was an elench in the Illinoisan's logic, but he was not skilful enough to analyze it. Now the mulatto began to see that Farquhar was right. The negro question was a matter of individual initiative. Critics forgot that a race was composed of individual men.

Peter had an uneasy sense that this was exceedingly thin logic, a mere smoke screen behind which he meant to retreat back up North. He walked on down the poor village street, turning it over and over in his mind, affirming it positively to himself, after the manner of uneasy consciences.

An unusual stir among the negroes on Hobbett's corner caught Peter's attention and broke into his chain of thought. Half a dozen negroes stood on the corner, staring down toward the white church. A black boy suddenly started running across the street, and disappeared among the stores on the other side. Peter caught glimpses of him among the wretched alleyways and vacant lots that lie east of Main Street. The boy was still running toward Niggertown.

By this time Peter was just opposite the watchers on the corner. He lifted his voice and asked them the matter, but at the moment they began an excited talking, and no one heard him.

Jim Pink Staggs jerked off his fur cap, made a gesture, contorted his long, black face into a caricature of fright, and came loping across the street, looking back over his shoulder, mimicking a run for life. His mummery set his audience howling.

The buffoon would have collided with Peter, but the mulatto caught Jim Pink by the arm and shoulder, brought him to a halt, and at the same time helped him keep his feet.

To Peter's inquiry what was the matter, the black

fellow whirled and blared out loudly, for the sake of his audience:

" 'Fo' Gawd, nigger, I sho thought Mr. Bobbs had me!" and he writhed his face into an idiotic grimace.

The audience reeled about in their mirth. Because with negroes, as with white persons, two thirds of humor is in the reputation, and Jim Pink was of prodigious repute.

Peter walked along with him patiently, because he knew that until they were out of ear-shot of the crowd there was no way of getting a sensible answer out of Jim Pink.

"Where are you going?" he asked presently.

"Thought I'd step over to Niggertown." Jim Pink's humorous air was still upon him.

"What's doing over there? What were the boys raising such a hullabaloo about?"

"Such me."

"Why did that boy go running across like that?"

Jim Pink rolled his eyes on Peter with a peculiar look.

"Reckon he mus' 'a' wanted to git on t'other side o' town."

Peter flattered the Punchinello by smiling a little.

"Come, Jim Pink, what do you know?" he asked. The magician poked out his huge lips.

"Mr. Bobbs turn acrost by de church, over de Big Hill. Da' 's always a ba-ad sign."

Peter's brief interest in the matter flickered out.

Another arrest for some niggerish peccadillo. The history of Niggertown was one long series of petty offenses, petty raids, and petty punishments. Peter would be glad to get well away from such a place.

"Think I'll go North, Jim Pink," remarked Peter, chiefly to keep up a friendly conversation with his companion.

"Whut-chu goin' to do up thaiuh?"

"Take a position in a system of garages."

"A position is a job wid a white color on it," defined the minstrel. "Whut you goin' to do wid Cissie?"

Peter looked around at the foolish face.

"With Cissie?—Cissie Dildine?"

"Uh huh."

"Why, what makes you think I'm going to do anything with Cissie?"

"M-m, visitin' roun'." The fool flung his face into a grimace, and dropped it as one might shake out a sack.

Peter watched the contortion uneasily.

"What do you mean—visiting around?"

"Diff'nt folks go visitin' roun';
Some goes up an' some goes down."

Apparently Jim Pink had merely quoted a few words from a poem he knew. He stared at the green-black depth of the glade, which set in about half-way up the hill they were climbing.

"Ef this weather don' ever break," he observed sagely, "we sho am in fuh a dry spell."

Peter did not pursue the topic of the weather. He climbed the hill in silence, wondering just what the buffoon meant. He suspected he was hinting at Cissie's visit to his room. However, he did not dare ask any questions or press the point in any manner, lest he commit himself.

The minstrel had succeeded in making Peter's walk very uncomfortable, as somehow he always did. Peter went on thinking about the matter. If Jim Pink knew of Cissie's visit, all Niggertown knew it. No woman's reputation, nobody's shame or misery or even life, would stand between Jim Pink and what he considered a joke. The buffoon was the cruelest thing in this world—a man who thought himself a wit.

Peter could imagine all the endless tweaks to Cissie's pride Niggertown would give the octoroon. She had asked Peter to marry her and had been refused. She had humbled herself for naught. That was the very tar of shame. Peter knew that in the moral categories of Niggertown Cissie would suffer more from such a rebuff than if she had lied or committed theft and adultery every day in the calendar. She had been refused marriage. All the folk-ways of Niggertown were utterly topsyturvy. It was a crazy-house filled with the most grotesque moral measures.

It seemed to Peter as he entered the cedar-glade that he had lost all sympathy with this people from which he had sprung. He looked upon them as strange, incomprehensible beings, just as a man will forget his own childhood and look upon children as strange, incomprehensible little creatures. In the midst of his thoughts he heard himself saying to Jim Pink:

"I suppose it is as dusty as ever."

"Dustier 'an ever," assured Jim Pink.

Apparently their conversation had recurred to the weather, after all.

A chill silence encompassed the glade. The path the negroes followed wound this way and that among reddish boulders, between screens of intergrown cedars, and over a bronze mat of needles. Their steps were noiseless. The odor of the cedars and the temple-like stillness brought to Peter's mind the night of his mother's death. It seemed to him a long time since he had come running through the glade after a doctor, and yet, by a queer distortion of his sense of time, his mother's death and burial bulked in his past as if it had occurred yesterday.

There was no sound in the glade to disturb Peter's thoughts except a murmur of human voices from some of the innumerable privacies of the place, and the occasional chirp of a waxwing busy over clusters of cedar-balls.

It had been five weeks and a day since Caroline Siner died. Five weeks and a day; his mother's death was drifting away into the mystery and oblivion of the past. Likewise, twenty-five years of his own life were completed and gone.

A procession of sad, wistful thoughts trailed through Peter's brain: his mother, and Ida May, and now Cissie. It seemed to Peter that all any woman had ever brought him was wistfulness and sadness. His mother had been jealous, and instead of the great happiness he had expected, his home life with her had turned out a series of small perplexities and pains. Before that was Ida May, and now here was her younger sister. Peter wondered if any man ever reached the peace and happiness foreshadowed in his dream of a woman.

A voice calling his name checked Peter's stride mechanically, and caused him to look about with the slight bewilderment of a man aroused from a reverie.

At the first sound, however, Jim Pink became suddenly alert. He took three strides ahead of Peter, and as he went he whispered over his shoulder:

"Beat it, nigger! beat it!"

The mulatto recognized one of Jim Pink's endless stupid attempts at comedy. It would be precisely Jim Pink's idea of a jest to give Peter a little start. As the mulatto stood looking about among the cedars for the person who had called his name, it amazed him that Jim Pink could be so utterly insane; that he performed some buffoonery instantly, by reflex action as it were, upon the slightest provocation. It was almost a mania with Jim Pink; it verged on the pathological.

The clown, however, was pressing his joke. He

was pretending great fear, and was shouting out in his loose minstrel voice:

"Hey, don' shoot down dis way, black man, tull I makes my exit!" And a voice, rich with contempt, called back:

"You need n't be skeered, you fool rabbit of a nigger!"

Peter turned with a qualm. Quite close to him, and in another direction from which he had been looking, stood Tump Pack. The ex-soldier looked the worse for wear after his jail sentence. His uniform was frayed, and over his face lay a grayish cast that marks negroes in bad condition. At his side, attached by a belt and an elaborate shoulder holster, hung a big army revolver, while on the greasy lapel of his coat was pinned his military medal for exceptional bravery on the field of battle.

"Been lookin' fuh you fuh some time, Peter," he stated grimly.

Peter considered the formidable figure with a queer sensation. He tried to take Tump's appearance casually; he tried to maintain an air of ordinariness.

"Did n't know you were back."

"Yeah, I 's back."

"Have you—been looking for me?"

"Yeah."

"Did n't you know where I was staying?"

"Co'se I did; up 'mong de white folks. You know dey don' 'low no shootin' an' killin' 'mong de white

"Naw yuh don't," he warned sharply. "You turn roun' an'
march on to niggertown"

folks." He drew his pistol from the holster with the address of an expert marksman.

Peter stood, with a quickening pulse, studying his assailant. The glade, the air, the sunshine, seemed suddenly drawn to a tension, likely to break into violent commotion. His abrupt danger brought Peter to a feeling of lightness and power. A quiver went along his spine. His nostrils widened unconsciously as he calculated a leap and a blow at Tump's gun.

The soldier took a step backward, at the same time bringing the barrel to a ready.

"Naw you don't," he warned sharply. "You turn roun' an' march on to Niggertown."

"What for?" Peter still tried to be casual, but his voice held new overtones.

"Because, nigger, I means to' drap you right on de Main Street o' Niggertown, 'fo' all dem niggers whut 's been a-raggin' me 'bout you an' Cissie. I 's gwine show dem fool niggers I don' take no fumi-diddles off'n nobody."

"Tump," gasped Jim Pink, in a husky voice, "you ought n't shoot Peter; he mammy jes daid."

" 'En she won' worry none. Turn roun', Peter, an' when I says, 'March,' you march." He leveled his pistol. "'Tention! Rat about face! March!"

Peter turned and moved off down the noiseless path, walking with the stiff gait of a man who expects a terrific blow from behind at any instant.

The mulatto walked twenty or more paces amid a

confusion of self-protective impulses. He thought of
whirling on Tump even at this late date. He thought
of darting behind a cedar, but he knew the man behind him was an expert shot, and something fundamental in the brown man forbade his getting himself
killed while running away. It was too undignified a
death.

Presently he surprised himself by calling over his
shoulder, as a sort of complaint:

"How came you with the pistol, Tump? Thought
it was against the law to carry one."

"You kin ca'y 'em ef you don' keep 'em hid," explained the ex-soldier in a wooden voice. "Mr. Bobbs
tol' me dat when he guv my gun back."

The irony of the thing caught Peter, for the author-
ities to arrest Tump not because he was trying to kill
Peter, but because he went about his first attempt in
an illegal manner. For the first time in his life the
mulatto felt that contempt for a white man's technical-
ities that flavors every negro's thoughts. Here for
thirty days his life had been saved by a technical law
of the white man; at the end of the thirty days, by
another technical law, Tump was set at liberty and
allowed to carry a weapon, in a certain way, to murder
him. It was grotesque; it was absurd. It filled Peter
with a sudden violent questioning of the whole white
régime. His thoughts danced along in peculiar excitement.

At the turn of the hill the trio came in sight of the

squalid semicircle of Niggertown. Here and there
from a tumbledown chimney a feather of pale wood
smoke lifted into the chill sunshine. The sight of
the houses brought Peter a sharp realization that his
life would end in the curving street beneath him. A
shock at the incomprehensible brevity of his life rushed
over him. Just to that street, just as far as the curve,
and his legs were swinging along, carrying him forward at an even gait.

All at once he began talking, arguing. He tried to
speak at an ordinary tempo, but his words kept edging
on faster and faster:

"Tump, I'm not going to marry Cissie Dildine."

"I knows you ain't, Peter."

"I mean, if you let me alone, I didn't mean to."

"I ain't goin' to let you alone."

"Tump, we had already decided not to marry."

After a short pause Tump said in a slightly different
tone:

"'Pears lak you don' haf to ma'y her—comin' to yo'
room."

A queer sinking came over the mulatto. "Listen,
Tump, I—we—in my room—we simply talked, that's
all. She came to tell me she was goin away. I—I
didn't harm her, Tump." Peter swallowed. He
despaired of being believed.

But his defense only infuriated the soldier. He
suddenly broke into violent profanity.

"Hot damn you! shut yo black mouf! Whut I keer

whut-chu done! You weaned her away fum me. She
won't speak to me! She won't look at me!" A sudden insanity of rage seized Tump. He poured on his
victim every oath and obscenity he had raked out of the
whole army.

Strangely enough, the gunman's outbreak brought
a kind of relief to Peter Siner. It exonerated him.
He was not suspected of wronging Cissie; or, rather,
whether he had or had not wronged her made no
difference to Tump. Peter's crime consisted in mere
being, in existing where Cissie could see him and desire
him rather than Tump. Why it calmed Peter to
know that Tump held no dishonorable charge against
him the mulatto himself could not have told. Tump's
violence showed Peter the certainty of his own death,
and somehow it washed away the hope and the thought
of escape.

Half-way down the hill they entered the edge of
Niggertown. The smell of sties and stables came to
them. Peter's thoughts moved here and there, like
the eyes of a little child glancing about as it is forced
to leave a pleasure-ground.

Peter knew that Jim Pink, who now made a sorry
figure in their rear, would one day give a buffoon's
mimicry of this his walk to death. He thought of
Tump, who would have to serve a year or two in the
Nashville Penitentiary, for the murder of negroes is
seldom severely punished. He thought of Cissie. He
was being murdered because Cissie desired him.

And then Peter remembered the single bit of wisdom that his whole life had taught him. It was this: no people can become civilized until the woman has the power of choice among the males that sue for her hand. The history of the white race shows the gradual increase of the woman's power of choice. Among the yellow races, where this power is curtailed, civilization is curtailed. It was this principle that exalted chivalry. Upon it the white man has reared all his social fabric.

So deeply ingrained is it that almost every novel written by white men revolves about some woman's choice of her mate being thwarted by power or pride or wealth, but in every instance the rightness of the woman's choice is finally justified. The burden of every song is love, true love, enduring love, a woman's true and enduring love.

And in his moment of clairvoyance Peter saw that these songs and stories were profoundly true. Against a woman's selectiveness no other social force may count.

That was why his own race was weak and hopeless and helpless. The males of his people were devoid of any such sentiment or self-repression. They were men of the jungle, creatures of tusk and claw and loin. This very act of violence against his person condemned his whole race.

These thoughts brought the mulatto an unspeakable sadness, not only for his own particular death, but that this idea, this great redeeming truth, which burned so brightly in his brain, would in another moment flicker out, unrevealed, and be no more.

CHAPTER XVIII

THE coughing and rattling of an old motor-car as it rounded the Niggertown curve delayed Tump Pack's act of violence. Instinctively, the three men waited for the machine to pass before Peter walked out into the road. Next moment it appeared around the turn, moving slowly through the dust and spreading a veritable fog behind it.

All three negroes recognized the first glimpse of the hood and top, for there are only three or four cars in Hooker's Bend, and these are as well known as the faces of their owners. This particular motor belonged to Constable Bobbs, and the next moment the trio saw the ponderous body of the officer at the wheel, and by his side a woman. As the machine clacked toward them Peter felt a certain surprise to see that it was Cissie Dildine.

The constable in the car scrutinized the black men by the roadside in a very peculiar way. As he came near, he leaned across Cissie and almost eclipsed the girl. He eyed the trio with his perpetual menace of a grin on his broad red face. His right hand, lying across Cissie's lap, held a revolver. When closest he shouted above the clangor of his engine:

"Now, none o' that, boys! None o' that! You 'll prob'ly hit the gal if you shoot, an' I 'll pick you off lak three black skunks."

He brandished his revolver at them, but the gesture was barely seen, and instantly concealed by the cloud of dust following the motor. Next moment it enveloped the negroes and hid them even from one another.

It was only after Peter was lost in the dust-cloud that the mulatto really divined what was meant by Cissie's strange appearance with the constable, her chalky face, her frightened brown eyes. The significance of the scene grew in his mind. He stood with eyes screwed to slits staring into the apricot-colored dust in the direction of the vanishing noise.

Presently Tump Pack's form outlined itself in the yellow obscurity, groping toward Peter. He still held his pistol, but it swung at his side. He called Peter's name in the strained voice of a man struggling not to cough:

"Peter—is Mr. Bobbs done—'rested Cissie?"

Peter could hardly talk himself.

"Don't know. Looks like it."

The two negroes stared at each other through the dust.

"Fuh Gawd's sake! Cissie 'rested!" Tump began to cough. Then he wheezed:

"Mine an' yo' little deal's off, Peter. You gotta he'p git her out." Here he fell into a violent fit of coughing, and started groping his way to the edge of the dust-cloud.

In the rush of the moment the swift change in Peter's situation appeared only natural. He followed Tump, so distressed by the dust and disturbed over Cissie that he hardly thought of his peculiar position. The dust pinched the upper part of his throat, stung his nose. Tears trickled from his eyes, and he pressed his finger against his upper lip, trying not to sneeze. He was still struggling against the sneeze when Tump recovered his speech.

"Wh-whut you reckon she done, Peter? She don' shoot craps, nor boot-laig, nor—" He fell to coughing.

Peter got out a handkerchief and wiped his eyes.

"Let's go—to the Dildine house," he said.

The two moved hurriedly through the thinning cloud, and presently came to breathable air, where they could see the houses around them.

"I know she done somp'n; I know she done somp'n," chanted Tump, with the melancholy cadence of his race. He shook his dusty head. "You ain't never been in jail, is you, black man?"

Peter said he had not.

"Lawd! it ain't no place fuh a woman," declared Tump. "You dunno nothin' 'bout it, black man. It sho ain't no place fuh a woman."

A notion of an iron cage floated before Peter's mind. The two negroes trudged on through the crescent side by side, their steps raising a little trail of dust in the air behind them. Their faces and clothes were of a uniform dust color. Streaks of mud marked the runnels of their tears down their cheeks.

The shrubbery and weeds that grew alongside the negro thoroughfare were quite dead. Even the little avenue of dwarf box was withered that led from the gate to the door of the Dildine home. The two colored men walked up the little path to the door, knocked, and waited on the steps for the little skirmish of observation from behind the blinds. None came. The worst had befallen the house; there was nothing to guard. The door opened as soon as an in-inmate could reach it, and Vannie Dildine stood before them.

The quadroon's eyes were red, and her face had the moist, slightly swollen appearance that comes of protracted weeping. She looked so frail and miserable that Peter instinctively stepped inside and took her arm to assist her in the mere physical effort of standing.

"What is the matter, Mrs. Dildine?" he asked in a shocked tone. "What's happened to Cissie?"

Vannie began weeping again with a faint gasping and a racking of her flat chest.

"It's—it's— O-o-oh, Peter!" She put an arm about him and began weeping against him. He soothed her, patted her shoulder, at the same time staring at the side of her head, wondering what could have dealt her this blow.

Presently she steadied herself and began explaining in feeble little phrases, sandwiched between sobs and gasps:

"She—tuk a brooch— Kep'—kep' layin' it roun' in —h-her way, th-that young Sam Arkwright did,—a-an' finally she—she tuk hit. N-nen, when he seen he h-had her, he said sh-sh-she 'd haf to d-do wh-whut he said, or he 'd sen' her to-to ja-a-il!" Vannie sobbed drearily for a few moments on Peter's breast. "Sh-she did fuh a while; 'n 'en sh-she broke off wid h-him, anyhow, an'—an' he swo' out a wa'nt an sont her to jail!" The mother sobbed without comfort, and finally added: "Sh-she in a delicate fix now, an' 'at jail goin' to be a gloomy place fuh Cissie."

The three negroes stood motionless in the dusty hallway, motionless save for the racking of Vannie's sobs.

Tump Pack stirred himself.

"Well, we gotta git her out." His words trailed off. He stood wrinkling his half-inch of brow. "I wonder would dey exchange pris'ners; wonder ef I could go up an' serve out Cissie's term."

"Oh, Tump!" gasped the woman, "ef you only could!"

"I 'll step an' see, Miss Vannie. 'At sho ain't no place fuh a nice gal lak Cissie." Tump turned on his mission, evidently intending to walk to Jonesboro and offer himself in the place of the prisoner.

Peter supported Vannie back into the poor living-room, and placed her in the old rocking-chair before the empty hearth. There was where he had sat the evening Cissie made her painful confession to him. Only now did he realize the whole of what Cissie was trying to confess.

Peter Siner overtook Tump Pack a little way down the crescent, opposite the Berry cabin. The thoroughfare was deserted, because the weather was cold and the scantily clad children were indoors. However, from every cabin came sound of laughing and romping, and now and then a youngster darted through the cold from one hut to another.

It seemed to Peter Siner only a little while since he and Ida May were skittering through wintry weather from one fire to another, with Cissie, a wailing, wet-nosed little spoil-sport, trailing after them. And then, with a wheeling of the years, they were scattered everywhere.

As the negroes passed the Berry cabin, Nan Berry came out with an old shawl around her bristling spikes. She stopped the two men and drew them to her gate with a gesture.

"Wha you gwine?"

"Jonesbuh."

"Whut you goin' do 'bout po-o-o' Cissie?"

"Goin' to see ef the sheriff won' take me 'stid o' Cissie."

"Tha' 's right," said Nan, nodding solemnly. "I hopes he will. You is mo' used to it, Tump."

"Yeah, an' 'at jail sho ain't no place fuh a nice gal lak Cissie."

"Sho ain't," agreed Nan.

Peter interrupted to say he was sure the sheriff would not exchange.

The hopes of his listeners fell.

"Weh-ul," dragged out Nan, with a long face, "of co'se now it's lak dis: ef Cissie goin' to stay in dat ja-ul, she's goin' to need some mo' clo'es 'cep'n whut she's got on,—specially lak she is."

Tump stared down the swing of the crescent.

"'Fo' Gawd, dis sho don' seem lak hit's right to me," he said.

Nan let herself out at the rickety gate. "You niggers wait heah tull I runs up to Miss Vannie's an' git some o' Cissie's clo'es fuh you to tote her."

Tump objected.

"Jail ain't no place fuh clean clo'es. She jes better serve out her term lak she is, an' wash up when she gits th'ugh."

"You fool nigger!" snapped Nan. "She kain't serve out her term lak she is!"

"Da' 's so," said Tump.

The three stood silent, Nan and Tump lost in blankness, trying to think of something to do for Cissie. Finally Nan said:

"I heah she done commit gran' larceny, an' they goin' sen' her to de pen."

"Whut is gran' larceny?" asked Tump.

"It's takin' mo' at one time an' de white folks 'speck you to take," defined the woman. "Well, I'll go git her clo'es." She hurried off up the crescent.

Peter and Tump waited in the Berry cabin for Nan's return. Outside, the Berry cabin was the usual clapboard-roofed, weather-stained structure; inside, it was dark, windowless, and strong with the odor of black folk. Some children were playing around the hearth, roasting chestnuts. Their elders sat in a circle of decrepit chairs. It was so dark that when Peter first entered he could not make out the little group, but he soon recognized their voices: Parson Ranson, Wince Washington, Jerry Dillihay, and all of the Berry family.

They were talking of Cissie, of course. They hoped Cissie wouldn't really be sent to the penitentiary, that the white folks would let her out in time for her to have her child at home. Parson Ranson thought it would be bad luck for a child to be born in jail.

Wince Washington, who had been in jail a number of times, suggested that they bail Cissie out by signing their names to a paper. He had been set free by this means once or twice.

Sally, Nan's little sister, observed tartly that if Cissie hadn't acted so, she wouldn't have been in jail.

"Don' speak lak dat uv dem as is in trouble, Sally," reproved old Parson Ranson, solemnly; "anybody can say 'Ef.'"

"Sho am de troof," agreed Jerry Dillihay.

"Sho am, black man." The conversation drifted into the endless moralizing of their race, but it held no criticism or condemnation of Cissie. From the tone of the negroes one would have thought some impersonal disaster had overtaken her. Every one was planning how to help Cissie, how to make her present state more endurable. They were the black folk, the unfortunate of the earth, and the pride of righteousness is only to the well placed and the untempted.

Presently Nan came back with a bundle of Cissie's clothes. Tump took the bundle of dainty lingerie, the intimate garments of the woman he loved, and set forth on his quixotic errand. He tied it to his shoulder-holster and set out. Peter went a little of the way with him. It was almost dusk when they started. The chill of approaching night stung the men's faces. As they walked past the footpath that led over the Big Hill, three pistol-shots from the glade announced that the boot-leggers had opened business for the night.

Tump paused and shivered. He said it was a cold night. He thought he would like to get a kick of "white mule" to put a little heart in him. It was a long walk to Jonesboro. He hesitated a moment, then turned off the road around the crescent for the path through the glade.

A thought to dissuade Tump from drinking the fiery "singlings" of the moonshiners crossed Peter's mind, but he put it aside. Tump was a habitué of the glade. All the physiological arguments upon which

Peter could base an argument were far beyond the ex-soldier's comprehension. So Tump turned off through the dark trees. Peter watched him until all he could see was the white blur of Cissie's underwear swinging against his holster.

After Tump's disappearance, Peter stood for several minutes thinking. His brief crusade into Niggertown had ended in a situation far outside of his volition. That morning he had started out with some vague idea of taking Niggertown in his hands and molding it in accordance with his white ideas; but Niggertown had taken Peter into its hands, had threatened his life, had administered to him profound mental and moral shocks, and now had dropped him, like some bit of waste, with his face set over the Big Hill for white town.

As Peter stood there it seemed to him there was something symbolic in his attitude. He was no longer of the black world; he was of the white. He did not understand his people; they eluded him.

He belonged to the white world; not to the village across the hill, but to the North. Nothing now prevented him from going North and taking the position with Farquhar. Cissie Dildine was impossible for him now. Niggertown was immovable, at least for him. He was no Washington to lead his people to a loftier plane. In fact, Peter began to suspect that he was no leader at all. He saw now that his initial success with the Sons and Daughters of Benevolence had been effected merely by the aura of his college training. After his first misstep he had never re-habilitated himself. He perhaps had a dash of the artistic in him, and the power to mold ideas often confuses itself .subjectively with the power to mold human beings. In reality he did not even understand the people he assumed to mold. A suspicion came to him that under the given conditions their ways were more rational than his own.

As for Cissie Dildine, his duty by the girl, his queer protective passion for her—all that was surely past now. After her lapse from all decency there was no reason why he should spend another thought on her. He would go North to Chicago.

The last of the twilight was fading in swift, visible gradations of light. The cedars, the cabins, and the hill faded in pulse-beats of darkness. Above the Big Hill the last ember of day smoldered against a green-blue infinity. Here and there a star pricked the dome with a wintry brilliance.

Then, somehow, the thought of Cissie looking out on that chilly sky through iron bars tightened Peter's throat. He caught himself up sharply for his emotion. He began a vague defense of the white man's laws on grounds as cold and impersonal as the winter evening. Laws, customs, and conventions were for the strength-ening of men, to seed the select, to winnow the weak. It was white logic, applied firmly, as by a white man. But somehow the stars multiplied and kept Cissie's image before Peter—a cold, frightened girl, harassed with coming motherhood, peering at those chill, distant lights out of the blackness of a jail.

The mulatto decided to spend the night in his mother's cabin. He would do his packing, and be ready for the down-river boat in the morning. He found his way to his own gate in the darkness. He lifted it around, entered, and walked to his door. When he tried to open it, he found some one had bored holes through the shutter and the jamb and had wired it shut.

Peter struck a match to see just what had been done. The flame displayed a small sheet tacked on the door. He spent two matches investigating it. It was a notice of levy, posted by the constable in an action of debt brought against the estate of Caroline Siner by Henry Hooker. The owner of the estate and the public in general were warned against removing anything whatsoever from the premises under penalty exacted by the law governing such offenses. Then Peter untwisted the wire and entered.

Peter searched about and found the tiny brass night-lamp which his mother always had used. The larger glass-bowled lamp was gone. The interior of the cabin was clammy from cold and foul from long lack of airing. In the corner his mother's old four-poster loomed in the shadows, but he could see some of its covers had been taken. He passed into the kitchen with a notion of building a fire and eating a bite. but everything edible had been abstracted. Even one of the lids of the old step-stove was gone. Most of the pans and kettles had disappeared, but the pretty old Dutch sugar-bowl remained on a bare paper-covered shelf. Negro-like, whatever person or persons who had ransacked Peter's home considered the sugar-bowl too fine to take. Or they may have thought that Peter would want this bowl for a keepsake, and with that queer compassion that permeates a negro's worst moments they allowed it to remain. And Peter knew if he raised an outcry about his losses, much of the property would be surreptitiously restored, or perhaps his neighbors would bring back his things and say they had found them. They would help him as best they could, just as they of the crescent would help Cissie as best they could, and would receive her back as one of them when she and her baby were finally released from jail.

They were a queer people. They were a people who would never get on well and do well. They lacked the steel-like edge that the white man achieves. By virtue of his hardness, a white man makes his very laws and virtues instruments to crush and mulct his fellow-man; but negroes are so softened by untoward streaks of sympathy that they lose the very uses of their crimes.

The depression of the whole day settled upon Peter with the deepening night. He held his poor light above his head and picked his way to his own room. After the magnificence of the Renfrew manor, it had contracted to a grimy little box lined with yellowed papers. His books were still intact, but Henry Hooker would get them as part payment on the Dillihay place, which Henry owned. On his little table still lay the pile of old examination papers, lists of incoherent questions which somebody somewhere imagined formed a test of human ability to meet and answer the mysterious searchings of life.

Peter was familiar with the books; many of the questions he had learned by rote, but the night and the crescent, and the thought of a pregnant girl caged in the blackness of a jail filled his soul with a great melancholy query to which he could find no answer.

CHAPTER XIX

TWO voices talking, interrupting each other with ejaculations, after the fashion of negroes under excitement, aroused Peter Siner from his sleep. He caught the words: "He did! Tump did! The jailer did! 'Fo' God! black man, whut 's Cissie doin'?"

Overtones of shock, even of horror, in the two voices brought Peter wide awake the moment he opened his eyes. He sat up suddenly in his bed, remained perfectly still, listening with his mouth open. The voices, however, were passing. The words became indistinct, then relapsed into that bubbling monotone of human voices at a distance, and presently ceased.

These fragmentary phrases, however, feathered with consternation, filled Peter with vague premonitions. He whirled his legs out of bed and began drawing on his clothes. When he was up and into the crescent, however, nobody was in sight. He stood breathing the chill, damp air, blinking his eyes. Lack of his cold bath made him feel chilly and lethargic. He wriggled his shoulders and considered going back, after all, and having his splash. Just then he saw the

Persimmon coming around the crescent. Peter called to the roustabout and asked about Tump Pack.

The Persimmon looked at Peter with his half-asleep, protruding eyeballs.

"Don' you know 'bout Tump Pack already, Mister Siner?"

"No." Peter was astonished at the formality of the "Mr. Siner."

"Then is you 'spectin' somp'n 'bout him?"

"Why, no, but I was asleep in there a moment ago, and somebody came along talking about Tump and Cissie. They—they are n't married, are they?"

"Oh, no-o, no-o-o, no-o-o-o-o." The Persimmon waggled his bullet head slowly from side to side. "I heared Tump got into a lil trouble wid de jailer las' night."

"Serious?"

"I dunno." The Persimmon closed one of his protruding yellow eyes. "Owin' to whut you call se'ius; maybe whut I call se'ius would n't be se'ius to you at all; 'n 'en maybe whut you call se'ius would be ve'y insince'ius to Tump." The roustabout's philosophy, which consisted in a monotonous recasting of a given proposition, trickled on and on in the cold wind. After a while it fizzled out to nothing at all, and the Persimmon asked in a queer manner: "Did you give Tump some women's clo'es, Peter?"

It was such an odd question that at first Peter was at loss; then he recalled Nan Berry's despatching Cissie some underwear. He explained this to the Persimmon, and tacked on a curious, "Why?"

"Oh, nothin'; nothin' 'tall. Ever'body say you a mighty long-haided nigger. Jim Pink he tell us 'bout Tump Pack marchin' you 'roun' wid a gun. I sho don' want you ever git mad at me, Mister Siner. Man wid a gun an' you turn yo' long haid on him an' blow him away wid a wad o' women's clo'es. I sho don' want you ever cross yo' fingers at me, Mister Siner."

Peter stared at the grotesque, bullet-headed roustabout. "Persimmon," he said uneasily, "what in the world are you talking about?"

The Persimmon smiled a sickly, white-toothed smile. "Jim Pink say yo' aidjucation is a flivver. I say, 'Jim Pink, no nigger don' go off an' study fo' yeahs in college whut 'n he comes back an' kin throw some kin' uv a hoodoo over us fool niggers whut ain't got no brains. Now, Tump wid a gun, an' you wid jes ordina'y women's clo'es! 'Fo' Gawd, aidjucation is a great thing; sho is a great thing." The Persimmon gave Peter an apprehensive wink and moved on.

There was no use trying to extract information from the Persimmon unless he was minded to give it. His talk would merely become vaguer and vaguer. Peter watched him go, then turned and attempted to throw the whole matter off his mind by assuming a certain brisk Northern mood. He must pack, get ready for the down-river gasolene launch. The doings of Tump Pack and Cissie Dildine were, after all, nothing to him.

He started inside, when the levy notice on the door again met his eyes. He paused, read it over once more, and decided that he must go over the hill to the Planter's Bank and get Henry Hooker's permission to remove certain small personal belongings that he wanted to take with him.

The mere clear-cut decision to go invigorated Peter. Some of the energy that always filled him during his college days in Boston seemed to come to him now from the mere thought of the North. Soon he would be in the midst of it, moving briskly, talking to wide-awake men to whom a slightly unusual English word would not form a stumbling-block to conversation. He set out down the crescent and across the Big Hill at a swinging stride. He was glad to get away.

Beyond the white church on the other side of the hill he heard a motor coming in on the Jonesboro road. Presently he saw a battered car moving around the long swing of the pike, spewing a trail of dust down the wind. Its clacking became prodigious.

The mulatto was just entering that indefinite stretch of thoroughfare where a country road becomes a village street when there came a wail of brakes behind him and he looked around.

It was Dawson Bobbs's car. The fat man now slowed up not far from the mulatto and called to him.

"Yes, sir," said Peter.

Dawson bobbed his fat head backward and upward in a signal for Peter to approach. It held the casualness of one certain to be obeyed.

Although Peter had done no crime, nor had even harbored a criminal intention, a trickle of apprehension went through him at Bobbs's nod. He recalled Jim Pink's saying that it was bad luck to see the constable. He walked up to the shuddering motor and stood about three feet from the running-board.

The officer bit on a sliver of toothpick that he held in his thin lips.

"Accident up Jonesboro las' night, Peter."

"What was it, Mr. Bobbs?"

"Tump Pack got killed."

Peter continued looking fixedly at Mr. Bobbs's broad red face. The dusty road beneath him seemed to give a little dip. He repeated the information emptily, trying to orient himself to this sudden change in his whole mental horizon.

The officer was looking at Peter fixedly with his chill slits of eyes.

"Yeah; trying to make a jail delivery."

The two men continued looking at each other, one from the road, the other from the motor. The flow of Peter's thoughts seemed to divide. The greater part was occupied with Tump Pack. Peter could vision the formidable ex-soldier lying dead in Jonesboro jail, with his little congressional medal on his breast. Some lighter portion of his mind flickered about here and there on trivial things. He observed a little hole rusted in the running-board of the motor. He noticed that the officer's eyes were just the same chill, washed blue as the winter sky above his head. He remembered a tale that, before electrocution became a law in Tennessee the county sheriff's nerve had failed him at a hanging, and the constable Dawson Bobbs had sprung the drop. There was something terrible about the fat man. He would do anything, absolutely anything, that came to his hands in the way of legal sewage.

In the midst of these thoughts Peter heard himself saying.

"He—was trying to get Cissie out?"

"Yep."

"He—must have been drunk."

"Oh, yeah."

Mr. Bobbs sat studying the mulatto. As he studied him he said slowly:

"Some of 'em say he was disguised as a woman. Others say he had some women's clothes along, ready to put on. Now, me and the sheriff knowed Tump Pack purty well, Peter, and we knowed that nigger never in the worl' would 'a' thought up sich a plan by hisself."

He sat looking at Peter so interrogatively that the mulatto began, in a strained, earnest voice, telling the constable precisely what had happened in regard to the clothes.

Mr. Bobbs sat listening impassively, moving his toothpick up and down from one side to the other of his small, thin-lipped mouth. At last he nodded.

"Well, I guess that's about the way of it. I did n't exactly understand the women's clothes business,—damn' fool disguise,—but we figgered it might pop into the head of a' edjucated nigger." He sucked his teeth, reflectively. "Peter," he said at last, "seems to me, if I was you, I 'd drift on away from this town. The niggers around here ain't strong for you now; some say you 're a hoodoo; some say this an' some that. The white folks don't exactly like you trying to get up a cook's union. It's your right to do that if you want to, of course, but this is a mighty small city to have unions and things. The fact is, it ain't a big enough place for a nigger of yore ability, Peter. I b'lieve, if I was you, I'd jes drift on some'eres else."

The officer tipped up his toothpick so that it lifted his upper lip in a little v-shaped opening and exposed a strong, yellowish tooth. At the moment his machine started slowly forward. It gave him the appearance of accidentally rolling off while immersed in deep thought.

The death of Tump Pack moved Peter with a sense of strange pathos. He always remembered Tump tramping away through the night to carry Cissie some underclothes and, if possible, to take her place in jail. At the foundation of Tump's being lay a faithfulness and devotion to Cissie that reached the heights of a dog's. And yet, he might have deserted her, he would probably have beaten her, and he most certainly would have betrayed her many, many times. It was inexplicable.

Now that Tump was dead, the mantle of his fidelity somehow seemed to fall on Peter. For some reason Peter felt that he should assume Tump's place as Cissie Dildine's husband and protector. Had Tump lived, Peter might have gone North in peace, if not in happiness. Now such a journey, without Cissie, had become impossible. He had a feeling that it would not be right.

As for the disgrace of marrying such a woman as Cissie Dildine, Peter slowly gave that idea up. The "worthinesses" and "disgraces" implicit in Harvard atmosphere, which Peter had spent four years of his life imbibing, slowly melted away in the air of Niggertown. What was honorable there, what was disgraceful there, somehow changed its color here.

By virtue of this change Peter felt intuitively that Cissie Dildine was neither disgraced by her arrest nor soiled by her physical condition. Somehow she seemed just as "nice" a girl, just as "good" a girl, as ever she was before. Moreover, every other darky in Niggertown held these same instinctive beliefs. Had it not been for that, Peter would have thought it was his passion pleading for the girl, justifying itself by a grotesque morality, as passions often do. But this was not the correct solution. The sentiment was enigmatic.

Peter puzzled over it time and time again as he waited in Hooker's Bend for the outcome of Cissie's trial.

The octoroon's imprisonment came to an end on the third day after Tump's death. Sam Arkwright's parents had not known of their son's legal proceedings, and Mr. Arkwright immediately quashed the warrant, and hushed up the unfortunate matter as best he could. Young Sam was suddenly sent away from home to college, as the best step in the circumstances. And so the wishes of the adolescent in the cedar-glade came queerly to pass, even if Peter did withhold any grave, mature advice on the subject which he may have possessed.

Naturally, there was much mirth among the men of Hooker's Bend and much virulence among the women over the peculiar conditions under which young Sam made his pilgrimage in pursuit of wisdom and morals and the right conduct of life. And life being problematic and uncertain as it is, and prone to wind about in the strangest way, no one may say with certitude that young Sam did not make a promising start.

Certainly, over the affair the Knights of the Round Table launched many a quip and jest, but that simply proved the fineness of their sentiments toward a certain delicate human relation which forms mankind's single awful approach to the creative and the holy.

Tump Pack became almost a mythical figure in Niggertown. Jim Pink Staggs composed a saga relating the soldier's exploits in France, his assault on the jail to liberate Cissie, and his death.

In his songs—and Jim Pink had composed a good many—the minstrel instinctively avoided humor. He always improvised them to the sobbing of a guitar, and they were as invariably sad as the poetry of adolescents. It was called "Tump Pack's Lament." The negroes of Hooker's Bend learned it from Jim Pink, and with them it drifted up and down the three great American rivers, and now it is sung by the roustabouts, stevedores, and underlings of our strange black American world.

This song commemorating Tump Pack's bravery and faithfulness to his love may very well take the place of the Congressional medal which, unfortunately, was lost on the night the soldier was killed. Between the two, there is little doubt that the accolade of fame bestowed in the buffoon's simple melody is more vital and enduring than that accorded by special act of the Congress of the United States of America.

When Cissie Dildine returned from jail, she' and her mother arranged the Dildine-Siner wedding as nearly according to white standards in similar circumstances as they could conceive. They agreed that it should be a simple, quiet home wedding. However, as every soul in Niggertown, a number of colored friends in Jonesboro, and a contingent from up-river villages meant to attend, it became necessary to hold the service in the church.

The officiating minister was not Parson Ranson after all, but a Reverend Cleotus Haidus, the presiding elder of that circuit of the Afro-American Methodist Church, whose duties happened to call him to Hooker's Bend that day. So, notwithstanding Cissie's efforts at simplicity, the wedding, after all, was resolved into an affair.

Once, in one of her moments of clairvoyance, Cissie said to Peter:

"Our trouble is, Peter, we are trying to mix what I have learned in Nashville and what you have learned in Boston with what we both feel in Hooker's Bend. I—I'm almost ashamed to say it, but I don't really feel sad and plaintive at all, Peter. I feel glad, gloriously glad. Oh, my dear, dear Peter!" and she flung her arms around Peter's neck and held him with all her might against her ripening bosom.

To Cissie her theft, her jail sentence, her pregnancy, were nothing more than if she had taken a sip of water. However, with the imitativeness of her race and the histrionic ability of her sex, she appeared pensive and subdued during the elaborate double-ring ceremony performed by the Reverend Cleotus Haidus. Nobody in the packed church knew how tremendously Cissie's heart was beating except Peter, who held her hand.

The ethical engine that Peter had patiently builded in Harvard almost ceased to function in this weird morality of Niggertown. Whether he were doing right or doing wrong, Peter could not determine. He

The bridal couple embarked for Cairo

lost all his moorings. At times he felt himself walking according to the ethnological law, which is the Harvard way of saying walking according to the will of God; but at other times he felt party to some unpardonable obscenity. So deeply was he disturbed that out of the dregs of his mind floated up old bits of the Scriptures that he was unaware of possessing: "There is a way which seemeth right unto a man, but the end thereof are the ways of death." And Peter wondered if he were not in that way.

The bridal couple embarked for Cairo on the *Red Cloud,* a packet in the Dubuque, Ohio, and Tennessee River trade. Peter and Cissie were not allowed to walk up the main stairway into the passengers' cabin, but were required to pick their way along the boiler-deck, through the stench of freight, lumber, live stock and sleeping roustabouts. Then they went through the heat and steam of the engine-room up a small companionway that led through the toilet, on to the rear guard of the main deck, and thence back to a little cuddy behind the main saloon called the chambermaid's cabin.

The chambermaid's cabin was filled with the perpetual odor of hot soap-suds, soiled laundry, and the broader smell of steam and the boat's machinery. The little place trembled night and day, for the steamer's engines were just beneath them, and immediately behind them thundered the great stern-wheel of the packet. A single square window in the end of the chambermaid's cabin looked out on the wheel, but at all times, except when the wind was blowing from just the right quarter, this window was deluged with a veritable Niagara of water. The continual shake of the cabin, the creak of the rudder-beam working to and fro, the watery thunder of the wheel, and the solemn rumble of the engines made conversation impossible until the travelers grew accustomed to the noises. Still, Cissie found it pleasant. She liked to sit and look out into the main saloon, with its interminable gilded scrolls extending away up the long cabin, a suave perspective. She liked to watch the white passengers dine—the white napery, the bouquets, the endless tables all filled with diners; some swathed in napkins from chin to waistband, others less completely protected. It gave Cissie a certain tang of triumph to smile at the swathed ones and to think that she knew better than that.

At night a negro string-band played for the white excursionists to dance, and Cissie would sit, with glowing eyes, clenching Peter's hand, every fiber of her asway to the music, and it seemed as if her heart would go mad. All these inhibitions, all this spreading before her of forbidden joys, did not daunt her delight. She reveled in them by propinquity.

The chambermaid was a Mrs. Antolia Higgman, a strong, full-bodied *café-au-lait* negress. She was a very sensible woman, and during her work on the boat she had picked up a Northern accent and a number of little mannerisms from the Chicago and St. Louis ex-

cursionists, who made ten-day round trips from Dubuque to Florence, Alabama, and return. When Mrs.
Higgman was not running errands for the women
passengers, she was working at her perpetual launder-
ing.

At first Peter was a little uneasy as to how Mrs.
Higgman would treat Cissie, but she turned out a
good-hearted woman, and did everything she could to
make the young wife comfortable. It soon became
clear that Mrs. Higgman knew the whole situation, for
one day she said to Cissie in her odd dialect, burred
with Yankeeish "r's" and "ing's."

"These river-r towns, Mrs. Siner-r, are jest like one
big village, with the river-r for its Main Street. I
know ever-r'thang that goes on, through the cabin-boys
an' cooks, an'—an'—you cerrtainly ar-re a dear-r, Mrs.
Siner-r," and thereupon, quite unexpectedly, she kissed
Cissie.

So on about the second day down the river Cissie
dropped her saddened manner and became frankly,
freely, and riotously happy. After the fashion of
village negresses, she insisted on helping Mrs. Higgman
with her work, and, incidentally, she cultivated Mrs.
Higgman's Northern accent. When the chambermaid
was out on her errands and Cissie found a moment
alone with Peter, she would tweak his ear or pull his
cheek and provoke him to kiss her. Indeed, it was all
the hot, shuddering little laundry-room could do to
contain the gay and bubbling Cissie.

Peter thought and thought, resignedly now, but persistently, how this strange happiness that belonged to them both could be. He was content, yet he felt he ought not to be content. He thought there must be something base in himself, yet he felt that there was not. He drank the wine of his honeymoon marveling.

On the morning before the *Red Cloud* entered the port of Cairo Mrs. Higgman was out of the cabin, and Peter stood at the little square window, with his arm about Cissie's waist, looking out to the rear of the steamer. A strong east wind blew the spray away from the glass, and Peter could see the huge wheel covered with a waterfall thundering beneath him. Back of the wheel stretched a long row of even waves and troughs. Every seventh or eighth wave tumbled over on itself in a swash of foam. These flashing stern waves strung far up the river. On each side of the great waterway stretched the flat shores of Kentucky and Ohio. Here and there over the broad clay-colored water moved other boats—tow-boats, a string of government auto-barges, a snag-boat, another packet.

Peter gave up his question. The curves of Cissie's form in his arm held a sweetness and a restfulness that her maidenhood had never promised. He felt so deeply sure of his happiness that it seemed strange to him that he could not aline his emotions and his mind.

As Peter stood staring up the Ohio River, it occurred

to him that perhaps, in some queer way, the morals of black folk were not the morals of white folk; perhaps the laws that bound one race were not the laws that bound the other. It might be that white anathemas were black blessings. Peter thought along this line peacefully for several minutes.

And finally he concluded that, after all, morals and conventions, right and wrong, are merely those precepts that a race have practised and found good in its evolution. Morals are the training rules that keep a people fit. It might very well be that one moral régime is applicable to one race, and quite another to another.

The single object of all morals is racial welfare, the racial integrity, the breeding of strong children to perpetuate the species. If the black race possess a more exuberant vitality than some other race, then the black would not be forced to practise so severe a vital economy as some less virile folk. Racial morals are simply a question of having and spending within safety limits.

Peter knew that for years white men had held a prejudice against marrying widows. This is utterly without grounds except for one reason: the first born of a woman is the lustiest. Among the still weaker Aryans of India the widows burn themselves. Among certain South Sea Islanders only the first-born may live and mate; all other children are slain. Among nearly every white race marriage lines are strictly drawn, and the tendency is to have few children to a family, to conserve the precious vital impulse. So strong is this feeling of birth control that to-day nearly all American white women are ashamed of large families. This shame is the beginning of a convention; the convention may harden into a cult, a law, or a religion.

And here is the amazing part of morals. Morals are always directed toward one particular race, but the individual members of that race always feel that their brand of morals does and should apply to all the peoples of the earth; so one has the spectacle of nations sending out missionaries and battle-ships to teach and enforce their particular folk-ways. Another queer thing is that whereas the end of morals is designed solely for the betterment of the race, and is entirely regardless of the person, to the conscience of the person morals are always translated as something that binds him personally, that will shame him or honor him personally not only for the brief span of this worldly life, but through an eternity to come. To him, his particular code, surrounded by all the sanctions of custom, law, and religion, appears earth-embracing, hell-deep, and heaven-piercing, and any human creature who follows any other code appears fatally wicked, utterly shameless, and ineluctably lost.

And yet there is no such thing as absolute morals. Morals are as transitory as the sheen on a blackbird's wing; they change perpetually with the necessities of the race. Any people with an abounding vitality will naturally practise customs which a less vital people must shun.

Morals are nothing more than the engines controlling the stream of energy that propel a race on its course. All engines are not alike, nor are all races bound for the same port.

Here Peter Siner made the amazing discovery that although he had spent four years in Harvard, he had come out, just as he went in, a negro.

A great joy came over him. He took Cissie wholeheartedly in his arms and kissed again and again the deep crimson of her lips. His brain and his heart were together at last. As he stood looking out at the window, pressing Cissie to him, he wondered, when he reached Chicago, if he could ever make Farquhar understand.